William's Wife

y of the Husband.—Apart from all financial relationship as
and and wife, there are matters over which the husband has
undisputed control. It is for him to decide what companion-
shall keep, where she shall resort, and to what individuals
ll be open. He is within his rights if he forbids his wife to
any given person; he may decline to receive whomsoever he
guest beneath his roof, and he is not bound to give his wife
or any decision to which he may come. But if his wife be
o his commands in these particulars, he will not obtain the
any court to which he may be driven to obtain relief if he
ably and without sufficient cause debarred, or attempted to
e from the usual and innocent diversions or friendships.

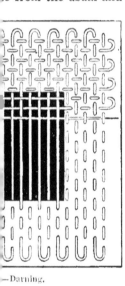

—Darning.

HRIFTY HOUSEWIFE SHOULD BUY

Refined Beef Suet. It replaces Butchers'
ard, and Cooking Butter for Puddings,
d cooking. Absolutely pure, goes further
s sweet for months. Ask your grocer for
n blocks and refuse substituted brands.

William's Wife

Gertrude Eileen Trevelyan

Introduction by Alice Jolly
Afterword by Ann Kennedy Smith

RECOVERED BOOKS
BOILER HOUSE PRESS

Contents

Introduction
by Alice Jolly

A bold and interesting work of literature often balances precariously on the edge of failure. Part of the reader's interest in such a book derives from the tension of watching as the book might rise up and fly, or stumble and plunge. Sometimes books do both. Flaws, imperfections and contradictions are essential to a good novel.

All of this is demonstrated clearly by the reactions we might have to *William's Wife*, the penultimate novel of Gertrude Trevelyan (1903-1941). Gertrude Eileen Trevelyan was born into an affluent family and studied at Oxford University. She then spent eight years writing eight novels, all of which have been largely forgotten.

She died aged 37 from injuries sustained during the Blitz. Why has her work been so neglected? Perhaps partly because there is no distinctive "Trevelyan" novel. Also, she made no effort to become a presence in the literary world of her time. Leading a quiet life (possibly due to ill health), she spent her days experimenting with what the novel can do.

At first glance, it appears that *William's Wife* is one of Trevelyan's more conventional books. Certainly, its subject matter is not inherently dramatic. Set in the early part of the nineteenth century, the book tells the story of Jane Atkins, a lady's maid who marries a prosperous widowed greengrocer named William Chirp.

They live together in the fictional town of Jewsbury. Their house, The Elms, is a "solid, dark red brick villa with gabled roofs, well shut in by high trees." Jane initially feels that she has done well to marry William, with his silk hat, "heavy black broadcloth suit and gold watch-chain." William is "comfortably off" and "much respected in the parish."

Jane initially believes that William isn't "as open-handed as some" but it soon becomes apparent that he is "the most tight-fisted man in Jewsbury." The problem begins with the crooked blind in the upstairs window and progresses to the handle which has fallen off the kitchen door. William won't "lift a finger to get things seen to in the house."

He controls the money, so there is little Jane can do. She saves a few coins from the housekeeping, puts three pence instead of sixpence in the church collection. She hides these clandestine coins in "screws of paper" under the sheets, tucks them into the thumbs of her gloves or conceals them in her Sunday shoes.

She becomes obsessed by how to "get some stuff for a new dress" or a "yard of fine meshed black veiling" for a hat. William will give her nothing. "My first wife didn't go spending money on new gowns, not once in ten, no, fifteen years." Increasingly thwarted emotion and repressed anger poison the already chilly atmosphere of The Elms.

All of this might sound small, domestic, dreary and it is. Yet strangely it is also gripping. Jane's furtive attempts to save money, fix things in the house, buy a new dress start to have the suspense and thrill of major military manoeuvres. The repeated details of marital suffocation and domestic alienation are mesmeric in their effect.

How is this done? The reader doesn't quite know. The book is all told from Jane's point of view, in a myopically close third person. The liberal use of interior monologue might suggest the influence of Richardson and Woolf. However, in those writers the assumption is that the "stream of consciousness" has flow, rhythm, a touch of poetry.

In contrast, Trevelyan renders Jane's thoughts in short and repetitive sentences. The tired aphorisms of the time are repeated. "Waste not want not." "Saving for a rainy day." She worries about fabrics which are "not what they used to be" and won't "wear." She is constantly "turning out a room" or "scolding the girl" or worrying about gossip.

It feels as though even language itself must be "turned out" and kept in order. The effect of this may not be poetic but Jane's voice does have its own unique and relentless power. The reader can only marvel at how Trevelyan gives voice to this small life in a way which is totally captivating and immersive and avoids even the smallest hit of satire or condescension.

As the book progresses, the modern reader realises that Jane's marital situation would now be classified as "coercive control," but this does not make us feel sympathetic to her. This dismal situation endures for many years. Gas lamps arrive, Jewsbury is enlivened by the First World War and the arrival of troops.

Jane enjoys an hour a week at the vicarage, knitting for the war effort. People buy gramophones, take buses and go to the cinema. Women of all classes start to take jobs. Yet life at The Elms continues unchanged – until suddenly Jane is released.

She has always said she will "give herself a treat one of these days" and she has long speculated as to what she might do if she "had the handling of it." How will she take advantage of her new situation? "What a relief to get away from Jewsbury."

Jane lives in a series rented rooms, buys a new umbrella stand. She enjoys "going out now on her mornings and seeing new faces all around her!" She walks out in the evenings. "It was like a fairyland, with the shops lit up; and things so cheap!" But soon Jane wants a place where "everyone couldn't get at her so easily."

She moves again and again. "Get right away from the lot of them." But from whom must she escape? There is no-one. Jane becomes paranoid, obsessive. William's small-minded and controlling concerns have transferred themselves to her. She needs worry, she needs minor problems.

Soon she is putting unnecessary bolts on doors and drawing the blinds against imagined intruders. She starts carrying all her possessions with her when she goes out, even the teaspoons. Money is sewn into the hems of her skirts. She moves from enjoying a bargain to becoming a woman who is picking up discarded food from the gutter.

She appears to be in a process of erasing herself from her own life. The modern reader understands this as incipient mental illness. But why has this happened? What is Trevelyan telling us about human nature, about ourselves? Perhaps she is issuing a bitter reminder that change is not always possible. Too often habits cannot be broken.

Cramped ideas of life can spread and stick. Are human beings imprisoned or do they imprison themselves? The reader does not want to be reminded that no-one is betrayed as thoroughly as they betray themselves. But Trevelyan never relents, never swerves from the narrative path she has chosen.

Is her book boring and bitter or is it brilliant? I find that it is all of those things – and more. Certainly, it is a book which lingers in the mind, which leaves the reader unsettled and disturbed. How does Jane's life become so small, damaged, wracked by paranoia? Was there never a possibility of salvation?

William's Wife
by Gertrude Eileen Trevelyan

Chapter I

Jane Atkins was doing up her dress collar in Miss Miniver's best bedroom. Her head was inclined over the muslin-skirted toilet-table while she dabbed anxiously at the high back hooks; the whalebone supports in front dug into her chin. It was kind of Miss Miniver to allow Jane Atkins to use the best bedroom for dressing in before the ceremony. The toilet-table had a bright pink underskirt, very grand, with the pincushion muslin-over-pink to match, and behind a row of china trays and little pots shoehorn and buttonhook were laid head to toe like knife and fork. However would Miss Miniver manage with that new girl. Jane mistrusted young girls.

There. The top hook was done at last. Jane's head went up, she craned her neck in front of the glass. The lace, stretched between its bone supports, swept down from her chin and out into a taut, splendid circle over her chest and shoulders, almost to the high puffed purple sleeves. It did look nice. You couldn't wear white for a widower, could you; and not only that, but she hoped she knew what was fitting to her station, for all Miss Miniver's kindness. Letting her use the best bedroom.

She stooped and lifted her skirts to do up the high new boots. It was a pity, in a way, she couldn't have put on the smart slippers she'd bought, with the beads sewn all over the toes; but they never would do for out-of-doors, even with going in the cab. Have them nice and new for afterwards. She laid the buttonhook back, head to toe with the shoehorn; breathing a little sharply from stooping in the new tight stays. Downstairs she could hear the new girl laying out the glasses in the best parlour, where Miss Miniver was going to allow Jane, very kindly, to bring in Mr. Chirp afterwards for a glass of port wine.

All in a flutter now, she turned to the open cardboard box on the ottoman and lifted from its tissue paper wrappings the hat, fancy straw and one rose, nothing loud, and set it reverently, tilted forwards, on her head. She'd been right to save, hadn't she. Miss Miniver had been very kind to her all these years — fifteen she'd been when she came, and twenty-eight now: fifteen and ten makes twenty-five, and three twenty-eight, that's thirteen years — and Jane had a nice little nest-egg put by. Not like these young girls, here today and gone tomorrow, easy come easy go. Jane had worked for her money, she knew the value of it. Knew how to save, and knew how to spend, too. All good quality, all of the very best. Mr. Chirp might have done worse for a manager. Gone further and fared worse.

From among the paper wrappings she drew a yard of fine meshed black veiling and fitted its upper edge closely and lovingly over the fancy straw brim. She couldn't help an almost guilty thrill of pleasure as she drew the knot tight behind. She turned her thin, long face this way and that, pinching up her mouth behind its close-meshed black curtain. She hoped she knew her place, she wasn't one to be aping gentry, but she owed it to herself to look nice; Mr. Chirp — William — would expect it of her. She owed it to *him*, as you might say. Trembling with excitement she collected the dangling lower edge of the veil and twisted it into a tight screw and tucked it in under her chin, the mesh taut against her cheek, taut from chin to brim. Really, anyone might take her for a gentlewoman in that veil! She gave a little, daring giggle. All at once she heard a crunch of gravel under the window as the cab turned into the drive, and the new girl running. From the bottom of the stairs Miss Miniver's thin, anxious voice called, "Jane?"

"Coming, Mam."

She dug the heavy gold brooch, which was what Miss Miniver had given her, into the lace at her throat, in her hurry pricking herself with the pin; shook out the feather boa, lifted it over her hat, let it drop, light and elegant, across her shoulders.

With a quick, final screw of the head from side to side, Jane Atkins dragged at the new, tight primrose kid gloves with the heavy black braiding on the back and ran downstairs with the fingers not quite to the tips, work them on in the cab, and went to church, and came out Jane Chirp.

Chapter II

Jane Chirp was dusting the front parlour at The Elms. There was a girl for rough work, but Jane dusted the parlour herself, she mistrusted young girls. She had been married three weeks and she was dusting the front parlour for the third time, on a chilly Saturday morning in October. By this time she knew the furniture well: the plush suite and horsehair sofa and the yellowish wood, tinkly upright piano and the inlaid occasional table by the fireplace and the pair of round, beaded footstools on dumpy wooden legs. She handled all these things, and the ornaments, fondly, with pride: the clock under its glass dome and the pair of china vases and the candlesticks hung with bunches of gilt grapes: it was her furniture now, her ornaments, hers, Jane Chirp's. When she had time, in the long evenings, she'd crochet some new antimacassars and a runner for the piano, she hadn't any patience with other folks' stuff. She hadn't ever seen his first wife, but it didn't make much difference what she'd been like. This furniture hadn't been hers, it was William's, and his

17

father's before him, and now it was Jane Chirp's, seeing Jane had married William.

The air was chilly near the window, the garden damp seemed to strike up through the glass. Outside, there was the drive in a semicircle, with two gates, and between them a line of damp *arbor vitae* and a monkey puzzle hiding the road. A yucca stood in the centre of the semicircular grass patch edged in by the drive. The Elms was quite a big house. Mr. Chirp — William — had always been comfortably off, always much respected.

There was the bookcase, between the window and the grate, with his books in: a tall, narrow bookcase with rows of dark calf-bound sermons and the Decline and Fall and Bohn's translations of the classics: a well-read man. Mr. Chirp. And up on the top shelf, out of reach, behind the stuffed parrot in a case, a lot of piled up rubbish Jane hadn't had time to clear yet. She fetched the piano stool now and, lifting her skirts, got up gingerly on its embroidered seat. Dust, she flicked it off. Old photograph albums of his family: that couldn't be Her, must be his mother. And the first Mrs. Chirp's workbasket, pushed to the back; crammed up there most likely before the funeral, by someone clearing up.

Jane's mouth tightened. Don't want *that* rubbish here. Collecting dust. She wiped the albums and pushed them in a pile behind the parrot's case and got down from the stool with the basket grabbed firmly in her hand. She pushed out the wooden rod which held down the top and looked inside. Some reels of thread and mending and a broken pair of scissors and a few needles rusted into the worn, rusty holed red silk of the padded lid. The fire's the best place for such rubbish. With the basket in her hand she went out of the room and down the narrow hall to the kitchen. At the last moment, just before she pushed the basket into the round, red hole of the stove, she took out the reels and slipped them in her pocket.

The girl followed her back to the parlour. "Will I lay the fire in here, Mum?"

"Why isn't it laid," she asked haughtily, "this time of year?" All alike.

"The master wouldn't never have it laid, not unless someone come. Will I lay it now, Mum?"

Jane turned round sharply. "And quite right too. Wasting coal. No, certainly not."

She wasn't going to have any young girl answering back about Mr. Chirp. She was grateful to Mr. Chirp, he'd made her the mistress of The Elms, she hoped she knew her duty by him.

In the evening they sat in the small back parlour, when Mr. Chirp came home from the shop. The back parlour, wedged in between the parlour and the kitchen, was Mr. Chirp's study. It had a big leather-topped writing desk with his ledgers and pipes, and a big, horsehair armchair, and a smaller horsehair chair, without arms, for Jane, and a very small grate. On the mantelpiece there was Mr, Chirp's tobacco jar and the Grocers' Almanack.

Mr. Chirp pulled at his pipe and looked at Jane, out of his little, hidden-in blue eyes.

"It's turning chilly," she said, getting up to draw the heavy plush curtains. "Time for a fire almost."

Mr. Chirp grunted. "Light it if you want," he allowed, a bit ungraciously.

"Ah," he said, rubbing his hands as the flames licked up. He hitched his chair across the hearth, the worn castors grated on the carpet. "Cosy, eh?" He twitched his head sideways and looked at Jane over his short moustaches. Sandy. Pepper-and-salt.

Cosy he said. That was right. Jane knew how to make a man cosy. She kicked out her skirts round her feet and went on with her darning with a little, pleased nod. Don't tell Jane he'd ever been cosy with *Her*. It took a bit of thought to make a man comfortable. It was a knack, what Jane had got. *She'd* been dead for years, Jane never saw her; right back before Miss Miniver started dealing with Chirp's.

He was reaching up for his tobacco jar, neck stretched so that the folds were smoothed out: lined neck straining from the worn greenish velvet collar of his smoking jacket. His red lined wrist strained from the worn cuff.

"Emily was here today," she said, casual sounding. Funny him having a daughter nearly as old as her. Emily, that was it. Called after Her.

He jerked round with the heavy lead jar in his hand, half-way from mantelpiece to knee. "Eh? What she want?"

"Her and Jim want to come here Sunday."

"They do, do they?" He brought the jar down to his knees and balanced it between them, flaking out the tobacco with hands that shook a bit as he chuckled. He was a humorous man, Mr. Chirp. "Then I'm very much afraid," he chuckled, the brush of his moustache twitching as he shook, "that Want must be their master."

She gave a little, cosy giggle. "Poor Emily," she said happily. William was a funny one! His own daughter, too. But he wasn't one to put up with any nonsense. He knew when he was comfortable. "She wants to see her Pa, I expect. It's the best part of month since they were here for Sunday dinner. Since we was married."

"See her Pa, eh? Fat lot she cares about her Pa till it comes dinnertime. And that great Jim, a pretty knife and fork *he* can play. Eating me out of house and home."

"I didn't rightly know what to tell her," she said with a happy, smooth smile. "So I told her so far as I knew they'd be welcome.".

He planted his feet apart and rapped his pipe on the top bar of the grate. "Well don't you tell her any such thing again."

"I didn't like not to," she said, meekly, with a secret, happy look in her eyes. "Seeing I'm strange here."

He twisted around at her with a distant, puzzled look. "Strange, eh?"

"Well..." she said, deprecating.

He pulled at his pipe and seemed to consider it.

"Look here," he said, turning suddenly, his boots crunching the cinders in the grate. "If she should come here again asking…" he pointed the pipe stem at her and shook it triumphantly; a bead of saliva dropped from it on to the floor. "You tell her I say *NO*!" He looked at her for a moment over the pipe and rammed it back between his teeth; the toes of his boots pivoted back, crunching, to face the fire.

"Yes, William," she said meekly.

William wasn't standing any nonsense from Emily, she could see that, nor from that Jim either, with his check suit and his loud ways and his big, dirty boots on the parlour carpet. Emily was trying to make up to Jane, with her chit-chat and her needle-work. Show me that stitch, won't you? Knew which side her bread was buttered. But Jane wasn't having any, she could see through it all right and so could William. You could tell by the way he'd been sharp with Jim at dinner: cutting bread and leaving it, wasting good food. "We haven't *all* come into a fortune," he'd said, in his humorous way. Humorous, but meaning it, you could see that. "Waste not want not," he'd said. And he wasn't going to have the parlour fire laid for *them*, either.

"You might let us have a bit of fire, Pa," says Emily. Just on account of she, Jane, having given a bit of a shiver, all through not having changed yet into her flannels for winter. "Ma's cold."

Thought that would fetch him. Called her Ma though. Glad she showed *that* much respect.

"Cold? Who's cold. *I'm* not cold. You cold?"

"I'm not any such thing," Jane said indignantly.

Emily leaned over to her on the sofa. "You'll have to look out for yourself. Pa never did notice a thing like that."

Jane gave her a look. "I can look after myself all right, thank you."

Glad I told her that. Hope she saw it.

They wouldn't be coming here much more, that was one thing.

21

William could see through them all right, see through Jim with his flash ways and his here-we-are-together. And Emily, trying to be all honey. They wouldn't have the face to show themselves here again, not for a month of Sundays, not after the hint William had thrown out when they were going. "Well," he'd said, showing them to the door, "we won't be seeing you for a good bit."

"I don't know about that," says Jim. "You may have us back like a bad penny."

"Eh?" William says. "What's that? I've got no use for bad pennies. I'm a busy man, and a poor man, I've got my bread to earn. I've got no time to sit tongue wagging." All in his humorous way, but you could see he meant it.

"Cosy, eh?" he said now, rubbing his hands over the tiny fire in the back parlour grate. He hitched round the big armchair across the hearth and his boots crunched the embers. He toasted his hands close over the small flame.

Jane sat straight in her chair against the heavy plush curtains with her skirt drawn primly around her feet. "It's sort of home-like," she ventured, "isn't it?" Happy and timid, almost afraid of being happy like that; secure, yet with a kind of timid daring. "Cosy, just us two."

Chapter III

William went to the shop every morning, five days a week and half-day Wednesday, and kept the ledgers in a little back room. Nowadays he had three young men to serve at the counter, he hardly came forward himself excepting for old and valued customers: like when Jane used to go, shopping for Miss Miniver, "I trust Miss Miniver enjoys good health?" Quite the gentleman, bowing her out.

Jane never went near the shop nowadays, William wouldn't hear of it. The shop was no place for Mrs. Chirp, with its vulgar blue paper packets and cheeses and sides of bacon. William had too much respect for her, and for himself too. He'd never hold up his head again if any of the neighbours was so much as to think Mrs. Chirp was helping in the shop. A boy was sent down to The Elms on Saturdays with provisions for the week. When Jane went along the High Street, at eleven o'clock her three mornings a week, to give her orders at the butcher's and the baker's, she always walked on the other side of the street from Chirp's; and very neat and ladylike she felt, with the velvet-banded skirt swinging round her feet, and her gloved bands, and the knotted veil tucked in snugly under her chin. She never even looked round when passing Chirp's across the street, but out of the corner of her eye she could see it well enough: the display of mottled plenty in the big double window on either side of the open door, and the big brass sign CHIRP & SON.

"Who's Son?" she asked him once. Didn't know he ever had a son. Only Emily.

"Son?" He took his pipe from between his teeth and wiped his mouth with the back of his hand. "Son, eh? That's me!" He began to chuckle. "Chirp, that was my old Pa. Bit of a shop down Market Street it was when he started. And Son, that was me."

He put the pipe back into his mouth and pulled at it. "And now," he said, taking it out, "I'm Chirp! And Son too, as you might say. And have been, these twenty years." He gave a small, private chuckle, knocking out the pipe against the grate. "Chirp. And Son." Almost to himself. He brought the pipe back between his teeth and clenched it, pressing in the tobacco with a short, red forefinger. "Chirp," he muttered and chuckled to himself between his half clenched teeth. "*And* Son, eh? Chirp and Son."

Jane would go on past Chirp's, her high buttoned boots rapping genteelly on the opposite pavement, past the draper's and the bank and round the corner into Market Street, to the butcher's. Peel, the butcher, was very polite to Mrs. Chirp. There was another, larger butcher's in the High Street, near Chirp's, where gentry went, but Mr. Chirp had always dealt at Peel's. Penny a pound, very often, between them, and you wouldn't know the difference. Jane didn't believe in waste either. She went on dealing with Peel's. Mr. Peel would come forward himself, in his blue and white apron, rubbing his hands, when Mrs. Chirp came into the shop. Chirp's was a much larger shop, and an older established shop, than Peel's, and Mr. Peel was very respectful, as was fitting. Jane liked to give her custom where it was appreciated. When she came out of Peel's she smiled graciously and would have to pause in the doorway to compose her face and take her haughty air before stepping out past Maggit's, next door; Maggit was a small, cheap-and-nasty grocer, for the common people. Jane Chirp swept past Maggit's without so much as a look, head up and skirts swinging, and back along the street to the Market Place. If it were a Saturday she would have to pick her way between knots of loud-voiced, leather-gaitered farmers gathered near the doorway of the Jewsbury Arms, and drovers and idlers shifting and prodding among the pens by the Market Cross. Jewsbury market was known for miles around. Holding her skirts daintily, almost to the top of her boots, Jane would hurry round the corner into the High Street choked with farmers' traps[1] and dog carts and the governess-cars of the more prosperous farmers' wives and an occasional carriage, and tap her ways down the pavement across the road from Chirp's, back to The Elms.

The Elms stood right at the end of the little town, past the empty, straight cross-road with dusty hedges which led to the railway station a mile away. It was one of half a dozen smallish, solid, dark red brick villas with gabled roofs, well shut in by high trees and inhabited by the better class Jewsbury tradesmen and the dentist. Just before The Elms, a milestone let into the wall said: London 45 miles. Jane had never been to London, nasty, dirty, noisy place. And didn't want to. She turned in at the gate of The Elms and noted that the girl was laying the table in the crampy dining room on the left-hand side of the door. An upstairs blind was crooked in the end window.

She spoke sharply to the girl about dishing up the minute Mr. Chirp got in — only yesterday he'd had to wait ten minutes — and went upstairs and straightened the blind before she took off her

---

1 A light two- or four-wheeled horse-drawn carriage.

hat. Mr. Chirp never did have much to say for himself at dinner-time, he had his work to think about. He chipped a bit off the joint for the girl's dinner and Jane ladled out greens and potatoes and rang the bell for the girl to come in and fetch the plate; then he ate up quickly, and so did Jane: the bit he had passed across to her. She was a small eater, and it wasn't often she asked for more. When she did he would grunt and chew at his moustache while he chipped it off. Then he ate up his pudding and Jane saw him off, back to the shop. He never allowed himself a pipe until the evening. When he had gone Jane settled herself in the stuffy back parlour to mend the house-linen or darn William's socks, and about half past five she began to scold at the girl to have the kettle boiling for Mr. Chirp's tea, and see that the eggs weren't done too hard.

On Sundays they went to church. Mr. Chirp was vicar's warden and much respected in the parish. When he got up he put on his heavy black broadcloth and gold watch-chain and the boots the girl had shined bright — after a bit of telling — the night before, and Jane put on her purple dress. After breakfast Jane went up again to put on her wedding hat, and a heavy black cloth jacket over her dress now the cold weather was setting in. She liked the busy, excited feel of that hour after breakfast, getting ready for church; with the bells beginning to ring in the distance and knots of prim, clattering Sunday School children going past in the road. Then Mr. Gilpin, the dentist, and his wife would set out, early, from The Laurels, two doors up, and pass slowly in front of The Elms, she holding on to his arm; on account of her being poorly with the rheumatics and taking a longer time than anyone to get to church. Jane often watched them over the toilet tidy hung at the side of the glass, while she fastened the heavy gold brooch at her throat.

William would clump upstairs in his tight boots to get his silk hat out of the cardboard box under the bed, and stand there, as often as not, polishing the hat with his sleeve, and watch her while she put on her veil: pinching up her mouth and twisting the screw of veil tight and snug under her chin. "Saucy Jane" he called her and chuckled, in his humorous way, and stumped off downstairs chuckling; and her long face would get pink and pleased. Then they both put on straight, cold faces and walked slowly, in a proper manner, to church through the empty Sunday streets, she with her hands in her muff; saying very little; speaking, when they spoke, out of the corners of their mouths, sideways, at one another. Miss Miniver would be there, greeting friends in the churchyard, leaning on her cane, with the new girl, very prim, in black, walking little to the side and two steps behind her. Jane gave a little bob of the knee to Miss Miniver, she hoped she knew her place — just as she would never have dreamt of bringing her own girl to church, which would be aping gentry — and sailed on haughtily down the aisle, looking neither to right nor left, to the Chirp pew. The Chirps were among the most respected people in the parish. She stood and knelt and dug her nose in its prickly veiling into the fur of her muff, and stood and sang with head erect and hymnbook held low, well out over the back of the pew in front — the vicar's wife had a new bonnet on, with violets — and sat stiffly at attention during the sermon, and sang, lids lowered, pink and proud, while William stepped out of the pew to take the collection. Resting the hymnbook on her muff she felt with a right-hand finger in the round hole above the button of her left-hand glove and drew out the sixpence William had given her and dropped it into the bag, and turned to hand the bag to the pew behind, her eyes avoiding Mr. Chirp waiting in the aisle in his best broadcloth and his hair sleeked down with water, and turned back and went on singing. When they came out of church she spoke kindly to Mrs. Gilpin, asking after her rheumatism, and respectfully to the vicar's wife who called her to speak about the sale-of-work, and she and Mr. Chirp walked back to The Elms;

then, because this was not the vicar's Sunday for coming to tea, she took off her purple dress and laid it on the bed, to save it, until evening service.

In the morning she saw him off after breakfast, holding his hat for him in the hall while he stamped and grunted into his overcoat. She shut the front door behind him and turned back to the kitchen to bustle up the girl over the Monday wash, and went upstairs to make the bed.

The window cord was broken in their room. Must mention it. She put down the upper sash an inch to air the room and looked out over the lace curtain at the patch of road in front of each gate. Cold and wet, December already. She straightened the things on the chest of drawers, her brush and backglass and William's case of razors, and emptied the toilet tidy, and went across the passage to give the second bedroom its weekly airing. The room was small, over the dining room, and stuffy, shut up. Emily's room, that must have been. Jane pinched her mouth in the small mirror over the chest and gave the window, grudgingly, a couple of inches at the top. Well, Emily hadn't bothered them much, not since that Sunday back in October. Have them coming round Christmas time, most likely. She went down to watch the girl at her mangling and see about the dinner: the cold joint and the remains of yesterday's pudding.

"The window cord's gone, upstairs," she told William, watching him chip warily at the gaping mutton leg.

"Eh? Ah?"

He ate up quickly and was off back to the shop. Busy day, Monday. When the door had slammed she went out to see to the girl's hanging out the linen in the garden and took a cup of tea, with her mending, into the back parlour. Presently she went upstairs to shut the windows before it got dark.

"Expect we'll have Emily round for Christmas," she said chattily when he'd got his pipe going.

"Eh? Don't want them round."

He never wanted to be talked to much of an evening. You couldn't expect it, tired like he was.

But when they were walking back from church next Sunday, he in his silk hat and she with her hands prim in her muff, her eye went up as they got to the gate and rested on the upstairs window. "How about that window cord," she said in a low, Sunday voice, straight forward into her collar. "Did you tell someone to come about it?"

"Cord? Eh?" He shut the gate behind them and they went on around the drive, still talking in low voices in case one of the neighbours should overhear, or someone in the road.

"Yes," she said. "What I told you. It's gone in the lower sash."

"Don't want to open the lower sash." He fitted his key in the door. "That don't matter."

Jane was shocked. She never did want to open the lower sash, but you didn't leave things unmended like that. Letting property deteriorate. Soon go to rack and ruin.

"It would be nice if we could have that window mended," she suggested cautiously on Tuesday, when he was going out after lunch. He wasn't so busy on Tuesdays.

"Window? Oh-ah."

"It's only the cord," she said apologetically.

"Well, you see to it then. That's right, you see to it."

"I don't know who to get," she said. "If you could call in somewhere on your way."

"Oh, all right." He snatched the hat from her. "I'll drop in and send him up." He went out and the door slammed.

He wasn't too pleased, but you had to keep him up to the mark, for his own good as you might say. It was just that he was so busy, William was, that he hadn't got time to think of things.

"Did you tell anyone to come about the window?" she asked timidly at breakfast.

"Coming round today."

It was Emily's letter that had put him out. Emily writing to ask could they come Christmas Day. He pushed it over at her, looking the other way. "Here."

"I thought they'd want to," she said, putting the letter unfolded beside her plate and glancing down at it between mouthfuls. "What will you say to her?"

"Tell her they can't."

As he was going out he said, "You can write that letter. Say we can't do with them."

He said no more about it at dinnertime, and when he'd gone out again Jane went in and dusted the front parlour, although it was the middle of the week, because she hadn't got anything much to do and she wanted to think about Emily's letter.

After all it was his own flesh and blood, it didn't seem right in a way. Christmastime too. It wasn't as if they ever had much in the way of company. Parlour hadn't been opened up since that day back in October, excepting for the twice Mr. Peat had come in to tea Sunday. Come to think of it, William hadn't chick nor child excepting Emily. It didn't seem right cutting her off in that way.

"I been thinking," she said when he had lit his pipe and warmed himself. "About Emily. It hardly seems right not to let her come here for the once, seeing it's Christmas."

He looked round at her, the pipe between his teeth and his bent hands cupped over the flames. "What's that? Emily? You want her here?"

Her hands, with the crochet, dropped to her knee. "It isn't that, William, but it doesn't seem kind, your own daughter. Christmas too."

"Christmas, eh?" He turned back to the fire, pulled at his pipe. "Look here, we don't want any rubbishing holly and geegaws."

"No, William."

The pipe stem nodded at her. "No rubbishing non-sense, see? If they like to come here and eat their dinner, quiet and decent, well...." He paused and pointed. "They can come."

"Yes, William."

Her hands picked up the crochet and went on busily. Get the antimacassar done for the big chair anyhow, before Christmas, and a bit of a runner for the piano. Curtains want washing. Get the place looking nice. It isn't as if we ever had a lot of company. Once in a while like that.

At ten o'clock William got down to rake out the fire. When he got up his little blue eyes searched Jane with a distant, puzzled look, as if there were something to be done and he couldn't remember what. "You write that letter then," he said, getting up stiffly from the hearth and dusting the knees of his trousers. "Tell her I say they can come."

It wasn't as if they had people every day. It was quiet enough, when they were alone. It made a bit of a change when she went out to shop now with the shops all trigged up with bits of holly and coloured paper, to pick up a little thing here and there, so as it wouldn't make much of a hole in the house-keeping money, to brighten the place up for Christmas. A pink, crinkly frill for the ham, and some red ribbon to make bows for the parlour candlesticks. She hadn't got much to buy, for William sent down the things, a big bag of flour and little, tight packets of fruit and peel; she set the girl to work stoning raisins and fussed after her while she boiled the pudding.

She had the parlour fire laid without asking William and put a match to it herself when she came back from church, just before they were due. And there were the red bows on the candlesticks and little bunches of holly in the two vases on the mantelpiece, well away from the wallpaper.

"My word, Ma," said Emily, "you've made the old place look quite gay."

Emily wasn't so silly as she'd been before. She and Jane sat together after dinner, whilst William and Jim were smoking in the back parlour; and it was quite a change really having Emily to talk to. It was a pity she and Jim lived so far off, over at Toddleton.

Presently William came in with Jim after him. Jim said he'd go and see to his horse he'd left tied up in the drive, they'd have to be getting back soon.

"You aren't going yet?" said Jane. "We've only just lit up."

William came over to the fireplace. "Don't want these candles lit, with the lamp."

"Oh leave them, Pa," said Emily. "They look nice."

He grunted and settled himself in the armchair. Jim came back from seeing to the horse and Emily played a carol on the tinkly piano. William strolled about the room. After a few minutes he halted by the fireplace and blew out the candles. "Catch on fire," he muttered. "With these rubbishing ribbons."

After tea they went out to the door to watch Emily climb into the trap while Jim lit the lamps.

"Goodbye, Pa," said Emily. "Goodbye, Ma. Be seeing you sometime soon."

William strolled out on to the frosty drive. "You'll be able to drive over sometime," he muttered, "when the weather gets better. Getting on spring. Getting on for summer weather."

Jim got up and turned the trap into the road and leaned over to shut the gate. As soon as they had gone William went down the drive to make sure the gate was shut properly, then he came in and raked out the parlour fire. With a sigh Jane picked up her crochet from the sofa as William's hand went to the lamp. Funny how careful he was, she thought, going to her chair in the smoky back parlour. Funny, when he was quite well off as you might say, to be so careful. Not close, you couldn't call him close. Careful. Still, it was a good fault, a fault on the right side.

Chapter IV

With the spring, Jane put on the silk mantle over her dress, instead of the cloth jacket, when she went to shop. She tapped along the High Street, in her high buttoned boots, with her gloves buttoned tight, in the fine, spring sunshine; with downcast lids past Chirp's and head up round the corner into Market Street. When she had given her order at Peel's she tapped back, head up past Maggit's, to the Market Square. On Saturdays now the Square was busy and bustling, the pens full of lambs and young calves; earlier in the week it was large and empty, and on most days a carriage or two would be drawn up in the High Street, in front of Chirp's or the bank, horses waiting by the kerb, with an occasional, lazy chink of harness and a man in livery at their heads. Now and then, every few weeks, Jane stopped at the draper's for a skein of thick, white crochet cotton or a card of linen buttons.

She got back to The Elms in time to scold the girl on with the dinner, and sat and ate opposite Mr. Chirp and saw him off for the afternoon. As it grew warmer he left off his overcoat, but she still took the hat down for him from the rack and waited in the hall until the door had slammed. When he had gone she took her mending into the back parlour which looked out over a row of laurel bushes at the garden: spring greens and potatoes and on Monday and Tuesday the weekly wash. She shut the upstairs windows before William came in and gave him his tea and sat with him in the back parlour, with her crochet, while he smoked his pipe. At the end of April they stopped having the fire laid; the grate was filled in with crinkly blue paper in a fan. William sat with his feet in the fender and his hands, when he forgot, cupped over the paper fan. At ten o'clock they went up to bed. In the morning Jane gave William his breakfast and saw him off and scolded the girl and made the bed and opened the window an inch at the top, and on Saturday she dusted, carefully, the front parlour. In June the handle came off the kitchen door.

"It's something or other all the time."

"But the girl can't shut the door now."

"Don't want to shut it. Leave it open."

Jane sighed. It was getting on her nerves. It was the same with the washer in the scullery, a few weeks back. The tap left to drip day and night. "It's wasting water," she'd told him at last, and he *had* had that seen to.

The handle was still off the door by Sunday. Jane sailed into church with an almost imperceptible dip of the knee to Miss Miniver, and an inclination of the head — after all she was a married woman now, and come to that she'd been more of a companion really, even then, more than a servant — and up the aisle with her gloved hands clasped around her prayerbook and William's boots heavy behind her on the stone slabbed floor. She knelt, face nuzzled in between her hands, and stood and sang. It was getting on her nerves, this carefulness of William's. You couldn't call it carefulness hardly, letting the place go to ruin. He couldn't be like this at the shop, no repairs done nor anything. Look nice, with the gentry coming in. It wasn't as if he couldn't pay for things.

Mr. Peat was getting into the pulpit. His head came up and then his white surpliced shoulders. Jane closed her hymnbook and settled upright into her seat, feet together on the worn red dusty hassock and hands together in her lap. A pleasant gentleman, the Reverend Peat. "And He spake this parable unto them, saying...." You wouldn't think Chirp's was one of the biggest shops in Jewsbury, the way William went on. And it wasn't for what it would cost, putting a handle on a door. It wasn't so much what it cost, it was just the idea of the thing, he wouldn't lift a finger to get things seen to in the house if she wasn't after him every minute. It was enough to get anyone worn right down. "And I say unto you, my brethren...." And there, it was the Reverend Peat's day, and the kitchen door not mended, and what he'd think, with the door open and the girl peeking round at him and dinner smells all over the house.... Jane picked at a loose thread of cotton hanging from a finger of her glove. Mrs. Puller looked pleased with herself and well she might, they said Mr. Puller was sending her and all the family to the seaside for a fortnight. Minnie Hallet said that, Mrs. Puller had her in there sewing. Swaggering round at the seaside, and him nothing but a chemist in Jewsbury, don't know what people are coming to. Her and all those great boys, that'll cost him a pretty penny, some people don't mind parting, it isn't like others....

"And now to God the father...."

She was getting up, everyone was getting up, with coughs and rustles and a dropped hymnbook. William was out in the aisle, taking the collection, and Jane was fishing in the palm of her glove, without looking, mouth pinched up, singing, and dropping the sixpence silently into the embroidered velvet folds of the bag.

He was standing in the aisle, facing up to the altar, side by side with Mr. Luff, the people's warden, holding his full bag reverently as if he loved it. A stocky, short man, shorter than Jane, with the hair brushed over the bald patch on top of his head, in his broadcloth, with his gold watch-chain, stepping up, side by side with Mr. Luff, to lay his bag heavy with coppers on the silver salver Mr. Peat held out for it at the chancel steps. His heavy boots were coming back down the aisle, and as he turned in beside her his voice rose throatily in the last verse of the hymn.

They walked back in silence to The Elms, through the warm, deserted streets, and as William put his key in the lock and swung the door open a hot, Sunday smell of meat and cabbage came out to meet them on the steps.

Jane went through the hall and then stopped with her foot on the bottom stair, her long, meek face quite pink and angry. "I hope you like having dinner smells about for the Reverend Peat," she said, and tossed her head. As soon as she had done it she couldn't believe it.

She never saw how William looked because she went on quickly upstairs, breathing a lot and feeling frightened. Whatever have I done, she asked herself, quite pale now, as she took out her hatpins and stabbed them into the pincushion in front of the glass. I oughtn't ever to have spoken to William like that. As if it wasn't for him to say, in his own house too. Oh dear.

She took up a hatpin again and with its point tucked in a wisp that had escaped from the bun laid flat on top of her head. It's too bad of him though, she thought, her eyes filling with tears, and she went slowly downstairs.

She was grateful to William for not mentioning it. He said nothing at dinner. He looked through her in a hurt way and grunted, while he ate, into his moustache. Jane hardly ate anything. She sat opposite him, pale and sniffing, and picked at her food. After dinner she went out to whisper to the girl to put a chair against the door as soon as she'd shown in the Reverend Peat, and then she sat pale and silent behind the tea-tray in the parlour while Mr. Peat and William talked parish business.

Monday was washing day and the steam of boiling linen filled the house, but by Tuesday Jane had plucked up heart. She couldn't be worrying William any more to get the handle mended, but if she saw to it herself he couldn't mind. Not if she was to get it out of the housekeeping and not ask him any extra. There was a shilling or two over from last week's money after she'd paid up the bills, and it was quite a little adventure dropping in at the carpenter's on her way back from the shops and asking them to send up a man that afternoon: not before two, while William was out, so that he wouldn't be worried.

His eyes went round the hall while he hung up his hat. "Who had that door mended then?"

"I did, William," she said, all in a flutter. His little eyes were hard on her. "I thought you wouldn't mind, I thought it would save you troubling, I thought if I did it out of the housekeeping and I had some left over, William, and they only charged a shilling, I thought...."

"You did, did you."

He went out to the scullery to wash his hands and had tea before he'd say any more. Jane was all in a flutter, pouring the tea over the edge of the cup. "Oh dear," she said, flustered, trying to wipe the tray with her handkerchief, behind the teapot, so that he wouldn't see, William was so angry with her when she was stupid and clumsy. But he said nothing, which put Jane in a worse fluster than ever. She went on dabbing at the tray with her wet handkerchief, in between sips of tea.

William went from the dining room to the back parlour and planted himself down in the armchair, over the empty grate, and filled his pipe. "When you want anything done in the house," he said slowly, when he had got it going, not looking at her, "just tell me, will you. I'm master here."

"Yes, William," she said quickly. She didn't dare to say any more.

At the end of the week he asked for her housekeeping bills

and totted them up and deducted the balance from the amount he usually gave her.

Emily and Jim drove over for the day, in August, and soon after it was autumn: there was a nip in the air when Jane went out to shop, and William took to his greatcoat. It began to rain heavily at the end of October and Jane had to ask William for a shilling to get her boots mended. In November a patch of damp appeared in the bedroom ceiling.

Jane saw it one morning when she was making the bed. It was a lucky thing William wasn't there for she would have been sure to say something. And only bite my head off. She wondered whether he hadn't seen it. It would mean getting someone to go right up on the roof, with ladders. Now she had noticed it she could hardly keep her eyes off the widening wet patch while she was getting up and going to bed, but she didn't say anything — no good saying anything — until the rain was dripping right through one night and she had to put a bowl to catch it. "It seems as if there was a tile blown off."

"Hu, these bothering winds." Must have seen it then, already. "Get a spell of fine weather, soon dry up." Jane left him alone — after all it's his property, if he likes all to go to rack and ruin — and put the bowl underneath to catch the drippings when it rained. It was still there on Christmas Day when Jim and Emily drove over.

"Why, whatever's that for, Ma," asked Emily, when she came upstairs to take off her things and as near as near tripped over the basin.

"It's nothing but a tile that's off," Jane grumbled. It wasn't often she had somebody to talk things over with, even if it was only Emily. "Anyone but Mr. Chirp would have had it seen to weeks back. But it's always the same, if I don't keep on at him...."

Emily laughed. "Pa was always a bit like that. You ought to hear Jim...."

William's heavy boots came partway up the stairs. "You coming down?" Tired of being left alone with Jim.

On New Year's Eve Jane lay awake watching the dark wet patch on the ceiling in the flickering candlelight. The window had been put down half an inch to let in the sound of the bells when they started. William had dropped off already, she could tell by his breathing. His head was dug into the pillow and the brushed-over hair had come unstuck from his bald patch. A bell was tolling faintly in the distance. After a bit a long, thin whistle sounded, from the railway station a mile away, because the wind was in that direction, and the church bells began to peal. The turn of the year.

She dug William with her elbow. "Nineteen hundred."

"Eh?" He sat up, blinking. "Oh-ah." He got out in his night-shirt to shut the window.

Near the end of January a patch of plaster fell from the bedroom ceiling. Jane swept up the plaster into a dustpan and carried it downstairs and threw it out on the rubbish heap, and William sent a man on to the roof to put back the tile that was blown off.

Jane left off her cloth jacket and took to the silk mantle, and left off the mantle on fine days and took to the feather boa over her cloth dress in the fine spring sunshine. The purple dress, she'd taken to now for shopping; the old one, the old black, she'd had it she didn't know when, it wasn't fit to be seen in walking through Jewsbury. Time she had new Sundays. Summer coming on. Calling in at the draper's for a skein of mending she would linger by the counter near the door where the bales of stuff were laid out. But where was the use. She'd turn over a corner between finger and thumb, careless as it were, and pass on and out with a haughty sweep of the head. William wouldn't ever let her have the money they asked. But there was her own money, she'd forgotten that, slipped right out of her mind. What she'd saved while she'd been with Miss Miniver. A nice little bit too. What she hadn't spent on clothes for the wedding.

Not that *that* had been an extravagance, seeing she'd worn them ever since. Not bought a stitch since then, the best part of two years. And the purple was good still, only a bit faded. The stuff was hardly worn, it would stand turning. Do for years for everyday.

"I've been thinking, William," she said, all in a rush so that she wouldn't be nervous, "I ought really to get some stuff for a new dress before the summer."

She couldn't be sure whether he said something or whether he only grunted. He'd pushed himself as far as he could over the fire: the last of the fire for that year, it was nearly the end of April.

"If I got the stuff from Porter's," she went on in a nervous rush, for there was something about the back of his neck, where it was pink in a roll over his collar — I really don't see why he should mind; after all he can't mind when it's my own money — "Minnie Hallet won't charge much for making up, glad to have the work I daresay, if I got the stuff, if you could let me have, I thought you might let me have some of that money."

"What d'you want now. What's wrong with what you've got."

"I only meant, I thought, if you could let me have some of my own money, William, that I saved from Miss Miniver's, that you put in the bank."

"What's wrong with it, eh?"

"N-not much, only...."

"Well then."

"But I've worn it for so long, William. Best part of two years, ever since we was married, I feel so shabby in it for best, it would go on for everyday for years if I had something different for Sundays. And it isn't as if I was asking you, I only thought, I wondered if you'd let me have a bit of my own money."

William smoked deliberately for half a minute. Jane could feel her heart beating up against her stays.

"Your own money, eh?"

"Oh I know, William, it isn't really mine by rights now, what you'd call mine, but I did save it working at Miss Miniver's before we was married, and I did think you might go so far as to let me have a bit, it wouldn't take much getting the stuff at Porter's if Minnie Hallet was to do the making up and I wouldn't mind if I didn't feel so shabby for church, Sundays."

And he wasn't even looking round. Pointing with his pipe. "Waste not, want not."

"I know, William, but it's the best part of two years and...."

"Save something for a rainy day."

He drew at his pipe for some minutes, then he looked round at her. "My poor wife...." He cleared his throat. "My first wife didn't go spending on new gowns, not once in ten, no, fifteen years." He put the pipe in his mouth and turned back to the fire.

"No, William?"

He didn't want to be talked to any more. It wasn't any good talking to William when he'd once turned away like that, it only made him angry.

Jane took up her crochet and picked at it with a fumbling hook, blinking back her tears. It was too bad of William. It was all very well saying it was his money now. So it was. But she'd worked for it, and worked hard enough too, all those years, denying herself every pleasure, rolling up her little nest egg, her little bit of savings. It was different with *Her*. Daresay she didn't bring him anything. Came to him empty handed, as you might say. All very well for *Her* to wear the same for fifteen years. She didn't have the same position Jane had. Chirp's hadn't been anything like the business then that it was now. It wasn't that William was badly off either, he ought to have a pretty penny put by, what with the County custom and the shop full every market day. And keeping three young men to serve over the counter. It didn't look like someone who didn't know where to turn for a pound or two. He couldn't have troubles, could he, that he didn't let her know of? Don't see how he could have, not keeping up the business the way he does. And it isn't as if I asked for much, you'd think I'd asked for a hundred pounds to hear him. It couldn't be much, getting the stuff at Porter's, and Minnie Hallet'd be glad enough of a shilling or two with her mother taken bad like she is, five or six shillings I daresay, she'd think she was in clover. Say thirty shillings the lot, that would be about the outside of it. You'd think he'd never miss it, a man in his position.

"William," she said, timidly and desperately, "are we very poor?"

She sat and wished she hadn't said it, until they went to bed. Never opened his mouth or so much as looked at her, the best part of two hours. He went down on his knees, then, to rake out the fire, and when he got up he looked at her hard while he rubbed his hands together. "We'll say no more about it," he said, forgiving, with a hard look.

She picked up her crochet, saying nothing. She didn't feel like it.

"Eh?" His hand went to the lamp to turn it down. He peered at her over the fading globe, angry and suspicious. "Say no more about it."

"No, William," she answered mechanically.

It was almost as if he looked relieved. "That's right, say no more about it," he muttered. The lamp popped and went out.

Jane got ready for bed. Her mouth was set tight. It wasn't any good saying any more to William when he was like that. That was his way. If he didn't want to be told about something you might as well talk to a brick wall.

She lay down and got up and went about her duties with her face set tight; when William was in and she sat opposite him and poured out his tea she could feel her upper lip drawn down stiff and tight over her teeth. She didn't speak to him half a dozen times in the week. She did her duty by him, but after the way he'd spoken she didn't feel called upon to do more.

Then after breakfast on Sunday while she was hooking up her purple dress and the bells were starting, she heard him clumping on the stairs. She went on deliberately fastening the gold brooch, perching the hat on her hair and spearing it with a hatpin. She could hear him stamping uneasily, clearing his throat, behind her.

"That's a smart hat you've got there."

"It's the same," she said coldly. With the second pin she tucked in a wisp of back hair and pushed the pin into the hat.

"Hu."

Don't see why I should make myself pleasant.

She took up the veil and lowered her head to fit it round.

"Tell you what, how about a new veil, eh? Brighten it up for the summer. Smart new veil, eh? How about that?"

She picked up the hand glass and turned round, looking not at him but into the glass, around her face, at the hair smoothed up high into a thick segment of coil under the hat brim — not a grey hair, and she thirty-seven last birthday — and the mended wings of the veil clasping the worn fancy straw.

"Eh, how about that?"

"Well," she said ungraciously, "it might be better than nothing."

She saw her face set again over the words, straight and lady-like. A good-looking woman, a fine, well-set-up woman, and knew how to get herself up like a lady. It was a crying shame.

She turned and put down the glass.

William was fishing in his pockets. "See here, how much would that cost? A real smart veil, see, and no expense spared. What would that come to now?"

"About half a crown," she said contemptuously, laying a folded pocket handkerchief beside her prayerbook and drawing on her gloves.

William dragged a half crown from his pocket and turned it over as if torn between wisdom and generosity. Generosity won. "Here," he said, planting it on the chest of drawers and pushing it towards her. "Here you are. Half a crown. Now you mind you

43

get something smart with that. That'll get something first rate, eh?" He peered at her.

"Yes," she said lifelessly.

Can't think what I said that for.

William stumped out of the room, pulling modestly at his moustache.

She slipped the half crown quickly under a pile of handkerchiefs and her everyday gloves and followed him downstairs. They set out for church.

On Monday morning she went out earlier than usual to pay the weekly bills. She had the half crown in the shut, centre compartment of her purse. When she'd got the house shopping done she'd see about it. It seemed a pity to spend it today, when she was in a hurry. After all, half a crown was something, better than a smack in the eye. Having half a crown to spend on what you liked was something to think about, when you had someone like William to deal with. It wasn't the kind of thing that happened every day. She might have a look round today and decide on Wednesday.

As she came out of Peel's she made sure the half crown was still safe in her purse. It was only twelve o'clock. Come to think of it, if she waited till Wednesday William might ask for it back. Better go into Porter's and make sure of it. Some of it anyhow. It seemed a pity to spend a whole half crown on a veil.

She asked for veiling by the yard. Come cheaper, and just as good. Pondered, drawing the webbing through her fingers: fine or coarse, wide or close mesh, with spots or diamonds, or fine, plain net with a heavily patterned border. Too fine, wouldn't wear. She chose a medium thick, close mesh with small white dots. Nothing loud, but a bit different. Go nicely if she got a black dress later on. Three quarters at one and eleven three, one and six, leave a shilling over. Might want something another day. Save long enough, might even get the dress. No need to tell William.

44

She went home with the two sixpences safe in the middle of the purse and the purse clutched in her gloved hand. Put it away somewhere. No need to spend it at once. It wasn't as if he couldn't afford it. Brought him a tidy bit of savings, too.

She wrapped the sixpences in a screw of paper and slipped it into the top drawer, under her gloves. "I got the veil, William," she said at tea, in a bit of a flutter.

"Oh-ah." After a minute he said, "Look all right?"

"Yes," she said, her hand trembling on the teapot handle. "Thank you, William."

"That's right."

When she went up to bed she moved the screw of paper to the bottom drawer, under her winter flannels. You never know, with that girl poking her nose in everywhere. Serve him right, she thought triumphantly, smoothing the flannels and pushing in the heavy drawer. Being so mean. Not even as if he'd asked how much it was. Not as if I'd told him it was more. And I could have got one dearer if I'd wanted.

On Sunday she took the new veil from the top drawer and fitted it over her hat. She drew it tight, enjoying, in spite of William's meanness, the new, crisp, prickly feeling of the white dots pressing her cheek. As she was twisting in the screw under her chin William seemed to remember about it. He came over, polishing his hat with his sleeve.

"That the new veil?"

"How do you like it?" She swivelled round, with the hand-glass.

"Eh? Bit of all-right. And that cost half a crown?"

"Yes." Well, she thought quickly, and so it could have if I chose.

He put his hat on, chuckling, and rubbed his hands. "Saucy Jane, eh? Ah-ha, Saucy Jane."

He went to the door, rubbing his hands, chuckling to himself. Saucy Jane. That's good. Hu-hu. Saucy Jane.

"I'll be down in a minute," she said. She bent down and felt

45

on the floor of the wardrobe: covered with a pair of goloshes the screw of paper with the sixpences that had been tucked into her Sunday shoes.

Chapter V

When Jane got the housekeeping money for the week she changed the two sixpences for a shilling: less chance of losing it. For some weeks, when she went shopping she took the shilling with her in the middle compartment of her purse, in case she saw something she wanted. But after a time she gave this up. Only lose it. And if she saw something she could always take a shilling from the housekeeping and put it back.

Not as if it wasn't owed to her, a hundred times over, even if she *wasn't* to put it back. If she *did* spend a shilling on something she took a fancy to. Like to see William's face if I so much as suggested it.

Come to that, she had a perfect right to all she could save. Taking all that trouble to bring the bills down, and him keeping back the change. No one else would take a quarter the trouble I do. He'd soon find the difference if he had some to deal with.

Save it in no time if I had a free hand. Thirty shillings. And that would be about the top of it, making and all. Wouldn't take much more than a month or two, being careful. Like to know how I'll ever save that with him mean like he is. Might as well spend the shilling and have done with it.

She took the receipt from Mr. Peel and counted the change and swept out of the shop with a gracious inclination of the head.

No point, come to think of it, in frittering it away on something she didn't want. Might get a bit of luck another day, you never knew. She paid the baker's bill and tapped back along the High Street. A carriage was pulled up outside Chirp's, with a man in livery holding the door. Jewsbury Park. That would be Lady Mallet herself getting out. From the corner of her eye she could see William hurrying to the open shop door, all bows and smiles and rubbing his hands. You'd think butter wouldn't melt in his mouth. Must make a pretty penny out of the Jewsbury Park custom. And me without two sixpences to rub together.

After dinner she put the receipts on the back parlour mantelpiece to wait for William. There was a pot of ink and a pen on his desk and she sat down to write out her weekly account: coal, paid at the door, and a card of buttons for his nightshirts, and the two bills. Pity she couldn't make it more. She reached for the bills. Peel's was three and ten, the three looked like a five. With a stroke of the pen she had it altered. He'd never know.

Oh dear, whatever have I done. Too late to change it now. He'd never see it. Wouldn't add up, only the totals. If he did, have to say it was a mistake at the shop.

She put the papers behind the clock for him with the change, all but the two shillings, and took up her mending and sat stiff, sewing, as if he might come in any minute.

After a bit she began to feel easier. Three o'clock, and he not due till six. She got up and looked again at the bill. It didn't show she'd altered it. If Peel's made a mistake, that wasn't *her* fault, anyone could make a mistake. He wouldn't see it though.

She went up to shut the windows, and saw to his tea, and then there he was, and as much as ever she could do not to look queer. More especially when he'd done and gone through into the back parlour, the way he always did, sucking the tea from his moustache. She didn't know how she dared to go after him. He reached for his tobacco jar and saw the papers and took them down.

"Hu," he said. "Hu-ah."

He had her list balanced on his knee and was looking it through while he filled his pipe. She was making a lot of fuss now over finding a reel in the bottom of her workbag, but though her face was down she could feel her ears going red. He never would add the bills, would he?

When his pipe was drawing he pushed back the tobacco jar and took the bills from underneath the list. He was adding up one of them. It was Peel's.

"Here. What's the meaning of this." Pushing it at her.

"What…." She dropped the scissors. "Oh dear. What is it, William," she asked, her voice all stifled sounding, bending and clutching after the scissors.

"Here, *take this.*"

She sat up, red faced, and took the paper he was shaking at her. A reel of cotton fell from her lap and rolled across the room. "Peel's," she said faintly.

"*Add it.*"

The figures were in a blur. "I-I make it three and ten. They must have made a mistake." William was horribly angry. "I ought to have seen it," she went on quickly. "I'm sorry, William. I'll take it back to them tomorrow morning, the first thing." She slipped the bill into her workbag.

"Hm. You'd better. You say I won't have it."

"Yes, William."

With a gasp of relief she got up and went across and crawled under the table to find her reel. She felt safer, coming back with her hair disordered and her face red. William wouldn't think anything now.

It always irritated him if she dropped something and had to pick it up, and he didn't look at her after that, which was a mercy. Next day she put the two shilling piece on the dinner table by his plate and he pocketed it without so much as a thank-you.

"I hope they apologised."

"Yes, William, they were very sorry."

So it wasn't so difficult after all. It was only that he'd happened to count. There must be other ways besides that.

The next week she added sixpence to the price of coal.

"Coal gone up, eh?"

"It's the time of year I expect." She could feel her skin pricking.

"Hu."

"But I'll get on the girl," she promised eagerly. "I'll see she saves it. I'll see she doesn't use so much. I'll get after her."

It was too risky, he might go in and ask. She wouldn't do that again. But if she could save a sack, say, in the fortnight, without him noticing, that would be a different matter. Then she'd have that for herself.

"I can't keep it in with no less, Mum."

"And no answering back. You don't half sieve the ashes."

All alike, these young girls. No sense to be knocked into them. The kitchen stove couldn't be let go out after dinner, on account of William's tea; so she took to saving the back parlour fire in the afternoons, lighting it just before he came in. She could take her mending into the kitchen, just as well. The girl could be getting on with her work out in the scullery. And if she didn't like it there were plenty more where she came from.

The back parlour grate was so small that it didn't seem to make much difference that she could see, it took her over a month to save the sack. But still, that was one-and-six. And she'd earned it, too. She didn't owe him a farthing on it. And with putting threepence on the list for a card of mending one week she didn't need anything, there was three and threepence in the screw of paper by the time Christmas came.

And then Emily was there, laughing over old times. "Pocket-money! Me! My word! The only pocket money *I* ever got was the penny Pa'd give me to put in the bag Sundays, and I'd put in a button!"

How Jane did laugh. Emily was good company for an afternoon, it made a bit of a change having someone to talk to. Even though you couldn't what you'd call talk to Emily: you never knew how far she might have her father's ear, for all he looked so glum when she was about. That was on account of Jim and the hole in the joint. Not that she'd ever want to talk confidences to Emily, or anyone else, come to that. She didn't believe in confidences. And come what might she was still Emily's stepmother, she had her position to keep up. And she didn't want anyone's sympathy either, she wasn't one for that: all she wanted was a bit of what was due to her. If Emily liked to talk that was another thing.

"I didn't know myself," Emily was saying, "when I got with Jim. I couldn't believe my luck."

"How's Pa treating you," she said. "We did wonder, Jim and me, how you'd get on, Pa being like he is and so much older and all. But poor Ma didn't half stick up for herself."

"Your father and I get on very well together," Jane said stiffly.

"Well, it's none of my business. Maybe he's got kind of softer, with age."

If it hadn't been that they hardly saw Emily now from one Christmas to another, and if it didn't make a bit of a break from the quiet way they lived, Jane would have got up and told her what she thought. A nice way to talk about her Pa. Calling William old. He was no age at all. He was, well, twenty, twenty-five years older than her, but what was that. Sixty, he'd be, sixty-two or three, and that was no age for a man. He was a fine figure of a man, too, when he was got up in his best. On the short side, but thick-set: with a presence about him. Of a Sunday, in his best broadcloth, with his watchchain showing and his silk hat on his head, waiting in the hall; when Jane came sailing downstairs, buttoning her gloves, and he stepped up and pushed the sixpence into her hand....

She could feel it there in her palm when she sat for the sermon; if she squeezed up her hand the milled edge dug into her fingers.

Emily and her button. Of all the ideas. Ought to have been well smacked, the little monkey.

And would have been too, if William had ever found out. It was a bit hard, never letting the child have so much as a penny for herself, a man in his position.

Come to think of it, sixpence a time wasn't much for him to give to the church, when you thought of the position he had in the parish. Close in that as in everything else.

Sixpence a time, shilling a Sunday, fifty-two shillings in the year. Well, if you came to look at it like that it was a tidy bit of money. Not much to William, but more than she'd handled herself all the time they'd been married. A lot more. Why half of that would be enough to get the length of stuff she wanted, and making up too. Almost enough. Enough with what she'd got put by, and the bit she could save.

With her face pink she got up for the hymn. She was almost glad when William came round with the bag. She dropped the sixpence in as if it were red-hot, glad to be rid of it. It didn't make much of a tinkle on the coins at the bottom of the bag. Half of sixpence, that was a threepenny bit, there wasn't much difference if you came to think of it.

Now what an idea. What a thing to think of.

All the same she couldn't resist giving a peep into the housekeeping purse when she went up to take off her hat. Just to *see* if there was a threepenny bit there. Just in case.

Not that she could do a thing like that. It was all very well for

Emily, being a child and kept short. Don't blame her, with her father mean with her like he was. She and her button!

It was funny what a little bit of difference there was between a sixpence and threepenny, when you came to put them side by side.

It would be more use in a way if she had some small change among her own money. Handier. She fetched the screw of paper from under the sheets in the wardrobe drawer: two shillings and two sixpences and three pennies. She changed one of the sixpences for the threepenny bit and three coppers and put the screw back and went down to dinner.

Fifty-two shillings in a year. It did seem a thousand pities, putting all that just into the bag. Lost, as you might say, in the big sums they got. Most likely think nothing of it. Wouldn't make a scrap of difference to them, I daresay. There were a number of wealthy families living round Jewsbury: must get a mint of money.

After all, half of it came to twenty-six shillings and that wasn't to be sneezed at. If they got that from everyone in the congregation they wouldn't do so badly.

When she went up to get ready for evening service she slipped the threepenny bit into the palm of her left-hand glove. Not that she was really going to do it, but just on the chance. In the hall, she pushed William's sixpence into her right.

Stepping out through the dusky streets, hands in her muff, she could feel with her thumbs through her best kid gloves the two coins snug in her palms. There wasn't any need yet to think which she'd put in. There they were, and she'd see when the time came.

The church was warmer in the evening, with the gas sizzling up in the roof, and not so light. People had to hold their books up closer to see the words, and for the sermon they snuggled back in their seats, a bit drowsy. The side aisles, where the Sunday School sat in the morning, were dark and empty, and there was more of a crowd around the centre aisle. Housekeeper and butler and a row of lower servants filled the Jewsbury Park pew, and many of the lesser gentry, too, sent their servants in the evening. The free seats at the back were all full. There was more of a comfortable, friendly feeling about at evening service.

When William came round with the bag Jane slipped the threepenny bit in without another thought. After all, he'd think it funny if she was to take it out of her right-hand glove instead of her left as she always had done, and for all the difference it made, falling. Catches on the side of the bag, as often as not.

When William started back up the aisle, side by side with Mr. Luff, with his bag held up so reverent as if he'd got a million in it, she could have laughed, really she could. To think of how he'd have looked he could have seen that sixpence sitting snug in her glove. Serve him right for looking so pleased with himself. Pleased as a dog with two tails. Marching up to hand his bag to the Reverend Peat. You'd think he'd put the whole lot in himself.

When she got back she took off her glove carefully and tucked the sixpence into the screw of paper under the sheets. Three and six. Only threepence really, hardly seemed worth it, but it would come to sixpence another week. After all, it wasn't as if she was defrauding the church of anything. She'd keep count, and put it back sometime when she got the chance.

Only a week or two later the Queen died, and Jane told William she'd have to go into black. "It doesn't look nice, in our position, not showing respect."

Everyone was, too, not only gentry. Minnie Hallet was up to her eyes with making, and Porter's had the window full of ready-made black. Not that ready-made was much of a catch. But anything was better than nothing, if William could be brought to part.

"What you got's purple, isn't it? That's mourning enough."

"What everyone in the parish knows I've had for years and years. It doesn't show proper respect. It doesn't do your credit any good," she cried, "looking as if you hadn't got two pennies to rub together."

"Hu. Get it dyed then."

"Dyed stuff," she sniffed.

She managed to charge him a couple of shillings over on the dyeing, and she hoped it didn't show it was the same dyed. She was almost ashamed to go out.

She swept into Peel's in her dyed black to pay her bill, and there, as luck would have it, was Mrs. Peel behind the counter. Not often she was there. How vexatious. She'd know fast enough, if he didn't. She drew herself up haughty and gracious to settle the bill with Mrs. Peel.

"Haven't you got anything smaller," she said, scooping up the change, and pushed back a sixpence.

Respectful enough, but then she couldn't well be otherwise, when you came to think of the standing of Peel's compared to Chirp's.

She picked up, delicately, the two threepenny bits and swept out of the shop.

After all it mightn't show. It was good dye. She'd paid to have the best, even though it meant charging William only a couple of shillings over instead of four or five. No one could say *she* was mean. She believed in having the best. The best was always the cheapest in the end.

They had some lovely stuffs now in Porter's. She stopped to have a look. Dear, too. But they'd come down after a bit when everyone had got their black. She'd get black when she did get it. Always looked good. Ladylike.

There was only sixteen shillings put away by Easter. That sixpence a week was so slow in coming in, it seemed she'd never get there. And she wouldn't be able to save any more on the coal now, now they were stopping fires. Not till next winter. And as for that wasteful hussy in the kitchen, you'd never get *her* to save a sack, not in six months, not even with going at her all the time. For two pins she'd do without a girl and save her wages and her keep, too if it wasn't for owing it to her position. And if it wasn't that *she'd* never see a farthing of it.

She wished she could hurry up and get the rest and spend that money, she lived in mortal fear William would stumble on it. Not that he was likely to go looking under the linen or among her clothes, but you never knew. And then there was that girl, you never knew what *she* was up to of a morning when she was left alone in the house. One day Jane put the screw of paper among her sewing last place William would ever look, and then she came hurrying back from the town in a prickly heat, for fear the girl might have been at her basket for a needle and thread. Just the sort of thing she'd be up to. But it was all there when she counted it.

She wondered where William kept his money. Up at the shop of course, in the safe in the back room. What he'd got that wasn't in the bank.

Wonder how much he's really got.

Turning out the cupboard in the second bedroom, full of old rubbish, she came across a small tin moneybox. Must have been Emily's. What someone gave her. That would be safer in a way than keeping it in paper. The box was locked and the key gone, but that would stop anyone from seeing what was inside. Easy get it out, when she wanted, with a knife.

She took the box back into their room and dropped in the coins and hid the box under the piled linen. The sheets were thick and heavy and it didn't make a bump, not to notice. But when she came to think about it afterwards she didn't much like that. Suppose William did get suspicious and go looking round. Best place really would be in the old cupboard where it was before, among the rubbish. Then if he did get nosing round and find it she could say she didn't know it was there.

And she could just see him gloating, slipping it into his pocket. All Sunday afternoon she was like a cat on hot bricks for fear he'd suddenly take it into his head to go turning out that cupboard, just because she didn't want him to. Next day she fetched it back again and hid it among her clothes, finding a new place every day or two; and each Monday morning, when she went up to make the bed, while the girl was shut away in the scullery with the wash, she slid the coins out along the blade of a knife and counted them, taking care to slide each of them separately into the bedclothes so that they wouldn't chink.

It was the end of October before she'd got the thirty shillings. She'd had to pay out once for new lace edging — it was a downright disgrace the way it was worn and frayed out under her chin, past mending — and that had put her back a week. It might be as well to wait a week or two more, there'd be the braid and a few extras, but if she made sure of the stuff she could take it along to Minnie Hallet's for her to get on with the cutting out.

She was almost afraid to go into Porter's, the day she'd got that thirty shillings in her purse, for fear William should see her going in from across the street.

What an idea! As if I couldn't be going for mending as well as any other time.

She turned over everything they'd got, she saw to that. She wasn't being put off with anything hurry. Silk: good silk was too dear, and cheap wouldn't wear. Cheap and nasty. And serge wasn't enough of a change. There was the new material, alpaca. Very new that was, and a bit dear, but she could just manage it. Have to cut her down over the making. To do him justice the young man was very civil and so he well might be, and asked if he could send. But she said no, she was in a hurry, and would he wrap it up small. There was just time to slip round and leave the parcel at Minnie Hallet's before dinner.

In the afternoon she went round again, the back way, behind Chirp's, to get measured.

"I couldn't reely, Mrs. Chirp," said Minnie Hallet, "I couldn't do it under five-and-six, not if it was ever so. Not with all the gor-ing[1], and sewing on the bands. I'm sure I'd oblige you if I could."

Jane drew herself up. "You know I wouldn't ask you anything but what was fair, Minnie, but I don't think it ought to be more than four-and-six, or five at the most."

Next Sunday, and the coal next week, that would do it.

"I'm sure Mrs. Chirp, I do wish...."

Jane held up her hand. "Very well," she said proudly. "I'm not one to stint expense."

She couldn't have Minnie Hallet working there at the house, for fear William should come in; but it really quite made something to look forward to, going round for her fittings. Minnie Hallet was so pleased and respectful, bustling up to wipe a chair for her in the little parlour with the big, shiny calico covered dummy and the fashion plates, and so grateful when Jane remembered to ask after Mrs. Hallet, who'd taken to her bed now, very bad, and she said Mrs. Chirp had got the very latest in the black alpaca, and it was going to look lovely, reely and truly. It was cut the new shape, not quite so full at the back, and two deep velvet bands going round above the hem. Jane couldn't help agreeing it looked nice. And well it might. Whatever William would say if he knew....

She let Minnie Hallet bring it home on the Saturday when it was finished, because she couldn't say to Minnie that she wanted to carry it herself, and Saturday being market day it was less likely than any other time that William would take it into his head to pop back to the house. When she'd put the dress away she gave Minnie Hallet a cup of tea in the back parlour, but she was in a fidget all the time for Minnie to go, so that she could go up and try it on again.

It really was a beautiful fit. Fitted her like a glove, all round where it ought to, and just a bit of a sweep out round the feet, not

---

1   To cut a piece of cloth into a tapering triangular form (as in for a skirt).

enough to call it a train but just so that it swished out when you walked. Lovely, it looked. She couldn't stop feeling the smooth face of the stuff — warm, too — and watching the way the light shifted on it when she moved. Whatever would she say to William? He'd never believe it was the same.

Pooh. No man 'ud ever see the difference.

She shrugged her shoulders and hung the new dress in the wardrobe, taking down the very old black, the one she'd had at Miss Miniver's, and bundling it into a drawer.

And if he did, well he did, that was all. Have to tell him she'd sold something, sold her brooch, anything. He'd never believe that, never mind. After all, he couldn't eat her.

"You there?"

She gasped and slammed the wardrobe door and ran downstairs. William back and she not there to meet him and his tea not on the table, such a thing had never happened before.

"I'm sorry, William," she twittered, "I was just seeing to something, I oughtn't to have left it so late, I was just coming down."

"Hu."

He hung up his hat and turned into the dining room. The table was laid but nothing to eat on it. He could hear her out in the kitchen, scolding at the girl. "I told you ten minutes ago. Don't answer me back." She came in, almost panting, with the teapot; the girl behind, flushed and sulky, carrying the kippers.

Thank goodness he seemed to be in a good temper. She did want to try to wear the new dress next day, if it was fine.

By the time he came upstairs after breakfast, she had got it on and was trying to see the back in the hand-glass. Pity she hadn't got a long glass like Minnie Hallet had for fitting. When she heard him she turned back quickly and put down the glass and settled her hat.

"What's that you've got on then?"

"This, William?" She thought she'd never be able to turn round and face him. But she heard her voice coming out: how she said it she never knew. "The old black. You know. I turned and altered it." As soon as she'd got it out she felt safe.

"Eh? Hu."

He had a notion there was something wrong, you could see that. But he didn't like to say any more because he didn't know, he couldn't put his finger on anything.

"Saucy Jane, eh?"

It was almost nasty, the way he said it. But he didn't say any more. He could think what he liked; even if he did think it was new he'd never find out how she got it. She drew on her left-hand glove, making sure not to drop out the threepenny bit that was there already, waiting in the thumb. As she went downstairs after him she worked it down, into the palm.

Chapter VI

It was almost as if he had a suspicious look about him sometimes, as if he were watching her. Not that he looked at her much, to take any notice of her: he never had done that. But the way he'd turn round sharp now and then, when he was sitting over the fire, and give her a look with his eyes half shut up, and stick his pipe back in the other side of his mouth. And when he went through the accounts at the end of the week. Balancing the bills on his knee one at a time and grunting over them, you'd think it was a matter of a million, instead of a few shillings, and counting out his change. It wasn't nice, the way he counted every penny as if he couldn't trust her.

She sat and watched him without looking at him; sat with mouth tight and lids lowered over her needlework, through the long winter evenings into the spring, and through the chilly, fireless days of early summer until it got hot and stuffy in the close shut back parlour and she'd have given a lot for a breath of air, and on into autumn, chilly again until they started fires. She didn't need to look up to see him, she could have told you at any minute what he was doing by the noises he made: the scrape of his boots in the iron fender followed by the knocking of his pipe on the grate, and the creak of chair springs and him breathing, Hu, when he reached up for the jar; and the ring of the pewter, dropped back. Presently she would begin to yawn. Must be getting on for bedtime.

"Sunday tomorrow." He took his watch from his pocket and compared it with the clock and put it back, turning on her. "Eh? Sunday tomorrow."

"Yes, William," she said mechanically, meaninglessly.

He turned back, satisfied.

She began to fold away her work.

Sunday made a bit of a break. There was the chance of putting on her best dress — the stuff wore well, she'd say that for it: good as the day it was made: it always paid in the end, getting the best — and the slow walk to church, with the bells ringing, and through the churchyard: a nod from Miss Miniver and shaking hands with Mrs. Peat, and smiles and bows from the smaller tradesmen's wives with their husbands pulling off their hats. Jane Chirp was still somebody, for all she was driven to scrape and save. Nobody was to know that. She wasn't one, thank her stars, to wash her dirty linen in public. If William didn't always treat her with the respect that was due — counting up his change as if it was his clerk he was dealing with and not his lawful wedded wife — and if he wasn't as open-handed as some, that was nobody's business, that reflected on himself. She would watch him sourly, going up with the bag; well, she might be worse off, be thankful for small mercies. And when she had got back and upstairs and had taken off her hat there was the excitement, for a moment or two, of listening where he was; kneeling by the wardrobe and pulling out the heavy drawer, listening for the creak of chair springs from the back parlour and digging her hand in under the linen, and listening, and dragging out the box, silently, with an eye on the door, and dropping the sixpence, with a small, breath-taking chink, through the slit. There was a tidy bit in the box by now, slow and sure, easy does it: easing in the drawer: she'd give herself a bit of a treat one of these days when she got half a chance.

And not before it was time either. For all the pleasure she ever got. Not that she was ever one for gadding about. But there was a difference. There was a long way between being a gada-bout, and the sort of life she and William led. There was hardly a family in Jewsbury nowadays of any standing, and not half the standing of Chirp's most of them, that didn't go to the seaside for a week in summer, at the very least. And there was William, wouldn't even take her to the flower show out at Jewsbury Park last year. Saying if she wanted to gape at prize marrows and suchlike she could wait for Harvest Thanksgiving. There wasn't a man among them wouldn't be ashamed to stint his wife the way William did her.

Saturday afternoon, and she having to lower herself to ask the girl for change; all through William having picked out her small money to pay for having the blind mended. And after she'd been at him for weeks and weeks, and the blind down day and night so you'd think there was someone dead in the house, and yet he couldn't have it seen to. And if it hadn't been that it was Saturday dinnertime and the Reverend Peat's Sunday next day he wouldn't have done it then. Saying he'd left his money up at the shop, and then picking all the small change out of her purse. And she not able to say a word, though he could just as well have handed the man a shilling to change.

And then having to demean herself to ask the girl.

Sailing out into the kitchen with her purse in her hand and her mouth pulled down. Don't suppose she's got it, either. No, just what I thought. These young girls, never got a penny to their names.

Having to go out again to pay the bill at the baker's, although it was only Saturday afternoon and she never had paid before the Monday morning, not so long as she could remember.

"Haven't you got something smaller?"

And pinching up the threepenny bits with her gloved fingers.

It wasn't nice, her having to go round asking for small change. It didn't look nice. It was too bad of William. It was a crying shame. That all through him being so mean she had to stint and scrape, letting herself down.

She stared after him marching past up the aisle, his broad-cloth getting baggy at the knees. For all his pressing under the mattress. Pressing won't make old cloth new. He ought to be ashamed. Thinks his credit's good enough to do what he likes, as if he was gentry. A lot he cares if I get a name for myself. stinting. And for all the pleasure he gets out of his money.

The things I could do, if I had the handling of it. In here for instance.

She moved systematically around the cold front parlour, dusting, putting back. Wiping the polished piano top and shaking out the runner. *My* work, that. Like the antimacassars and the curtains. Like anything else that's any good in the house. A bit of something to brighten it up. If it wasn't for me it would be gone to rack and ruin by now. Look like a second-hand shop, lot of old stuff jumbled up together, and no roof on top hardly. A lot he cares what the house looks like. Paper coming away from the wall, and in the best parlour too. Whatever the Reverend Peat must think. Must think Chirp's isn't so flourishing as is said.

She shut the door upon the chill, dusted horsehair and moved into the back room.

Wonder what the turnover is. That's one thing I *would* like to know. He can't be so poor as he acts.

On his desk in the back parlour there were the big, dusty ledgers in a pile, their leather backs turned to the room. Rubbed at the corners. She had never looked inside, never thought of it. Come to think, what was to prevent her taking a peep. She was no scholar, but figures must be plain to all. Five o'clock. He wouldn't be back yet awhile.

And then, just when she's got her hand on the top one.... That girl, dropping something in the kitchen, up to her tricks. That's all.

For if she hadn't got a right to look, who had. His own wife. It wasn't right, him keeping it from her. He wasn't doing the right thing by her, keeping her in the dark.

She lifted down the top, heavy ledger and turned it round and opened it. There was a date at the top, February. Might be this year or last.

What...?

Only her again, opening the back door. Now what's she up to, the sly hussy. Slipping out. Knows I'm shut in here. I'll give her slipping out.

Steps came along under the window, and the laurels rustled: that hung so thick over the path she'd told William many a time.... She popped back the heavy book as if it were nothing at all. Ah. And stood waiting.

That would only be her though.

She stepped over quickly to the window, to the side, behind the deep curtain. Ha, my lady, that's it is it. Taking it out to the ash-heap, whatever it was you broke. Think I wouldn't hear. Think I'd believe it was ashes you was taking out, this time of day. You just wait, that's all.

The steps came back behind the laurel bushes, and a flicker of white apron. The back door shut.

Only just after five, she thought, moving back to the desk, and he'd never come back early of a Saturday, of all days.

She took down. the ledger again and opened it; the pages were gritty at the edge. March. Last year, then. There were several columns of figures to a page and she didn't know which to look at. Turning back to the beginning, for he must have brought forward a balance from the year before, she found the date 1888, and dropped the cover, disgusted. The next was 1887 and below that 1886, and earlier still. Going back to his father's time. So he kept all the newer ones up at the shop. Trust him. Ten years before they were married, what was the good of that. She pushed the pile angrily back against the wall and then wiped, slow and careful, across the track it had made on the dusty leather top of the desk. Trust William to leave anything about that was any good.

There were drawers in the desk, but she didn't like to look into them. You never knew when he might take it into his head. She put away her duster and went out to see to the girl. Ha, so I thought. And as if there wasn't hardly a cup and saucer left matching in the place, and even the best set chipped that I'm downright ashamed for the Reverend Peat to drink his tea. As if I wasn't slaving day in day out to keep the place nice, and you going behind my back. You just go out again and fetch in those pieces you threw away thinking I wouldn't know, and none of your back answers.

It was getting dark. She went and stood by the backparlour window, arms crossed at her waist, holding her elbows, and stared out across the laurels at wet patches of spring greens in the fading light, until it was time to draw the blind and see to William's tea.

She gave him his tea and his breakfast, and at dinner she sat quiet and ate what he passed to her.

"Muggy today," he'd say, looking up from his plate.

"Yes, William?"

Or she might say: "The girl broke a plate again today. What we're to do I don't know, and there I am on at her all the time and not a scrap of good, you might as well talk to a brick wall, and the china all smashed up I'm ashamed for anyone to see it, but they're all alike."

"Eh? Hu."

He never told her anything about the shop.

After meals, twice a day, every day except Sunday, she held his hat for him in the hall until he was ready to take it from her; while he felt in his pockets, and in winter pulled on his greatcoat: and summer or winter she waited by the hall stand until he had pushed the hat on his head and slammed the door behind him. Three mornings a week, Monday and Wednesday and Saturday, she changed into her best black, she was wearing it now Sunday and weekdays, and screwed the veil under her chin ready to go out. The veil with white spots tore and was mended and tore: she got a new one, plain black, it was cheaper and nothing William could notice. And one spring she even bought a new hat, like the old one as near as she could get it. Though how he ever thinks I've been all these years with the same....

She buttoned the boots she bought herself new every three years — and every second year William gave her a shilling for resoling — and took the housekeeping purse in her gloved hand and walked in a stately way up through the town, along the High Street, on the opposite side from Chirp's, to the baker's or Peel's: on Monday to pay the bills and on Wednesday to get in a bit of steak or a couple of chops if the Sunday joint hadn't lasted out, and on Saturday to order the joint. On the way back, most days, she had a look in Porter's windows.

Porter's had one window with furniture now. Quite a new departure. Lovely suites, they had, in red or green plush, all matching, a sofa and two armchairs: green or red plush, with a square full of pink roses on the seats and backs, and carved wood tops. Now wouldn't that make the parlour a different place. And bright, flowery hearthrugs.

If she had *her* way she'd soon brighten it up. All this old horsehair, soon get rid of that, if it lay with *her*. Let it go for anything it would make. Ugly, black, cold stuff, with the springs gone and the stuffing showing at the corners. There wasn't a respectable house in Jewsbury had the parlour so shabby. If it wasn't for the bits of crochet she'd worked herself she'd be ashamed for anyone to see it. When you thought of what lovely matching suites you could get at Porter's, and not dear either when you came to think. Not dear at the price. He could afford it easy. And never miss it. If she had the handling of the money for a bit she'd soon get the place smartened up. The first thing she'd do is get rid of these broken-down chairs, if ever it came to *her*.

She let the piano lid shut with a bang so that the strings rattled.

Well, we've all got to go sometime, after all. And I should like to know who else it should come to, if not his wife. Neither chick nor child but Emily, and not as if he set great store by *her*. Likely he'd leave her something to remember him by, but nothing to speak of. The bulk 'ud come to me. Must have a tidy bit put by.

Wonder if he's made a will.

She took off the china globe of the brass lamp and carried the lamp out to the kitchen to trim and fill it herself. Can't depend on these young girls. There was hardly a house in Jewsbury now hadn't got gas. It was a downright scandal her having to dirty her hands with oil lamps as if they lived in a cottage, all because William was the most tight-fisted man in Jewsbury. Any other man wouldn't like to think of his wife doing it. As if she was a common working man's wife. Oh, he had something to answer for. She wiped the lamp and pushed the oily rag into a dresser drawer that reeked of it and carried the lamp carefully back to the parlour. It was time to see about his tea.

First thing *I'd* do, if it ever came to *me*, is get this ceiling mended.

Bending forward to fasten the back hooks, she could see in the glass the unsightly patch of brown laths where the plaster had come down years before, that time the roof leaked.

And it wouldn't take a man more than an hour to put a dab of new plaster over that. No one but William would think anything of it. And even if it was to be done all over it wouldn't come amiss.

The bells were starting. Jane fastened her brooch, peering

over the toilet-tidy from. one to another of the twin patches of road across the weedy drive. Dry and sunny.

And I'd give those gates a coat of paint, and not before they want it. This weather shows them up.

While she was pinning on her hat William stamped in, puffing from the stairs. "Hu. Get off in good time. This heat. Go slow. Don't want to hurry." He bent down to get his hat from under the bed.

"No one's gone by yet." She fastened her veil.

And I'd get rid of this old chest of drawers with the glass you can't see into. Get a proper dressing table with a glass fixed on, and a separate chest....

"Want to go slow. This heat. Get off in good time." He was brushing the hat with his sleeve.

"They've only just gone by from The Poplars." She put out her gloves and prayerbook and a folded handkerchief.

Like they've got at Porter's. And washstand to match.

"And here's Mr. Gilpin," she said, peering. "It doesn't look too nice, if you ask me, the fast way he walks since poor Mrs. Gilpin was taken. When you think of the slow, quiet way they used to be. And swinging his umbrella, Sunday or not. For all the world as if he was glad to get the poor soul underground."

William put the hat on his head and went to the door. "Hu. This heat. No bothering hurry. Want to go slow."

She reached for the limp feather boa and pulled it around her neck.

A proper matching suite, with a glass to the wardrobe. I'd clear all this lot right out.

Chapter VII

Not one word did he ever say as to his intention, not one word. Sitting there night after night with his knees over the fire or over the blue crinkled paper fan, winter or summer. Winter again and then summer, and winter and summer and winter. Sitting there like a carven image, knocking out his pipe: you wouldn't ever have believed he had a deep-laid plan like that going on inside his head. Not until he turned round on her, one night, the way he had. "Shut up shop, week today."

"What did you say, William?"

"Going out of business. Sold out. Retiring."

"*Sold* the business?" She just stared at him. She couldn't believe her ears.

"Hu. Getting out week today."

And you could see he was pleased with himself, the way he chewed on his pipe. Thought he'd done something clever. Now whatever did he want to go and do a thing like that for.

Now what a funny thing for him to do. To go and sell the shop that had been his father's before him, that he'd always set such store by. He never meant to move away out of Jewsbury surely. He couldn't mean to set up fresh at his time of life.

"Are–are you going to buy another shop, William?"

His boots moved the fallen cinders. He wasn't to tell her anything, not he. No more than he ever had done before. Like he'd been over this: keeping it all to himself and then springing it on her when it was done so she couldn't say anything. Fat lot of notice he'd take if she did. A nasty, mean way of doing things. He must have been planning this for months past. Jump down my throat if I say half a word.

Her needle shook on the towel she was hemming. She put the work down in her lap. "Are you, William?"

"Eh? What?"

"Are you going to buy another shop?"

"Shop? No."

So she *had* got that much out of him.

That was it, then, he meant to retire. Felt himself getting past it, very likely. After all he was getting on. Not so young as he was. Found it a bit too much for him, the whole care of the shop: put a younger man in. Likely as not he'd be going up there just the same, keeping an eye on things.

"Who did you sell it to?" she muttered. Even if he does bite my head off. *She* knew well enough he wasn't wanting to be asked questions, but she had a right to know that much.

"Eh? Chap from London."

So it was a stranger, someone from away. Looked as if he was turning it over, lock, stock and barrel. But he might keep an interest in the business, you never knew.

Wonder how much he got for it, now.

She wondered, off and on, going about her work.

Must have fetched a tidy sum, a fine, old-established busi-ness like that. Must have been made worth his while or he never would have parted. I wonder now, whether he ever meant to sell, or whether someone didn't take a fancy to it, as you might say, passing through Jewsbury, and he got tempted to let it go. You never knew. He might never have meant to give up, might have meant to die in harness like his father before him. Not that old Mr. Chirp was any age, by all accounts, when he died. Not much more, I daresay, than what William is now. He might have thought it wisest to give up if he felt himself getting past things, wiser to pass the business on before it went downhill; him not feeling up to it and you know what these young fellows are, up to mischief the minute his back's turned I daresay. Better to pass it on and turn in the cash.

What will he do with that, now.

Lay it by, that goes without saying. Maybe invest it. Not that William would be one for making rash investments. More likely let it lay quiet in the bank or have the safe brought down here, if he hasn't sold that along with the rest. Wouldn't do him any harm if he spent a bit getting the house tidied up first. Things that are crying out for mending.

She dressed herself and went out to the shops, the thin, shabby housekeeping purse clasped in her worn glove. Up the High Street between Chirp's and the bank. Wonder if they'll keep the same name over the shop, wouldn't be surprised. An old respected name like Chirp's, they wouldn't hardly like to change it.

Mr. Peel came from behind the counter, rubbing his hands.

"I want two nice chops," she said graciously.

Enough left on the joint for the girl, quite as much as is good for her. She selected a piece of meat and watched the saw biting the bone as Mr. Peel respectfully detached the chops. Not likely he would know the news as yet. William was never one to let his business get about before he wanted. For a moment, while Mr. Peel's striped apron turned away to put down the chopper, it was on the tip of her tongue to tell him, just to hear what he'd say. How surprised everyone would be when they knew. Mr. Chirp retiring? Well I never. Just fancy. But habit, and her dignity — and whatever William would say, if it was to get round to him before he put it about! — would never let her do a thing like that. She saw the chops wrapped up and left them to be sent and sailed out into Market Street and home, around the corner, past the bank and Chirp's.

Come to that, he might have thought it would be easier for her another day, not being left with the shop on her hands. Handier to find the ready cash.

After dinner, when she had given him his hat and seen him off, she had the fire lit in the back parlour. It wasn't often she did that in the afternoon, but she'd give herself a bit of a treat for once. She went out to the kitchen to make herself a cup of tea and see that the girl wasn't up to her tricks, wasting coal; pushed in the dampers. She'd had an idea. She'd have a nice, quiet afternoon with those old ledgers; wouldn't have so much more time to herself, better make the most of it. Never mind how old they were, trade couldn't have changed so much in the last twenty years that she couldn't find out something from them. She took her cup of tea into the back parlour where the newly lit fire was putting up a feeble flicker at the bottom of the grate, and went over to set her cup down on the desk and found the ledgers weren't there.

Not there? Well, where were they then.

She stood and stared all round the room. She could feel herself going cold. Whatever William would say.... But he must have had them himself, who else would have. There was nothing on the table, nor on the old couch with a broken leg that ran down the opposite wall. There was only one cupboard, by the side of the fireplace, and nothing in it but a campstool and a straw boater and an old dog-basket.

He couldn't have known, how could he. How could he have known that she meant to take a look round, just this very afternoon. She hadn't even thought of it until now, when he went out.

Rubbish, how could he. The girl of course, it must be that girl. And whatever William would say....

"*What* have you done with the books that were on the master's desk. How *dare* you touch anything in there. *What* do you mean by it, where have you put them."

"Please'm, young man from the shop come for 'em, s'morning'm, when you was out."

Ah!

"And what do you mean, letting anyone that comes to the door take away what they like without asking me. No business to let anyone into the house. How often have I told you."

"Please'm it was the master sent 'im,' 'e said...."

Jane slammed the door. So that was it. He'd had them all taken back to the shop, so that she shouldn't know anything. Just to spite her. Just because she was going to have a nice quiet afternoon.

She sat and picked up her tea and stirred it. It was tepid and too milky and she could have cried. Just to spite her. Just to keep her from knowing. So afraid she'd have a guess at what he got for it.

She sat and sniffed over her tea in the stiff, highbacked chair sideways to the fire. His saddleback with the sagging leather seat was drawn across the hearth in front of her, shutting off most of the heat. She just wished she had him there then, she'd give him a piece of her mind, him and his nasty suspicions. The desk stood at her elbow, with a high patch of unfaded wallpaper at its back, to the left of the ink-stand, where the ledgers had been as long as she could remember. Shouldn't be surprised if he'd locked the drawers, only that there isn't any lock on them.

She put down the half empty cup and got up.

If he hadn't been so sly and nasty in his ways she would never have done it. But she would now, just to serve him out. She'd see what he'd got there if she died for it. There might be something that would tell her what he was up to with the shop. There might even be his will.

There were three drawers on each side of the desk. Do one side today thoroughly, there was still tomorrow and the day after. Take it slow and be sure not to miss anything. And stop half an hour before he ought to be home.

While she was thinking about it she had opened the top left-hand drawer, nearest the window. The drawer was full of papers. Ought to be something there. With a quick look round to make sure the door was shut she sat in his desk chair and took out the nearest bundle, long, thin slips, tied with tape. Receipts. Each, one folded, with the amount and date pencilled on the outside. 1900. She put it back and took out another bundle. They were all receipts, in this drawer: tied in neat bundles, a year to a bundle. They wouldn't tell her much. She drew one part-way from its tape and opened out a corner. Peel's. They were the receipts she gave him every week.

She pushed the drawer to impatiently and opened the next. More likely there'd be something here. Business letters in bundles. Dear Sir, re yours of the 21st.... And some long envelopes. Ah. But they were nothing but printed catalogues — wholesale firms — and price lists. The bottom drawer on that side was full of old tobacco pouches. Perished rubber, with the sides stuck together. It stank of rubber and tobacco. She shut it quickly.

On the right, at the top, there were the minutes of some church meetings and a bundle of parish magazines. More magazines in the next drawer and a broken-out envelope of old, yellow photographs: his first wife, with a placid, patient face and a bonnet — so *that* would be her — and Emily when she was so-high. And the last drawer was full of brown paper and string, paper nearly folded and string wound into tidy screws. Must be every bit that ever came into the house.

The sight of the tidy bits of paper and string made her angrier than the whole lot put together, she didn't know why. It was the idea of him picking up the bits from all over the house, what she'd thrown away very likely, and folding them up as if they were worth a hundred pounds apiece. She could see him at it: flattening the folded paper on his bent knee, stamping it flat with his fist. And then packing it away in his drawer, on the quiet, with that look he'd got as if he was doing something clever. Hoarding up old pieces of paper nobody'd ever want, and letting the whole place go to rack and ruin for the sake of a few shillings on a pot of paint. That was him all over. Just like he'd leave a tile off until the rain was through, and if there was a few lumps of sugar used too much you'd think the world was coming to an end.

She was so angry she hadn't seen how the time was going. She had to bustle up the girl to get the kettle boiling and the sausages on for his tea.

"There was a young man came this morning," she told him across the tray. Quite quiet, as if she didn't mean anything. But she wasn't going to let him off so easy. "Asking to take away some books of yours."

"Eh? Oh-ah."

"I didn't exactly like to let him have them, seeing I didn't know about it."

Busy with his knife and fork. Supping up gulps of tea through his moustache to wash down the sausage and fried bread.

"But he said you told him to come." She didn't feel like food herself. Couldn't have touched a crumb, not if you'd paid her.

He gave her a look, his little blue eyes peeking up at her from under his eyebrows; went on eating. "That's right" he said thickly. "I sent him."

So he didn't mean to say any more. *He* wasn't going to give away what he wanted those ledgers for. Might be for the young man who'd bought the business, or else it was just so that she shouldn't see them. It was all part of his close, sly ways.

If he hadn't done something silly over selling the shop it wouldn't be so bad. But you know what he is, always careful in the wrong place. Like as not he let himself be had over it. And won't be told, always knows best. If I told him once I have fifty times, that if he let the paint go so bad on the front of the house the woodwork 'ud warp, but you might as well talk to a stock or stone.

She wrenched at the parlour window, the sash went hard; went up at last, to let out the dust over the dark, shining laurels on to the drive. "You haven't got enough tea-leaves down. If I've told you once I have fifty times."

She watched the girl sprinkle them, brown and wet, over the carpet and left her to her sweeping; when it was done she went in again and turned out the girl and shut down the window, to dust.

She had the rooms turned out more carefully than usual. Shan't have so much time, with him about the house. She had the front parlour and dining room turned out on Saturday and the back parlour on Monday when he'd gone up to the shop to give up possession: and whatever is he going to do with himself all day, have him wandering round like a lost soul. But before she'd really had time to think what it would mean to her, his retiring, it had happened.

It seemed funny at first, him not getting off after breakfast. Or after dinner either, come to that. He went and shut himself in the back parlour in the morning, while she was busy in the kitchen and upstairs, and she hardly remembered he was there; but it did seem funny after dinner having him sitting, like a Sunday, and she had to take her sewing in there with him instead of in the kitchen like she'd done off and on for years. Shan't be able to save the coal, now. At four o'clock he'd get up and say he was going for a stroll to have an appetite for tea.

Most days he went out like that, but it wasn't like it used to be: she never knew now when he was going to come in when she was in the middle of something, and if he came in early and tea wasn't ready for him he put his empty pipe in his mouth and hung about like a lost soul, grumpy, though how he could expect her to know by magic when the fancy took him to turn back.... It was a relief the night a week he went up to the vicarage for parish meeting and she knew he was gone for a good hour or more.

"Mr. Chirp'll be finding the time heavy on hands," Mrs. Peel expected. She had come rustling out to the cash desk herself, in her best black, a thing she didn't do once in a month of Sundays. Curiosity. Killed the cat. "It was a surprise to us, I assure you, to hear how Mr. Chirp was retired. I remember, the very first thing I said, didn't I, Tim, whatever will he find to do with himself down there at The Elms all day."

Jane bridled. "Mr. Chirp has his interests. He can afford to take his ease."

It wasn't like an uneducated man, like Mr. Peel, that wouldn't be able to read a book if you were to pay him. Now William nearly always had a book by him from the lending library. He'd sit with it open on his knees while he was smoking of an evening. And as often as not if she went in even in the daytime it would be standing by him on the floor, with his chair leg marking the place, where he'd put it down to think. When she went in to him, disturbing him as it were, he'd give a grunt and pick it up. And once a week it gave him something to do, walking down to the lending library to change his book.

As summer came on he went out more. He hadn't got the young man from the shop now, to come down once a week and do the garden, he had to do it himself. On fine mornings he'd be out there after breakfast, sticking beans or earthing up the potatoes. It gave him something to think about. It was a pity he didn't do more to it. He was always in before her, on the days she went out to the shops, and if she was a minute or two over the usual time, having stopped to pass the time of day with Minnie Hallet if she ran into her up Market Street — and whatever Minnie must be thinking of her, not having brought her any more work all these years — or so much as turned aside to take a look in Porter's window, the front door would be open and him on the step with his watch out in his hand.

"Twenty-two past twelve," he'd say. Or "Seventeen minutes past." Giving her a look from under his eyebrows. "Hu."

He never said any more than that. Shut his watch with a snap and stamped in and shut the hall door behind her. He never would have said, "You're late" or "Where have you been to," but you could see that was what he meant. It put her in a fluster, coming down the road, wondering whether he'd be out there and what the time was. Some days she remembered to look at the clock in the window of the bank. Twelve ten was the time she got home most days, and if she was there to the tick she'd just get to the door before he opened it. "Twelve-ten," he'd say, peering at his watch, "as near as near." And click it to and stamp back to his chair while she went upstairs to take off her things. If she was later it would be because she'd bought some little thing, a card of mending for his socks or a yard of frilling or a bit of braid out of her own money; and if it was that she'd hurry upstairs in a flutter for fear he'd ask what it was, with the string of the parcel cutting her finger.

You wouldn't have known Chirp's had changed hands not to look at it. There was the name up over the door, Chirp and Son, the same as ever. The young men had been kept on, you could see them sometimes through the open door, or dressing the windows on a Monday morning. And once when the Jewsbury Park carriage was pulled up outside she saw the new man come out, coming in his white coat right across the pavement, while the footman held the carriage door open, and bowing Lady Mallet into the shop, the way William used to.

Must have got a pretty penny for the good-will.

A tall, fine young fellow. Wonder where he lives, then. Must have a wife most likely. Anyone but William would have asked them to the house, so that I could have a look at her. She'd have been glad, I daresay, being a stranger. Glad for me to put her up to a few things about the shops, tell her where to go for things. Anyone but William.

"What's the name of the new man up at the shop?"

"Eh? What's that?"

A lot of good, asking *him*.

"Him that bought the shop," she persisted, in a tremble. "Who is he? *I* never heard his name. Isn't he married then? Oughtn't we to have them here, him and his wife? It doesn't look nice, in our position, not asking in his wife for so much as a cup of tea, strangers here and all, poor young thing. I haven't seen anyone in church yet that could be her. Nor him, come to that."

"Eh? Hu. Name of Davis."

As if he grudged the price of a cup of tea.

The young man was only a manager, Minnie Hallet said. And chapel. Only put in to manage. Chirp's was bought by someone that had got two or three shops, in different towns. "That's what they're doing now." Mr. Davis lived in lodgings up past the market, but he'd bespoke one of the new houses Carter's were putting up on the road to the station, so it was most likely he was thinking of marrying. Four houses they were putting up. Semi-detached. Quite small. Not half such a house as The Elms, nothing like. If you stood on the corner and strained your neck you could see the walls going up, bright red, away down the road and they'd almost got the roof on one of them. Daresay he'll be furnishing at Porter's.

She almost had to run to get to The Elms in time, and even then William was walking up and down the drive like a caged thing.

"Hu. Twenty-six minutes past."

She panted, "I got kept."

After dinner she went in the parlour to dust, even though it was only Wednesday.

Furnish at Porter's most likely, everything new. Wonder what sort of a salary he'd get, now. And not half such a house as this either. A downright crying shame, when you think of what lovely suites. Anyone but him would have spent something on doing up the house when he got all that money for the shop. Must have got a tidy bit, selling out to a big firm like that. Must have been made worth his while. If only I had the handling of the money for a bit. No good talking to him.

"I was thinking," she said.

"Hu."

Shutting up his ears the way he does when he doesn't want to hear. Like a deaf adder.

She fiddled with her teaspoon. "I suppose you wouldn't be thinking of doing up the place a bit now, getting rid of some of the old things I mean. Smartening up the place a bit."

"Eh? What place? What for?"

"Well I mean, I was only thinking...." She tinkled the spoon nervously against her cup. When he's like that. Might as well talk.... This room was a sight, what with the armchair that had a caster off, and the old bamboo bookcase that had nothing in it but some of Emily's old lesson books, and whatever anyone put it there for.... Not that she'd bother with this room to start with, seeing no one came in here from one year's end to another, and the parlour in the state it was, crying out. Well if he didn't like it.... "Here, I mean. The house."

"House, eh? What's wrong with *that*, *now*."

As if she was always asking him for one thing or another. You'd think to hear him.... As if she didn't put up with what no mortal being would put up with.

"Well, I mean, the parlour, you must see what I mean, William, you must see what it's like." She'd scream in a minute, that way he shut up inside himself the minute she opened her mouth. The tinkling of the spoon against the cup was more than she could stand. She took it out of the saucer and put it down on the tray. "I'm ashamed for the Reverend Peat to see it, really I am, so dirty and shabby as it is, and what he must think, coming here month after month and nothing mended. And the stuffing coming out of the chairs and the old springs gone, and when you can get such lovely matching suites at Porter's and reasonable considering, and even the paper coming away from the walls. It can't have been done up for years and years, since the house was built hardly. And I did think, I wondered, whether you wouldn't think of doing something to it now you've sold the shop and got that money...."

"Tcha!"

"I mean to say, I know it might have been difficult with all the money tied up in the business but now you'd sold off I wondered whether you'd looked at the things they'd got in Porter's; no one has that old horsehair stuff now, and when you can get new so reasonable. I thought you might be willing to spend a bit getting it done up even if you didn't want to go so far as get a new suite, though they're what everyone has now and cheap at the money, but you might think of getting the old chairs done up now you've sold the shop, anyone might think of it."

William didn't speak for a minute. She could feel her heart in her mouth. Her mouth was so dry she couldn't say anything, but when she tried to lift her cup to wet her lips her hand was shaking so that she had to put it down again.

William wiped his moustache with his hand. "Any tom-fool might."

Well, she let him go his own way after that. She'd done all she could. If he liked to have the house looking like it did he must take the consequences. If he liked to look as if he hadn't got a penny to bless himself with. *She* couldn't do any more. It was nothing to do with *her*. You could talk to him till you were black in the face.

She took to working about the house more in the afternoons. It got on her nerves to see him sitting there in the back parlour morning noon and night. Sitting chewing at his pipe, and as often as not nothing in it. In the bad weather he wouldn't even go out and potter in the garden, or if he did he was in again before you could look round. It got on her nerves having to sit there so still, with him shuffling and mumbling to himself the way he'd taken to doing, and turning on her if she so much as dropped a needle or made a click with her scissors. Sitting there burning up coal. Doesn't care what he spends on his own pleasure. On the mornings she didn't go out she'd fetch the girl out of the kitchen and have the stair-rods up and give the place a good clean down, or turn out the bedroom, as often as once a week; and after dinner she'd wander about the house by herself, fiddling with things, and dusting. First thing *I'll* do, when it comes to *me*, is turn out this old bamboo thing. Put it on the fire and burn it, and the old books along with it. Nasty old things, collecting dust. And I'll have these old curtains down, nasty faded old things. Throw them out on the ash-heap. All they're fit for.

Now and then she'd hear William open the back parlour door and stand there, listening where she was, and then shut it again quietly. As if he couldn't bear to let her out of his sight. The only peace she got really was when he went out for his stroll at four o'clock, if it wasn't too wet. From where she was shut, in the parlour or the dining room, or if she'd gone into the kitchen to tell the girl about some little thing, she'd hear him stamp out into the hall and take his hat from the peg, and then, if it was winter, his feet shuffling while he got into his overcoat.

"Hey, you there?"

"Yes, William," she'd say, opening the door an inch.

"Get a breath of air. Back in time for tea."

"Yes, William."

When the door slammed she knew she had the best part of an hour. If she slipped upstairs at once she had half an hour for certain, if it didn't come on to rain, to do any little thing she wanted: sew a bit of new frilling on a collar without him asking what she was doing, or turn out a drawer, or just stand, drumming on the window, and look out at the road. Only bit of life she saw, passers-by now and then. Or count up her savings. There weren't very many days she didn't do that: it was the feeling that if she let a chance slip it might be wet next day; and the girl might get poking round, any time, you never knew. Got to keep your eyes open.

It was about the only bit of pleasure she got.

Making sure the girl was shut in the kitchen, and leaving the bedroom door ajar so that she'd hear William if he should come in, supposing she was to miss the sound of the gate, she knelt by the wardrobe and dragged at the heavy drawer — first thing I'll do is get rid of *this* great clumsy thing — and slid her hand blindly along the wood under the sheets, avoiding the place half-way along where she'd got a splinter once in her finger, until she felt the cold tin. She put the box down quietly on the carpet and felt at the side of the sheets for the old, thin knife she kept there. She got up and listened and took the box and knife over to the bed. The box was quite heavy now, there was a tidy bit in it. Six pounds and three shillings and twopence, it made a good few coins, even though she'd got bigger change as often as she could: changing sixpences for half crowns and half crowns for sovereigns or half sovereigns when she got the chance, out of the housekeeping. It wasn't so easy as you'd think to get it all out without a chink or rattle, even over the bedclothes: each coin separately, through the slit, along the thin, whippy knife-blade. The threepenny bits came out first, the two threepenny bits for next Sunday, and then the half sovereigns and a sixpence, and the two shilling piece, and the sovereigns, and then the half crowns and pennies. Separately, on to the bedspread. Three sovereigns and five half sovereigns and four half crowns and a florin, and the sixpence and two threepenny bits and two pennies. They were there all right. Six pounds three shillings and tuppence. It was a tidy sum, a tidy bit to have got put by. When you came to think how she'd had to scrape and save to get it. Nine years it had taken her to get that saved, and it would have come to more, a good bit more, if she hadn't had to spend now and then, getting little things for herself. Three times she'd had to buy herself boots, throwing out the oldest pair in the ashpit, when it was getting on for dark, and raking over the ashes so William wouldn't notice. Though it was a thousand pities, they'd have stood another mending; done just for slopping around the house; but William might smell a rat if he was to see too many pairs lying about. And now there was her best black alpaca, that she'd worn for Sundays and shopping the best part of nine years, so rubbed she was almost ashamed to go out in it. Beginning to give at the seams. She picked up a sovereign and turned it over, and a half sovereign. Thirty shillings that stuff had cost her. Come to that she could do it again easy. But it seemed a pity in a way, made such a hole. Take more than a year to get it back. And she never knew when she might want it worse. Hang on a bit longer.

She collected the coins and slid them back as quietly as she could into the tin box. Don't altogether like that box, now, with William about all the time. Might find something quieter. She put back the box and knife under the sheets and tidied her hair, tucking in the ends with a hat-pin, and got down into the hall before she heard the gate. She slipped into the back parlour and sat down and picked up her sewing.

She heard him shut the door and hang up his hat.

"You there?"

"Is that you," she said tonelessly, coming out. She went into the kitchen to tell the girl about the tea.

When she went up to bed she looked through her top drawer and hunted out an old glove, gone too bad for anything. A nice little bag that would make. And as soon as William had gone out the next afternoon she slipped up and got to work on it, cutting off the fingers and joining it up and running a string round the top. The gate went before she'd done. Next day was Sunday, but on the Monday afternoon she was able to get at it and finish, and put the money in, six pounds three and eight, out of the box; and slip the box back where she had found it years before, among the rubbish in the cupboard in the small bedroom. Next day she changed the florin and one of the sixpences for a half crown out of the housekeeping purse, and put the sixpence alone in the middle compartment to remember to change it for three-pennies when she went out on Wednesday.

After that it rained for two or three days and she had him about the house. She dusted the front parlour one afternoon and the dining room another, taking down the curtains to shake, and the plush cloth and underfelt from the dinner table. That's a nice bit of mahogany. Good solid piece of furniture. One of the most valuable things in the house, I shouldn't wonder. Wonder what that would fetch, now.

She dug a lump of wax out of the tin and polished the table.

Might sell that, another day. Shouldn't want a great heavy table like that if I was by myself. Turn in a bit that would come in handy for something else. Something wanted worse.

She heard him come out of the back parlour and stand and go in again. In a minute, passing the door to put away her wax and rag in the kitchen, she could hear him pushing at a drawer. The desk, that would be. In a mighty hurry, for fear I'd come in. So *that's* it. Looks out to see what I'm doing, so I won't hear.

She slipped her things away and tiptoed back to the dining room door and stood listening. She couldn't hear him do any more.

Of all the sly deceitful ways! Looking in his drawers and afraid I'll know. Then he's got something there wasn't there before, I'll be bound. Papers he brought from the safe most likely, when he gave up the shop. Might be anything. Might be his will, come to that.

I wonder now.

After tea she went and sat with him in the back parlour, with her needlework. Mending an old sheet, turning it side to middle. She sat upright on her high chair with the sheet draping her knees and snipped with her scissors at the centre edge of the thin, worn linen. At her elbow there was his desk, with the drawers shut tight.

Catch him leaving a chink.

She put down the scissors with a click and took hold of the sheet firmly to tear it downwards from the cut hem. William grunted and shifted his boots. The sheet divided in long, rasping tears; he moved his pipe from one side of his mouth to the other and edged forward on the sagging chair-seat, cupped his hands closer over the fire. Doesn't like that. Then he can lump it. Can't bear for me to be doing anything when he's in. Like to know when he expects me to do any work, with him sitting here day in day out, taking up the only room in the house. Sitting there burning up coal.

She gave a last, sharp tear and snipped through the bottom hem.

I wonder now, whether he ever made a new will.

Dropping one half of the sheet in a limp mound at her side she took up the other and began to hem the torn edge.

Likely he would, when he sold the shop. That altered things in a manner of speaking. Depend how he'd worded it, that's to say. "All my property" now, that wouldn't need any altering. "All of which I die possessed," that's how they put it. Wrap it all up so you can't make head or tail, all has to be put proper. Wonder if he ever had anyone to help him with the drawing up. Wouldn't pay a penny piece to the lawyers if he could help it, you can depend on that. "To my dear wife," that's how it ought to be. "All of which I die possessed."

He took up the poker and rattled the embers together in a small heap in the middle of the grate; pulled in his chair. The room was getting cold.

Jane shivered. Have a look one of these days and see what he's got there that he's keeping so quiet. I don't call it nice, hiding things away like that. Any other man would let his wife know what provision he'd made for her. Keeping me in the dark.

He pulled out his watch and stared at it, shuffling his feet. "Hu. Two minutes to."

She ran her needle in and out of the hem and began to fold the sheet.

"Hu. Hm." He held the watch to his ear, stared at it, waited. Listened, stared, pushed it into his pocket. "Ten o'clock. Hu. Time for bed." He got down on his knees, stiffly, and raked the faint embers into a thin layer over the bars.

No, I don't call it nice. She put her work, folded, on her chair with the work basket on top, and went out to light her candle on the hall table before William put out the lamp. She lit his candle for him from hers as she always did and took her own and went up the dim, steep stairs leaving William's to flicker in the dark well of hall while he saw to the fastening of the front door. First chance she got she'd have a look and put an end to this hole and corner way of going on.

Next morning he took himself off into the garden after breakfast. She could see him from the kitchen window while she was giving her orders: raking at a rough patch of ground where the potatoes had been dug up, with his old overcoat flapping round his legs and his pipe in his mouth. Burning up money.

When she went out into the hall on her way upstairs the back parlour door was standing open. Through the window she could see him with his back to her, getting down to pick up something from the ground. What an old man he was getting to look. It wouldn't take her half a minute to find out which drawer he'd put things in fresh. William straightened himself up and went on raking.

Hadn't been touched, not that one. The same old packets of bills, tied up with tape. William was getting to the end of a row, have to take care or he'd be turning round. She pushed the drawer in, crooked, and had to wrench it out again to get it in straight. Oh dear! But he never could have heard, with the window shut. Better leave the rest for another time. She went on upstairs and tidied the room quickly, pushing her brush and comb in the drawer, folding his nightshirt and her nightgown. When she had done she called down to the girl to come up and help her turn the mattress.

You would think she would have had the place to herself for a bit at four o'clock. Four to the tick, he always went out, regular as the clock. Watching for the hand to jerk up to the hour. "Breath of air before tea."

But by the time he'd got his hat on and the front door open the rain was spotting the steps and he turned in again. How vexatious. Hung up his hat and came back to his chair and sat himself there till tea was ready.

And she didn't really like to look through his drawers even when he went out the next afternoon. It was a dull, cloudy day; might come on to rain at any minute. And if he should take it into his head to come back, and come around by the garden, he'd see her standing there and want to know what she was doing. Not that he ever did do such a thing as come round the back way, but you never knew what he might take it into his head to do just to be contrary. And not that she hadn't a perfect right, if ever anyone had. But she didn't feel really safe until he'd got off to parish meeting the next night, in his broadcloth gone green at the collar, and then she did manage to take a good look at last, right through all: and believe it or not, there wasn't one single thing different from when she'd looked before.

All in the bank, will and all. If he ever made a will, that is.

Suppose he hadn't, now, just where did she stand? There wasn't any doubt about her rights, his lawful wife and all, but right wasn't Law, anyone knew that. She believed she'd heard once that in the case of a man like him dying intestate as they said, it would fall to his wife for her lifetime and after her to his children. Or it might be it would all come to her for good. Well, that wouldn't make much difference to her, either way, once she was dead and gone. Come to the same thing. So long as he hadn't made a will leaving all to Emily. But he never would do that.

She didn't like Emily so well, either, as she had done, come Christmas, and she and Jim there again. Emily'd changed for the worse this last year, sillier than ever she was. And didn't like the way she talked, it wasn't nice. Talking like that about her Pa.

"Seems to me Pa's showing his age." Bright as you please, bouncing on the parlour sofa so that the old springs twanged. Not that it took much to do that, nasty broken old things. Been putting on weight though. Come to the time of life she'll spread abroad. Too stuck-up and pleased with herself altogether. "Poor old Pa, it's breaking him up, having nothing to do with himself."

"He's got his interests," Jane said tartly. "Your Pa's an intelligent man. Not like some." Like that great Jim. A great hulking fellow like that, coming here with his check suits and whistling in the house. Ought to know better at his age. Breaking up, is he? You're ready enough to see it, I must say.

It wasn't too nice, when you came to think of it.

Not that he wasn't older than he had been, there was no getting away from that. You could tell by the way he'd taken to stooping. Even going up with the bag he didn't hold himself so straight as he used to. Getting quite the old man. All the same, it wasn't Emily's place to remark on it, as if she was glad her Pa was getting on, waiting to step into his shoes. Not that she was ever likely to come into much. William wasn't that sort of a man. He knew his duty too well for that. Had too much nice feeling.

Poor William, he wasn't so young as he had been. While she was dusting the back parlour sometimes she could see him out in the garden: picking up the hoe as if it was too heavy for him, as if it hurt him to bend. Too much for him altogether, all that heavy work, anyone else would get a man in to do it. Even if it was only a boy. Plenty of boys would be glad to come in for a day's work, or a half-day even a week, or even if it was after school of an evening now the days were longer, and thankful to do it, too. A man of his age working like a black slave for the sake of a shilling or eighteen pence a week. But that's William all over, you might as well save your breath.

She watched him going up with the bag, stamping up the aisle by the side of Mr. Luff. And Mr. Luff didn't look half so feeble as he did, and yet he wasn't a much younger man, nothing to speak of. I really do believe it's broken him up retiring as he did, as you might say before his time. Ah well, she sighed, holding the hymn-book well out over the pew top, pursing up her mouth for the last verse. We've all got to go sometime. None of us getting any younger.

It preyed on her mind, sometimes, the way she wasn't getting any younger herself. Sometimes while she did up her hair in the morning she would notice the grey that was creeping into it, in front, in the part that was put up over the pad. When she took the hand-glass and turned round, craning her neck to see in the small, blurred glass, her back hair and the bun that was coiled flat and neat on top was as brown as ever it was. Come to think of it she might as well get herself that new dress now, spend a bit on it while it was some good to her. If she waited much longer she'd be too old to spend it at all. Wouldn't make much difference to her once her hair'd gone white if she wore one thing or another.

Next time he was up at the vicarage for parish meeting she got out the bag and tipped her money on to the bed; with the candle by her on the commode: a wavering, sickly pool of light over the bed, fading on the carpet. She sorted the heap of spilt coins and laid them separate and flat on the greyish white counterpane: brown coppers and leaden silver pieces and dirty yellow gold. I don't know, she thought. Might want it worse another day. She couldn't make up her mind.

Grudgingly she pulled a sovereign towards her over the thick, matt cotton cover, and a half sovereign after it. Shan't have so many more chances to spend it perhaps. May as well make myself decent.

Resting on two fingers, a finger on each coin, she dug the cold, hard disks of metal into the yielding cotton. Keep it for a rainy day. Once it's spent it's spent. Always thought I'd give myself a bit of a treat one day. Don't know though, not much chance of that now. And if I was on my own I wouldn't need it.

Ten years, she'd had that alpaca.

If I had a decent dress to my back I *would* be able to hold my head up.

With sudden decision she pushed back the smaller coin and took up the sovereign, weighing it in her hand.

No need to spend so much, after all. Get cheaper stuff. Send Minnie Hallet to buy it. Ought to be able to get something off, being in the trade.

She put the money back in the bag, with the sovereign on top for the present, and felt over the counterpane to make sure she hadn't missed any, and tucked the bag away in the drawer.

Minnie oughtn't to charge so much either as she did. Didn't get the same class of work she used to. What with more people buying ready-made, and Minnie being a bit behind the times. She could remember when Minnie had her regular days working up at Jewsbury Park for old Lady Mallet, but now with the young ladies growing up and buying their clothes away in London it wasn't the same thing. Minnie ought to be glad to take a sovereign and make what she could on it. And thankful too, I daresay.

It wasn't so easy, either, even to slip around and see Minnie, with William there, watching her every out-going and in-coming like he did. She had to plan it ahead. If she was to give her Wednesday order to Peel's on the Monday, when she paid the bill, that would give her a minute or two on Wednesday: saying she didn't know, she mightn't be coming that way before the end of the week. As if she hadn't been, wet or fine, as long as she could remember. Mr. Peel might well wonder why it was, but he couldn't very well ask. Wouldn't like to.

And on Wednesday she was all in a twitter, all the way up the High Street, for fear William should have come out, contrary to his usual habits, after she'd gone, and see which way she turned at the Market Square: crossing by the bank, taking the opposite corner from Market Street, which was a gentlemen's outfitters, and a way she hadn't been more than two or three times all the years she'd lived in Jewsbury: all in a twitter up the smaller, shabbier street to Minnie Hallet's.

"You get me a nice bit of serge."

She didn't care if it *was* going out. Serge was reasonable and hard wearing and always looked good to *her* mind.

"You do me as well as you can for the sovereign, and you can have the difference for your trouble."

No one could say she was one to be mean. And if Minnie wasn't pleased with that she didn't know when she was well-off.

She pinched the sovereign from the middle compartment of her purse and put it down on the table as if it burnt her. Glad to be rid of it. Just suppose William had happened to pick up her purse and taken it in his head to look. She got Minnie to take her measurements then and there. Not that they were so very different from what they had been, she hadn't filled out much, thinner if anything, she wasn't the sort to put on flesh. But skirts weren't the same shape they were, not so full round, and shorter. Not that she could have it made too different, on account of William noticing. "None of these nasty hobble skirts, mind."

Minnie Hallett tittered. "Oh dear me no, Mrs. Chirp, I should think not indeed. I'll give you a nice bit of fullness at the hem."

Jane said she'd slip round again on Saturday week to see that it fitted right. Doing the same, giving her Saturday orders on the Wednesday. And then she wondered however she was going to get it home. It would never do to turn up with a parcel that size right under William's nose, and on the other hand if she was to tell Minnie to bring it down one afternoon you could depend upon it it would turn to rain and there he'd be. And whatever he would say she couldn't think. He'd have a fit, he really would.

In the end she asked Minnie in after tea on the Monday night, when he was safe up at parish meeting. To keep her company as it were. "Have another cup quiet to ourselves, and a cosy chat." Not that that wasn't going a bit beneath herself, but Minnie wasn't one to take advantage.

She took the parcel from her the minute she came in. "I'll just slip it upstairs. Mr. Chirp does dislike to see things left about." And if William should come in before his time it was easy enough then to say Minnie'd happened to drop in for a minute, but it wasn't likely he would.

All the same she was thankful when Minnie finished her tea and said she must get off home. She was able to slip the dirty cups out into the kitchen before he was due.

It didn't look as if he was going to notice the serge, but you never could tell. He hadn't said anything when he came up to get his hat for church. She slipped in the sixpence above the button of her right-hand glove and tripped out elegantly after him into the fine spring sunshine on the steps. It was only when he reached behind her to pull the door to that he seemed to give her a queer look, but she couldn't be sure.

She wondered during the sermon if he'd seen anything or not. He'd got so close now, he might never say.

Easy diddle him.

But she couldn't leave it alone. When they'd got home and he'd slammed the door after them, shutting out the white, bright steps and the warm gravel, shutting them in with the smell of Sunday dinner trickling out through the chinks of the kitchen door, she felt she couldn't stand it any longer. She had to know whether he'd seen or not. He was hanging up his hat.

She stopped at the bottom of the stairs, fussily peeling off a glove. The left-hand glove. "I'll just slip up and take off my dress.

Did you see I altered it?"

Just to see, you know, what he'd say.

"Eh?" Screwing up his eyes.

As if he could see any better with his eyes shut.

"Hu."

That was all. She went on upstairs. *That* was all. That was all the notice he took. So that was all the attention he paid to her nowadays. Don't believe he'd see if I hadn't got a stitch on. Oh dear, what a thing to think of.

She hung the serge carefully in the wardrobe and put on her everyday house dress, the one she'd had dyed for the Old Queen. And what a time ago that was. That was a time when he used to take more notice of what she looked like. Even if he'd never been one to put his hand in his pocket he used to like her looking nice. Ladylike. Used to chaff her about it, in his humorous way. Saucy Jane, that was what he used to call her. And now he wouldn't see it if she was to go in front of him in rags. It wasn't much encouragement to keep herself nice.

She went down and gave him his dinner.

Sunday evenings, when she couldn't sew, she sat with the bible on her lap, looking at it now and then, she never having been much of a one for reading, and watched him sitting there over the empty grate, muttering to himself, until he pulled out his watch and held it in his hand and pushed it back on the stroke of ten and got up stiffly to turn down the lamp. Other evenings she did her sewing and didn't look at him except when she couldn't help it. Listening to him shuffling his feet in the fender when he reached up for his tobacco; and later on, when they started fires, crunching the cinders under his boots.

On Monday mornings she sorted out the wash with the girl, and then put on the new serge and her jacket and hat and went up through the town to pay the weekly bills. She went just as fast as ever she could, and she wasn't going any faster: round the corner to Peel's and across to the baker's and back down the High Street with no more than a peep in at Porter's window on the way. She never got a chance to look in at Chirp's, even now, for William had settled with them to have things at cost price and even went so far as to make out the lists himself: a young man was sent down for it Saturday mornings and fetched back the goods. And William paid it, *she* never saw the money. Making out the list himself. What they must think of him. And what a nasty, mean thing to do.

And when she got back there he'd be, on the step, with the door open and the watch in his hand. "Hu. Twelve and a half minutes past." And shut the door behind her and walk up and down while she went up to take off her things.

Tuesday mornings she saw to the lamps and Wednesday she went out and Thursdays she had the stair carpet up and Friday was the day the girl did out the dining room and hall and Saturday she went out to give the orders. "Fourteen minutes past." And twice on Sundays she dressed herself and walked to church beside William and watched him, over her hymn-book, taking up the bag.

In the afternoons she worked about the house, dusting and fiddling. First thing *I'd* do…. At four o'clock if it was fine he'd take himself out, but you couldn't depend upon it, she'd given up doing that. She didn't try to do even so much as count her money except on Monday nights when he was safe for a good hour. And as time went on she got so low in spirits she hardly took heart even to do that. She knew how much was there, from week to week; it wasn't likely she'd ever get a chance to spend it on herself. Keep it for a rainy day. Don't suppose *I* shall ever get a chance to enjoy myself. She just slipped her hand in under the sheets and felt the bag; she knew the feel of it so well, what it ought to be: and pushed the heavy drawer in again. What *I'd* do, if I had *my* way….

Jim and Emily came at Christmas, but it didn't make much of a change, it was hardly worth the trouble. For all the thanks I get. After that there was a cold spell, and then it got a bit warmer, and in April they gave up fires. She sat and sewed in the evenings, darning old sheets and towels that had gone so bad they were hardly worth the mending, and patching up William's shirts, and listened to him scraping his feet in the bare fender. On Sundays she sat in church and listened to the Reverend Peat, not that she'd ever given much thought to what he had to say though he was a nice gentleman enough: but one hot Sunday, it would have been August, it seemed everyone was paying more attention than what they usually did, standing and talking after in the churchyard, over what he'd said, and then it seemed there was a war on.

William took to fetching a newspaper after breakfast every morning, marching it off with him into the back parlour. Wonderful to see him paying a penny a day for a paper, wonders will never cease. From what Jane could make out the war was abroad somewhere, out in France. It wasn't much to do with them. Though there was a lot of talk about all young men ought to join up. Jewsbury would be quieter than ever.

After a week or two, when the war was still going on, Mrs. Peat sent down from the vicarage to know if Mrs. Chirp would join her sewing party an afternoon a week, making comforts for the soldiers. She didn't mind if she did. It gave her a chance to get out. Except that it would mean William having his tea got by the girl, and he wouldn't like that. Not that he could say much, seeing it was Mrs. Peat who'd asked her. Wartime, too. Do him good for once, to see what it was like not having her at his beck and call.

It made a bit of a change going up there on Thursday afternoons. Almost everybody who was anybody in Jewsbury was there, and they all had something to talk about. Most had a brother or a son or if it was only a nephew, out in France where they were fighting, or else they knew someone who did. It made quite a little bit of excitement. Mrs. Peat was very pleasant and gave them tea, and she had Minnie Hallet there, cutting out. It made Jane laugh when they asked for everyone there to bring half a crown next time for materials. William would never be able to say no, seeing it was Mrs. Peat.

"Look nice, me saying I can't go any more for the sake of a half crown."

"Hu. Say you're wanted at home."

"And have everyone asking why."

He'd have to do it. She knew he would. If it wasn't for that she would never have asked him, she'd have found it herself. Sooner than give up her afternoons and not hear what was going on. But there wasn't any sense in that, seeing William would have to find it, willy-nilly. Besides, for all you knew, they'd be asking for more later on, if the war lasted.

The way he looked when he got out that half crown you'd have thought it was being cut out of him.

What the war was costing, that was what upset *him*. All those millions they wrote down in the papers. Though what was that to the government? The same as a few shillings to people like them. His face getting longer and longer, while he read about it. You'd think he was paying for it himself.

That and having his tea put on the table by the girl, Thursday afternoons. He couldn't stomach that. Face as long as a fiddle by the time she got in, stamping up and down the hall with his watch in his hand, and snapping her head off if she so much as told him anything she'd heard. It made her angry, to see him sitting there all the evenings so dull, as if there wasn't any war on. And half Jewsbury off doing war-work, and they said they were going to make a big camp for the soldiers out beyond the Park, if the war went on till the spring. But for all the interest he took....

She darned up his old socks the quickest way she could. Past mending, the nasty old things. Not worth the time and trouble. She pushed them away in the bag and went on with knitting a helmet[1] for Mrs. Peat's. William didn't like her knitting, he kept looking round at the noise the needles made. If he doesn't like it....

He frowned and looked up at the clock. Half past nine. He hitched-in his chair. His boots crunched the embers and he cupped his hands close over the fire. Under the ticking of the clock she could hear him muttering to himself. Bad business. Bad business.

Presently he looked round. "Hu. Bad business this war."

She went on clicking her needles.

"Hu."

He turned back. "Bad business." Bad business. Bad business. She could hear him muttering under his breath.

She snapped at him, she couldn't help it. "For all the difference it'll make to *us*."

---

1   A balaclava helmet or ski mask.

Chapter VIII

Jewsbury was different from what it had been. What with the war going on so long, all through the winter, though everyone had said it couldn't last till Christmas, but there you were. All the young men off joining up, all but those that were needed at home. Mr. Davis, from Chirp's-that-was, he hadn't gone, couldn't be spared. Jane could see him through the open door, in his white coat, serving at the counter. Had to do more himself now he'd let the young men go off. Only one he'd got there to help him. But that couldn't be young Tomkins. No, nor the other young fellow either. Shorter, and thicker set. Back behind, reaching something down from the shelves. Now who could that be.

It puzzled her, all the way round to Peel's, who Mr. Davis could have got in to help. If she could have caught sight of Minnie Hallet she would have asked her. Peel's wasn't changed, not in any way you could pick on. Mr. Peel was still there, they never would take an old man like him. And yet there was a difference, in a way of speaking. There wasn't the same amount of meat about for one thing: looked almost bare, the scrubbed boards so empty, and what there was was done up in small joints. Mrs. Peel was always in the shop now, sitting up in the cash desk, ready to pick up the news from anyone coming in, and knitting a helmet for their nephew that was out there. They had a photo of him in his khaki hung up behind the counter on one of the hooks along with the skewers and chopper. With a flag stuck in the corner of the frame. It was only when she'd got back into the High Street and crossed over, opposite the Gents' Outfitters — and their window was full of khaki too, mufflers and mittens and all sorts, the same as Porter's — that she realised what she was doing: going back down the High Street on the same side as Chirp's, a thing she never had done so long as she could remember. Well that was just what it came to in war-time, everyone having to act different to the way they always did. All but William. To look at *him* you'd think there never had been any war on, the way he'd sit....

Old Barton, that was who it was! Old Barton who'd given up years back, years before it stopped being Chirp's. Well now, fancy that. Fancy him getting old Barton in to help. Got quite the old man, too. Just think of that. That would show you what it was coming to, getting old men like Ned Barton back into harness. Just think of that. And if she hadn't happened to cross over the way she did, though she couldn't think whatever had come over her to make her do it, a thing she never had done since she could remember to come home down that side, she never would have known that about Ned Barton. It just showed you had to keep your eyes open nowadays. Fancy now, if it went on long enough they'd be asking William to come back and help carry on. Carry on, that was what they called it. Carrying on. Till the boys come home.

She didn't like to cross over again at once, it would look so funny, as if she'd gone that way on purpose. Not till she got down to the corner, by the road to the station. She went on past the shops she didn't know, except from across the street and that wasn't the same thing: the greengrocer's and a shoe shop and Puller's the chemist's: it made quite a change coming down this side, made it quite an outing. Until there was the long, bare wall of the Men's Institute, and then a row of cottages going on to the corner. A gramophone was on in one of them, playing Tipperary, out into the street. Everyone was getting gramophones now, you could tell by what a lot they had in Porter's window. In the furnishing window. Porter's had taken the sweet shop next door, wanted more room. Make a new department I daresay. She'd missed that today, coming back down this side, forgot to look on the way up. Remember to see on Wednesday. Chirp's, that was what it was, had taken her mind off it. Fancy that, about Ned Barton.

She crossed over opposite the new red houses on the turn down to the station. Half a dozen they'd put altogether, but the last one was never finished. There it was with the walls half up and the scaffolding, where the men had been taken off. Waiting for the war to be over.

And there was William, none too pleased, right out by the gate.

"Twenty-two minutes past."

Well and what if it was. She let him click his watch at her and went on into the house. Time he learnt it was wartime and things different from what they had been. "I had to wait," she said, "to get the meat. You can' t get things now the way you used to." It was as near as near she didn't toss her head at him.

She took her things off and sat down to table before she'd tell him anything about it.

"Who do you think they've got helping now in Chirp's?"

A lot of good telling him anything, for all the interest he took. Just staring at her and going on eating. But she couldn't resist telling him.

"Ned Barton. Old Ned Barton that you had, that gave up years ago, and now they've got him back to help."

"Hu."

With that blank look on his face, as if he didn't take in half of what was said. He didn't use to be like that. There was a time she used to think he had a sharp look about him, about his eyes.

She watched him picking about on his plate, the greying, sandy moustache twitching over the fork. He peered up and across at her, vacantly, and down again at his food. Bright blue, his eyes used to be, and now they'd got light, whitish looking. No need for him to look as old as he does. Can't be older than Ned Barton, if he's as much. And him working again, doing his bit.

"If the war goes on they'll be asking you to come back and help them out."

"Hu. Eh?"

"Up at Chirp's. They'll be asking you to give them a hand in the shop."

"Asking, eh. They can ask all they've got a mind to."

You'd think he didn't know there was a war on.

All the notice *he* took of the war was to make it a reason for saving, even more than he always did. As if it wasn't bad enough things being short in the shops without him buying less than he could have even. Economise, that was his cry, be patriotic. As if he was going to give it for the war, what he saved. And there were most people laying food by, what you could still get, in tins, for fear things would be shorter still, and he cutting her down so she could hardly buy what they had to eat from day to day. Grumbling every time the price of meat went up. Ought to be glad to get it at any price. Putting by, that was what he was doing, with all his talk of patriotic. She would watch him in the evenings, sitting over his two lumps of coal, and she having to knit to keep her hands warm: socks and helmets and mufflers to take up to Mrs. Peat's. Look nice if she couldn't do the same as the rest of them. And having to drag the money for the wool out of William as if it was a hundred pounds. As if he grudged half a crown for the poor young fellows in the trenches.

She heard a bit, going up there Thursday afternoons; it made you see what it was like, what was going on. There was Mrs. Bull, from the jeweller's, had had her son killed, such a fine young fellow too; and hardly one didn't know of someone that had been wounded. They were bringing the wounded back, to hospitals all over the country, and Mrs. Porter had been right up to Newcastle to see her brother who was in hospital there. Such a journey she had too, with the trains all slowed up, half the men taken off. It made you feel you were right in the middle of things. She wouldn't have missed her Thursday afternoons for anything.

She would hurry up over her housework and let things go a bit, what the girl couldn't do could wait, to get off early on the mornings she went out. But however early she was ready, and it didn't matter where William was, sitting over his pipe or pottering in the garden, he'd be out by the door when she went. Standing there with the door open, with his pipe in his mouth and his watch in his hand, peering round for her. How bent he'd got to look.

"What's the hurry then. Early off today, aren't you?"

"Am I? It takes me longer getting served than it did."

As soon as she was out of the gate she felt she could breathe. She'd have five minutes now for a chat with Mrs. Peel, and if she was lucky she might meet Minnie Hallet and hear something fresh.

She heard they were building the big camp they'd talked of, over the other side of Jewsbury Park. They'd be getting the soldiers there in another couple of months. That would make a bit of a change for Jewsbury!

And then in April, soon after they stopped fires, they got a letter from Emily to say Jim had joined up.

"My son-in-law, who's in camp." Down Salisbury Plain way he was. And Emily somewhere down there in rooms, to be near him. And then they came up, the two of them, one Sunday, for Jim to say goodbye before he went out to the front. In his khaki, sitting down to the piano to give them a tune. William needn't have been so short with him, even if it was the Sabbath, with him going out to the trenches the very next day. A fine looking young fellow he made in his uniform, and if he *was* a bit hearty in his ways where was the harm of that. Better be that way than like William was, moping in his chair without a word to say for himself except for going on about the war being a bad job, for all the world as if there was no one there. Come to think of it it hadn't been such a bad job for some. Look at young Jim. Made a new man of him. Made a man of him, that was what it had done.

"You're proud of Jim I expect," she told Emily. She showed her the work she was doing, a body-belt for Mrs. Peat's. "It isn't much I can do, shut up here in Jewsbury. Though Jewsbury isn't what it was, you'd be surprised. But I do what I can, though it's hard enough with your Pa and the house to see to, it's as much as you can do with one pair of hands. But I haven't missed one of my vicarage afternoons yet, and don't mean to."

"That's right Ma. Keep the home fires burning." Emily was improved from what she had been, the same as Jim. Done them both a world of good, the war had. Jane told her she must come over some time while Jim was away at the front, and they'd have a nice quiet afternoon together, with their work. Emily said she would, but the next they heard of her she'd gone for a V.A.D.[1]

They'd have the troops here in Jewsbury any day now. Minnie Hallet was saying they'd got the tents up, you could see from the road. Tents and huts: in case it lasts till the winter. All over the common out the other side of Jewsbury Park. Hundreds, they'd be having there. Hundreds of men. And what was more....

Jane was so excited she couldn't keep it back even over dinner. "What's more they're boarding men out, billeting as they call it. Out in people's houses, anywhere there's room."

---

[1] Voluntary Aid Detachment, a unit of civilian volunteers providing nursing care for military personnel.

William looked up from his knife and fork. "Better not come here. Pack of hooligans."

And that's a nice way to talk, of the poor young fellows that're fighting for him. But that's William all over, wear your fingers to the bone and all the thanks you'll get. And him with that nice little room lying empty upstairs, snug as you please. Be a godsend to some poor young fellow. Make a change too, to have someone fresh about the house. Not but what it'd make work, but I'm not one to complain. And the girl there half the time with nothing to do, twiddling her fingers in the kitchen. Show her what work is for once. If it was anyone but William they'd be falling over themselves for the chance to do their bit for the country.

But she wasn't going to say any more. That wasn't her way. And come to that it didn't make much difference what way William took it. It wasn't going to rest with him. *She* knew all about the forms that were being sent round — Minnie Hallet had told her all about *them* — asking what rooms anyone had empty and suchlike. William wouldn't put down something false on an official form like that, it wouldn't be like him, he'd never dare do that.

When William had gone out for his stroll she slipped up and had a look at the room. It wasn't a bad little room, not for wartime. They couldn't expect too much. If they didn't find anything worse than that they wouldn't hurt. The bed wasn't any too soft, and on the small side — little bit of a bed Emily had when she was a kid — but a healthy young fellow wasn't going to notice that. And if he wanted the cupboard cleaned out, all this old rubbish could go away in a box, what wasn't burnt. Good enough for any young fellow, don't care who it is. Ought to think himself in clover. They'd send an officer, I daresay, to a house like this.

Minnie Hallet said, "Oo they'd have to, Mrs. Chirp. They couldn't help themselves. They never could send *you* anything but an officer, could they."

107

Wouldn't that be funny? To see William's face? With a fine young officer in the house? William would have to mind his Ps and Qs, taking up all the fire the way he did, an officer would never put up with that. Not that he was likely to be about the house much, spend his days over at the camp most likely. But it would make a bit of a change, even having someone coming in and out. A smart young officer, too.

It was a nice little room, when you came to look at it, nice and snug. Better than these great barns of places. It was a pity the wallpaper had gone like it had, come away up at the top, but you'd never get William to do anything; If I had *my* way I'd soon get it looking different. And the marks where Emily had had pictures up and the paper hadn't faded back even now. Might find a picture or two to put up. Even if they weren't so big, hide a bit of it. And the mantelpiece looked bare, empty like that. Tell you what I'll do, I'll bring up those two candlesticks from the front parlour, never be missed. And there's the bows that used to go on them Christmas time, he might as well have them. Liven it up a bit. Make it more homelike for him.

Tuesday the troops were coming. Marching in. That's to say they'd come by train, but outside the station they'd line them up and march through Jewsbury, band and all. "You can depend on it, Mrs. Chirp!"

Everyone could talk of nothing else but how they'd go out to watch them march through. "Have half of Jewsbury after them right out to the camp, I shouldn't wonder."

There were a few of them about already, some that had come down ahead to see to things. A couple of smart young fellows in riding breeches outside the Jewsbury Arms when she went past on Monday morning. That would be the officers, now, wouldn't it.

Tuesday morning — if only it had been the Wednesday — she went up early after breakfast to make the bed. Ten o'clock, the troops were marching in. She could hear people out already down the road, by the corner, talking. You could tell at once there was something, it was always so quiet on a weekday. As soon as ever she'd got the mattress turned she sent the girl back down to the kitchen to get on with her work. Not going to have her up here, hanging out of a window the minute my back's turned. That's what she'd be up to.

You couldn't really see anything, even if the curtain hadn't been there: not without the window was open. The Elms was too far up from the corner.

She pushed the tight lace curtaining of the lower sash into puckers along its rods for an inch or two at the end. You couldn't really see up to the corner, not without looking right out. But you could hear them talking up there, waiting about. Where the men would have to turn round to go up the High Street. There was a good half-hour yet.

She straightened back the curtain for fear it should show from out in the road and went on tidying the room, giving a glance out now and then. Through the trees she could catch a glimpse of a cap and apron next door, out by the gate of The Lilacs. Mrs. Mace must be gone out. Catch *my* fine madam gallivanting out there, I won't half give her what for.

When the room was done, except for the sweeping and dusting which the girl could do later on — better where she is for the present, out of temptation's way — she went across the landing to take a look at the officer's room, to make sure everything was as it should be. She had a good mind to have the bed made up in case it was wanted tonight. You never could tell. They wouldn't know really, until they got them all there, how many they wanted to send out. The blankets that went with the bed were wrapped in newspaper, with mothballs, in the chest of drawers. In any case better come out and be aired. She hung them over the bedrail and went back to her room to get some sheets from the wardrobe. Put them out and she can make it when she comes up. Won't do her any harm, even if it shouldn't be wanted so soon.

At the bottom of the drawer she found some small, old sheets that would be big enough and slipped them out, taking care to cover her money again before she shut the drawer. Have to be careful with more of the linen in use. Find somewhere else to keep it. She took the sheets across and put them folded on the bare mattress for the girl to find.

Some of them were singing now, down the road. Children, come out from the cottages. It wasn't five to, yet.

It did smell terribly of mothballs in here. Dreadful. It really wanted the window opening.

It went up so stiff you'd think it hadn't been open for years. Generally speaking, you see, she only put the top down to let in a breath of air; but with all this smell of naphtha, whatever the young fellow would think.... It was enough to make anyone sick.

She took down one of the folded blankets and shook it vigorously. What did they want to be cheering for already, it wasn't.... Well, it was close on the hour. She hung the blanket back over the end of the bed and took down the other and began to shake it: and let it drop, anyhow, in a heap.

There, weren't they a fine lot of young fellows? And walking all in line! You wouldn't think they could with so many. Six to a row, wasn't it? Only the trees got in the way. By the right, WHEEL! My word, that young man had a voice on him. And the band striking up too. That would be the band in front, with their instruments. Leading them, that's it. Striking up for when they turned into High Street. Bm, bm, tramp tramp tramp. They didn't trouble to play all down from the station I expect, nobody there only those one or two houses. Tramp, tramp, by the right, WHEEL! Wouldn't have been worth their while. My word, if they send us one with a voice like that whatever William will say! Liking quiet the way he does. That would be the officers that say that, wouldn't it. What a tramping they do make, be a bit nearer and they'd shake the house. And look at that poor young fellow walking all by himself at the back. That would be an officer too I expect, they wouldn't let one of the men do that. By the right, WHEEL! What, another lot! Well however many of them have they got. They'll never get them all into Jewsbury. You'd think we ought to win the war wouldn't you with all that lot, and all the drilling they do to make them walk together like that. That's a fine looking young fellow walking behind that lot. And that funny little short one, well! I wonder when they'll know where they're going to send them. They might put them all in the camp for tonight, while they see about it. By the right, WHEEL! *And* some more.

Oh dear!

She drew back quickly into the room, knocking her head against the upper sash. Nobody could have seen her out there could they. Whatever she'd been thinking of to so far forget herself as to lean right out like that. Nobody could have seen, there wasn't anyone, they were all too busy watching down on the corner. And Mrs. Mace next door wasn't in, you could tell that, the way that hussy of hers was banging out there by the gate.

She felt so hot and put out that before she knew what she was doing she had taken the under blanket and was busy spreading it on the mattress.

May as well, she excused herself. Get it ready on the chance. Leave it to *her* it won't be done before nightfall, and you never know when they might take it into their heads to send one of the poor young fellows along. They must be tired after all that marching.

She pushed the pillow into the slip and shook it down. Some poor young fellow that would be glad of a bit of comfort.

The sheet was too narrow to tuck in on both sides, she spread the printed counterpane on top. Faded, too. But as for getting another.... I'd like to see William....

There.

She pushed the untucked side hard against the wall. Missing their homes very likely, some of them. Daresay some have never been from home before.

There was a towel wanted for the washstand. She went back across the landing to put one out herself; came back and hung it, folded, over the chipped brown paint of the rail. You have to do these things, in wartime.

Tell you what I'll do, she thought, looking round, and her cheeks went pink, I'll take a sixpence out of my own money and get the poor young fellow a bit of scented soap. Likely he wouldn't have brought it with him. Likely it would cheer him up a bit, being away from home.

It was as much as she could do to get through tea as if it was an ordinary day. With an ear to the front door in case the girl shouldn't hear the bell. And if they sent him down when it was dark, she thought later, keeping an ear open from the back parlour between the clicks of her knitting, he mightn't be able to find the bell. She stopped every now and then, at the end of a row, and listened for a knock.

They didn't send anyone that night. Likely they wouldn't know yet. They might have had room for all the first lot in the camp. They'd be having some more down, everyone knew that.

It was as much as she could do to wait for the next morning to see what was going on up in the town.

When she went up to make the bed she slipped a sixpence out of her bag and hid it in the middle of her purse, and put the bag away again without counting it. Not often she did that, but she was in a hurry, it would have to wait. She was in such a hurry to get out in good time that her hand was shaking when she stuck in the hatpins. If she could get down for once before William had done reading his paper. It would be just like him to have some silly excuse to make her late, today of all days.

He opened the back parlour door when she was halfway down, his pipe in his mouth and the paper in his hand.

"Early, aren't you?"

She fussed with her gloves. "Most likely I shall get kept, with the crowds in the town."

He took his pipe out of his mouth.

"I can manage the door," she said, coming on quickly.

"Hu. Wait a bit. No hurry."

He stumped back into the room and put his pipe down deliberately on the mantelpiece, picking up with his finger and thumb a bit of tobacco that had fallen out and getting down to put in the grate. As if he couldn't have come with his pipe in his hand like he always does. He bent to fold the paper, on his knee. "No hurry. No bothering hurry."

She could have screamed; she stood there buttoning and unbuttoning her gloves and waited for him to stump back and along the passage and put on his hat and fumble with the bolt and fasten back the catch. At last he had got the door open, and the bright, sunny air from outside rushed to her head.

He stood out on the step, peering at his watch. "Two minutes past eleven."

She brushed him by with her basket.

"I expect you'll be back early," he said, peering at her.

"I don't know." She hardly knew what she was saying. "I may get kept."

As she got to the gate she heard him shoot the bolt again behind her, and out in the road the air was so fine and light she felt she could have run.

The station road didn't look any different, you wouldn't think all those boys had marched down there only yesterday. But all the gramophones were playing in the cottages across from the turn, and through an open door she could see a khaki greatcoat hanging on the wall. And as soon as you got up into the High Street you could see things were changed, there was more of a bustle. You couldn't have said exactly there were more people about, but it was as if everyone had been livened up. She clutched the purse tight with the sixpence in the middle, but she wouldn't stop to get the soap now. Get her business done first and have plenty of time.

The Peels had had two Tommies billeted on them, and round at the baker's they'd had one. "Haven't you heard anything yet then, Mrs. Chirp? They'll be sending you an officer I expect."

It stood to reason they'd send to that class of house first, where they could send the Tommies.

When she came out into the Market Place there was a smart young officer making off up the street that went out to the camp, and then just as she ran into Minnie Hallet — of all people, just the very person I wanted to see — they heard a bugle call coming from right away the other side of Jewsbury Park. Just fancy, you can hear it right over here.

"They blow it ever so often," Minnie told her. "Out where I live you can hear it going all day long. For them to go to meals, and have their drill.

"I reely must run back," she said. "I wish I didn't have to, but I've got a lady coming."

Jane gave a glance at the clock over the Town Hall. "I'll just walk up a little bit of the way with you."

She hadn't been that way since she could remember, not for years back: not since she'd gone up to Minnie's for her fittings that time. Only three years it had been really, but stuff didn't wear like it used to; she'd be having to see about getting herself a new dress soon, with all that was going on.

"Don't you do it," Minnie said. "You take my advice and wait a bit. Materials aren't what they were, with the war on. What's coming in now is reely dreadful, no wear in it. There isn't the quality about.

"If you take my advice," she said, "you'll wait for the war to be over. It can't go on much longer now, can it."

"You wouldn't think so, to look at what a lot of young fellows they've got to fight." Jane went pink. "I saw them marching in," she said.

You wouldn't believe how this street had smartened up. It had always been a street of shabby little shops, where no one would think of going, but now there wasn't one that hadn't tidied up its window and stuck in a flag or two along with the goods. And one that used to sell out fried fish on Saturdays had opened up and called itself the Fish Café. All painted up white. And you could see the tables put about inside for people to eat at. "They'll be doing more trade out this way I expect, with the men from the camp."

"So I hear you've got an officer put next door, Mrs. Chirp? At Mrs. Mace's? Haven't you?"

"Next door?" said Jane. She felt quite funny. "Oh, Mrs. Mace's," she said quickly, for she didn't mean Minnie Hallet to see there was anything wrong. "We haven't had ours yet," she said stiffly, "they're evidently filling up that class of house first. I expect we shall be hearing very soon."

"Oo, I daresay they wouldn't like to trouble *you*, Mrs. Chirp, someone like you. Not unless they were put to it. I daresay yours'll be the last house in Jewsbury."

It was a funny thing, all the same, if they'd put one at Mrs. Mace's. You couldn't really call it a different class of house, like as two peas if it came to that; though Mrs. Mace being only the widow of a greengrocer, a little bit of a shop too, hadn't got half the standing. And that hussy of hers, she'd have to keep her eyes open. "Trouble or not," said Jane sharply, "you have to do these things in wartime." She didn't want Minnie Hallet going round saying....

She felt tired all at once. It was ages since she'd walked so far. "I'll turn off here," she said.

They'd got right out past the shops, to where there was nothing but rows of cottages. She could turn down here and go home round by the church, nearer than all the way back and down the High Street. She wouldn't bother about the soap for today, she was late enough as it was, and there wasn't any point as the young fellow hadn't turned up yet. It did seem funny, their not having heard anything.

Halfway home, by the vicarage, it struck her he might have been sent down there while she was out, and whatever William would have done with the poor young fellow.... She started to walk as fast as ever she could.

It was a mercy William wasn't out at the gate or he'd have seen her coming round the corner from the church instead of straight down High Street as she should have, even though she crossed over straight away to the corner of the station road and went up the right side to The Elms.

"Hu. Twenty-five past."

"There was a lot of people about."

The door thumped-to behind her.

So he hadn't come, or William would have said something.

She was still a bit breathless when she got down again to the table, but she couldn't wait before asking him. "Haven't you had one of those forms to fill up, about billeting out the soldiers?"

"Eh?"

"Those forms they've been sending round, to know what room everyone's got." Her fork clinked against her plate. She couldn't eat before she knew. He might have done it wrong and they didn't rightly understand.

"It seems funny they don't send anyone, when we've got that nice little room upstairs that no one ever uses. Better than most in Jewsbury. It seems a thousand pities. It might have got lost in the post," she said. "You ought to go and ask at the Town Hall."

"Oh-ah! I know what you mean." He chuckled. "Don't you worry, we won' t get any sent here."

Jane turned to stone. She seemed to know what he'd done.

"I soon settled that," he said. He was chuckling under his moustache. Soon settled that. Soon settled that.

She just sat staring at him.

He looked up, blinking and peered across at her. "I've *been* to the Town Hall," he said, his little moustache going up and down in a nasty sort of triumph. "See? Soon put a stop to that nonsense. None of their scallywags here."

Hu, hu, scallywags, bu. Put stop that nonsense. Hu.

She stared at him, she was quite cold.

"You mean you told them you wouldn't have anyone?"

She couldn't believe it, she really couldn't. How anyone, even William.... But they'd never listen to him. Soon as they wanted the room....

"Thompson knows me well enough. He soon had it put right. They aren't going to want half the room they been asking for."

Soon-put-it-right. Soon-put-it-right.

She couldn't help it. She said, "I should have thought you'd have been glad, with the war on, and those poor young fellows...."

It wasn't any good talking to him, you might as well talk to a brick wall. And to think that now in wartime he'd take a mean advantage just on account of knowing Mr. Thompson at the Town Hall. That would show you what he was. And if ever it was to get about Jewsbury, what he'd done, she didn't know how she'd ever lift up her head again. She really didn't know how she'd ever be able to lift her head up at the vicarage on Thursday afternoon, for fear someone should have heard.

When she went upstairs before tea, when he'd taken himself off — and he'd be back before you could look round — she took the sixpence from the middle of her purse and put it back in the bag. No point in having it about now, only get lost or mixed with the housekeeping and William stick to it like a leech if he got half a chance. She turned out the bag and counted over her money half-heartedly, she couldn't give her mind to it, she was so upset. Threepence short, she must have counted wrong. She put William out of her head for a minute and checked it over sharply. Seven pounds three and two, correct. She put it back in the bag and drew the strings tight and tied them. And to think, that she'd been ready to spend out of her own money to give some poor young fellow a bit of comfort, and there was William so mean he grudged even the use of a room that wouldn't have cost him a penny beyond a drop of oil or a few candles. So afraid he'd have to give the boy a bit to eat now and then, more than he'd been paid for. That was all he thought about, how he might have to spend something. A lot he thought about the poor young fellows that were fighting for him. Oh dear, she *was* upset. She hadn't got the heart to go in and take the sheets off the bed, she really hadn't. And she wasn't going to, either. It didn't follow they were going to listen to him, even if he had managed to get Mr. Thompson's ear. Come to that what was Mr. Thompson, only the Town Clerk, he wouldn't be able to help himself if he was told by someone higher up. If he got all those generals there, wanting the room, he wouldn't pay much attention to what William said. It wasn't even as if William was still Chirp's.

"You there?"

She went down and poured out his tea. He looked so pleased with himself she could have thrown it at him.

She really hardly liked to go up to the vicarage the next day. But when she got there she was glad she had. Everyone was so nice and friendly and they all had something to say. Most had had some Tommies billeted on them, and Mrs. Porter had an officer, but some hadn't heard yet. "I expect it'll be your turn next, Mrs. Chirp, when the new lot come in." It didn't seem as if anyone knew about William going to the Town Hall. And Mrs. Ted Ridge, from out the other side of Jewsbury, had had her son killed, poor young fellow. It made your heart bleed to see her, going on cutting out bodybelts[1] for some other young fellow that might be the next to go. "But there, you have to carry on." It was a nice, friendly little meeting, and it did you good to get out for a bit, hear what was going on. You didn't see much of the troops about in Jewsbury till

---

1 A knitted garment worn under clothes and around the midriff.

the evening, someone was saying, because they kept them doing their drill in the daytime, out at the camp. But they'd taken them out for a march this afternoon, out the other way towards Toddleton, and some days they'd bring them down through Jewsbury. It was pleasant with everyone sitting round and talking. A bit of a difference from sitting shut up there with William evening after evening. Him without a word to say for himself. If it hadn't been for her knitting that she tried to do as much of as she could each week to take up to Mrs. Peat's on Thursday, she really didn't know what she would have done.

And he grudging her the money even to get the wool. That was all he thought about, what he could save. Cutting down the rations smaller and smaller, trying to keep it down to less than even what you could get on the cards. Though there were times Mr. Peel had a joint over in the middle of the week and would have let her have a bit extra if she could have paid for it, and glad to. And she having to say they wouldn't think of it, she and Mr. Chirp were too patriotic. That was all the patriotism *he'd* got, making it an excuse to keep everyone short. Cutting down the coal that autumn when they started fires, making up the back parlour fire so small no one but he could see it. Though there was coal to be had if you were ready to pay for it, or wood in any case. And then as if it wasn't enough the girl must give notice to go off making munitions: and William saying she didn't need to get another one now wages were high like they were, she could do without till the war was over.

It didn't look as if it was going to be over this winter, the way they were bringing more and more men into the camp. They were building huts out there on and on, people said. Bringing in more than they sent out. And nothing but boys, some of them, poor young fellows. She could see them from the upstairs window, going by on their route marches. All those fine young boys going out to be killed, it did seem hard. And a lot of old men that weren't any good to anyone left at home. It didn't seem right.

She wasn't going to work herself to the bone, looking after William's comfort. It was his fault if he wouldn't let her get another girl. It was all nonsense to say there weren't any girls, there were plenty if you could give the wages. Plenty who'd be glad of a place in Jewsbury, to be near the camp. She heard enough up at the vicarage about the wages they were asking now, and the times out. Shameful, it was. But it was better than being without anyone. She didn't know how William could like to sit there knowing she was doing the work. But that just showed you.

"Mrs. Porter got a girl last week from out in the country."

"Hu. What she giving her."

"Thirty pounds a year."

"Thirty pound! Nothing but robbery. Hu."

Robbery. Nothing-but-robbery.

"If you hadn't stood out against having an officer living here you might have made a trifle."

"Ph!"

Scallywags. Robbery. Nothing but robbery. Better-without'em. Better-without'em.

Couldn't see further than his nose. William never could. Couldn't even see it would have been to his advantage. He'd sooner sit there and watch her working her fingers to the bone.

She wasn't going to have any of that. He could have his meals in the kitchen, with coal short like it was and she having to carry trays backwards and forwards. She shut up the dining room for the winter. If he didn't like it he could get a girl to do the work.

And she wasn't going to keep the front parlour cleaned, for all anyone ever went in there. It was enough if it was opened up once a month for the Reverend Peat's Sunday. She kept the door locked and the blind down, to save the dust, and William could grumble all he liked. It wasn't he who had the trouble, trying to keep things decent. And for all the attention he'd ever paid to what was thought, letting the place go to rack and ruin if it hadn't been for her, he needn't have anything to say now about the blind being down.

It didn't look too nice of a Sunday, all the same. After a bit she took to going in before church and putting up the blind; though the room smelt of damp and dust and they never sat in there.

It was bad enough with the kitchen to do. That and the back parlour and upstairs. She had as much as she could do to get the breakfast things washed up and the bed made on the mornings she went out, and the rest could wait. It wasn't many people who would have done as much.

She made the bed and straightened out the runner on the toilet table and put on her hat. She wasn't going to make herself late, for anybody.

"Twenty minutes past eleven."

And well it might be. She'd be out by ten past if she had her rights. It was worthwhile going out nowadays, there was hardly a day there wasn't something to see. High Street, that used to be so quiet, had so much traffic in it that sometimes you'd see people having to wait to cross over. What with the big lorries and trucks from the camp, with soldiers driving them, that went up and down to the station: and right on past The Elms, some of them, out on the London Road. And then the officers' motor cars. And the officers' wives that had come into the town: quite a lot of new faces, something wonderful for Jewsbury. They'd got the new houses finished up somehow, on the road to the station — and a big, shiny plate up on the corner saying STATION ROAD, though no one had ever needed to be told *that* before — and they said there were officers' families living in them. Some days you could see their cars standing outside. And Porter's had brought up the fancy-shop next door and opened a big new department for men's wear, next to their music shop: full of khaki and underwear and comforts for the troops. Porter's would be all down that side of the High Street if they went on much longer. Trade was looking up in Jewsbury, there was more money about.

Everyone was spending money except William. Everyone had plenty, you could tell that. With their separation allowances and such, and all the young ones off making munitions, getting their five and six pounds a week. Coming back in their fur coats. You could hear the gramophones and pianos going in the cottages, all the way up to the shops. Everyone meant to enjoy themselves in wartime. You could tell by the money Porter's were making, that would show you. And the troops coming down from the camp in the evenings, wanting their pleasure. You could hardly get by in the streets, Minnie Hallet said, and the Fish Café full night after night, and dances on Saturdays in the Town Hall. And they were building a cinema for them now, down Market Street, down past Peel's, as fast as ever they could get it up. Jane had to run down and see what they were doing there, she couldn't help herself. Even if it was to make her a few minutes late. A big, white place, my word, it was almost like a palace. And they said they were going to have dancing in the room over.

"You ought to open up an eating place," she told Mrs. Peel. "You'd do a fine trade with the crowds going to the new cinema."

"We had thought of it," Mrs. Peel admitted.

Everyone but William, knowing how to turn in a bit and enjoy themselves. And there was he walking up and down the drive with his watch in his hand, for all the world as if there wasn't any war on.

"Twenty-eight past twelve."

And what if it was *half* past, I'd like to know. She went in and took off her hat and dished up his cold dinner and watched him pick up his knife and fork at the kitchen table.

"They're building a big cinema down Market Street."

"Hu. Lot of clap-trap."

"They have to build it for the troops, I expect. Having them all turned loose about Jewsbury of an evening, with the money burning their pockets."

"Must have got more than what I have."

Clap-trap. Hu. More'n what I have.

"And Peel's are going to open up an eating place." She had to go on telling him about it, even though she knew he wasn't listening to her. If she'd once stopped on account of that she wouldn't ever have opened her mouth. "It's handy for them, being down there."

More'n what I have, hu.

When they had done dinner she put the plates in the sink and went up to dust the bedroom and watch the troops when they came marching past singing up the road on their afternoon march.

They didn't see anything of Emily that Christmas. If she got the day off from her V.A.D. work she spent it somewhere else, where she could enjoy herself. It wasn't likely she was coming to them, with William dull like he was and the place like the grave. And Jim was still out in France.

Early in the New Year they got the cinema finished, and all Jewsbury there for the opening performance. Jane slipped down to look at the outside: all whitewash and steps and big, coloured posters, and you could get in for as cheap as sixpence. She'd never seen one of those things. If only it had been on in the morning she would have gone in for a minute, even though it meant the price of a seat, just to see what it was like. Minnie Hallet said it made your eyes ache something dreadful, the way the pictures jumped about, but it was lovely what they showed. And in the evening, she said, you could see the soldiers and their girls queueing up to get in, standing all the way along the pavement almost back to Peel's.

Peel's had opened up their dining room, out behind, but they weren't the first to get in. Chirp's had branched out, too. A fine, big tea-room, up over the shop. You could see from the street the little tables they'd got, with flowers on them, and the officers' wives sitting in the windows taking morning coffee like the sign said. Morning coffee. Fancy. Now William would never have thought of that, if he'd still been there. That was that Mr. Davis. Go-ahead.

It wasn't so very long after that that they took Mr. Davis for the army. Even though they did say he was indispensable. And he wasn't such a very young man, either. It seemed a thousand pities, but there you were, the war had been going on for the best part of two years now, and they wanted all they could get. They didn't ask William to go back though, they knew too well for that. A quite elderly man was put in, sent down from another branch, and he carried on the tea room along with the shop. They said he even got an orchestra to play for teatime, so they were saying up at the vicarage. Put in a piano, and got that poor crippled boy of the Majors', that wasn't any good for the war, to play his violin.

Jane couldn't help thinking about it sometimes, when she was getting William's tea: how lovely it must be having tea up there over Chirp's, with the music playing. She gave William his tea in the kitchen and then they went and sat in the back parlour and she got out her knitting. "You might as well sit in the kitchen," she told him, "and save the fire altogether." But he wouldn't do that. And it wasn't long now before they'd be giving up fires.

In the summer Jim got leave from France and came up to see them. Emily wrote he and her would be coming that Wednesday, and as travelling was so bad they'd have to stop over: but Ma wasn't to worry, they'd stay the night at the Jewsbury Arms.

The letter didn't get there till the Wednesday morning, and lucky it *was* Wednesday, it gave Jane a chance to pick up something for dinner. Mrs. Peel would let her have a bit extra for once, seeing it was the middle of the week, "and my son-in-law coming on leave." And goodness knew what William would say when he saw the bill, but that wouldn't come in till the Saturday. She slipped back as soon as she could — no strolling this morning — to put the joint on.

It must have been the very first time she'd ever got to the door before William. She even had to ring the bell. She could hear him fumbling with the bolts inside.

"Eh? What's the hurry then."

"Why, you haven't forgotten Jim and Emily's coming?"

"Hu."

She had the joint in the oven before she went up to take off her hat; and the dining room opened up, airing. She couldn't help wondering what Jim would look like, after all this time at the front.

When they did come — and she'd just had time to lay the table and open the front parlour window a chink to freshen things up — she got the surprise of her life, she really did.

"Why, Ma, didn't you know Jim was made a lootenant?"

Jim an officer! Just fancy!

And what a smart young fellow he did look in his new uniform. Nicer quality they had, the officers. Why, you never would have known who he was, might have been anybody, and quite the gentleman. It gave her such a queer feeling to see him sitting there at dinner, looking just like a real officer, tucking into the pork and greens. And not a bit stand-off either, always had a joke ready.

"The war's done Jim a world of good," she told Emily, when they were out in the kitchen changing the plates.

She could hardly take her eyes off him. And to think that was Emily's Jim.

After dinner he said he didn't want to go and smoke in the back parlour. Quite quiet and nice, but knew his own mind. Just said he'd rather sit in with Jane and Emily and play the piano, if Ma didn't object. William went off by himself and Jim sat down and started to rattle them off a tune, and after a minute or two he pulled out a cigarette and stuck it in his mouth. "You don't mind," he said, quite polite, before he lit up.

Jane jumped. "Oh," she said. "Oh no." She really didn't know *what* William would say, if ever he came to know of it. She couldn't remember that he'd ever smoked a pipe in the front parlour all the years they'd been married. She gave Jim one of the china saucers off the mantelpiece for an ashtray, and he put it on top of the piano and went on playing, lively sort of tunes with bits of song to them, some of what the soldiers sang when they went out marching. And when he'd finished one cigarette he lighted up another.

"Give us one, Jim," Emily said. She went over and got it from him and came back and sat on the sofa by Jane, dropping her ash into the fender. "How about you, Ma?"

Jane went pink, she couldn't help feeling pleased. "Not for me, my word, I don't know what your Pa would say!"

"Pa'll have to learn to move with the times," Emily said, between puffing and taking bits out of her mouth. She was sitting there in her yellow fur coat that she hadn't taken off though it was too hot for the time of year, she was so proud of it, you could see that. But you could understand it.

Presently William came in, and he just stood by the door and looked at Jim.

"Want a smoke?" he said. "Just step this way, will you."

"No, thanks," said Jim, "I'm all right where I am. Know this one?" And he went on playing.

Jane hardly dared to look at William, she was so afraid of what he was going to say. But whether he didn't dare to, or whether it was that he couldn't on account of the noise Jim made playing, he just sat down on the edge of a chair, red in the face, and after a few minutes he got up and went off again by himself. What a mercy Emily had finished with hers before he came in. By the time it was all wet and chewed at the end and she'd got tired of taking the bits out of her mouth she'd put it out down in the fender and William hadn't noticed it.

Jim went on playing some more, and Emily gave them a song she'd learnt with the V.A.D.s, and then they both helped her to lay the tea on the dining room table.

William came out for tea, but he hadn't a word to say for himself. Jane said she didn't like the idea of them having to go to a hotel for the night, and why didn't Emily have her old room, it was all made up, and Jim could sleep on the sofa in the parlour. But Jim said they'd do fine at the Jewsbury Arms and she wasn't to think of it, and about half-past six he said they must be getting on because he was going to turn in early.

Going to the cinema, that was where they were going. And don't blame them either. Anyone but William would have suggested it, and then we could all have gone.

When she came back from seeing them out at the door William had got the saucer off the piano and was getting down to pick up Emily's end from the fender.

"Well," she said, "it was nice having them here, it made a bit of a change. And what a fine young fellow Jim's grown into."

He got up stiffly, red in the face from bending and finding the end in the fender. "Fine young scallywag. Smoking all over the house. If that's all they teach them out at the front." He went off grunting with the saucer, out to the kitchen fire.

It wasn't any good talking to William, you might as well save yourself the trouble. You never would get him to understand anything. Most people would be proud to have a fine young fellow like Jim for a son-in-law, fighting out there. Everyone up at the vicarage said that, when she told them how he'd been made an officer. "You ought to be proud of him, Mrs. Chirp."

And Mrs. Peat said, "I expect you'd like to have that last muffler you made, to send out to him, next time you send a parcel."

Jane went a bit pink. "Thank you, Mrs. Peat," she said, "I don't think I'll trouble you. He's got a muffler we sent out to him last time."

Because if ever anyone was to know that Jim had never had so much as a pair of socks from them all the time he'd been out there, she would never hold up her head again.

And it wasn't for want of telling. Time and again she'd told William they ought to send something out. Everyone up at the vicarage was talking of what they put in their parcels, and many of them that hadn't got half such close relations. But do you think she could get William to do it? And when you thought what nice things you could get in the shops. And even if it was a bit expensive it was wartime, and you had to do these things.

She reminded him again. "We ought to send Jim a parcel now he's gone back."

"Eh? Parcel? That young scallywag?"

"Whatever he is," she said, and she didn't know how she ever dared to say it, "he's Emily's husband, and he's never had so much as a pair of socks from us."

William scowled. "Socks, eh?" And then he began to chuckle. "*He* doesn't want any socks. What does *he* want with socks. Socks? He'd *smoke* them!" He burst into a loud chuckle, knocking his pipe on the bar of the grate.

Smoke-them. Hu. Hu. Smoke-them.

Trying to be funny. As if that was anything to do with it.

She didn't know how he could like to do it. How he could go walking up the aisle week after week like he did, when you thought what the Reverend Peat would say if he knew how he went on, grudging so much as the price of a parcel for his own son-in-law that was fighting for him....

She watched him taking up the bag. There weren't half so many people in the church as there used to be, with all the young ones gone, and half of those that were left and the new ones that had come in going up to the military service at the camp. Or nowhere, a lot of them, nowadays. Off enjoying themselves on a Sunday, and you couldn't blame them. There weren't more than two or three to a pew in front of her, spread about, and she could watch him all the way up. Mr. Luff had gone. He was in the reserve, and taken for home service. And William had Tom Higgs, poor young fellow, come from the war with a stiff leg, to walk up with him. It always gave her a shock to see him like that, walking away from her. It showed him up more, walking out there by himself, with nobody but that poor Tom Higgs, when everyone else was keeping still. It showed up how shabby he was, and what an old man he was getting to be. And it wasn't for want of telling. What the Reverend Peat must think of him, coming up to the altar with the velvet on his collar green with age, and he well able to afford new, it wasn't reverent. All the reverence *he* showed was for the bag, handing it up as if it was made of eggshells. Money, his god.

They were taking men older and older now, and younger too, poor young fellows. Three years the war had been on, no one ever thought it would last so long. It was as if they couldn't make up their minds to stop, no reason to stop one day more than another. They kept the poor fellows on at their marching, and it did seem as if they liked it almost, the way they went along singing, up past The Elms after dinner. It did you good to hear them. But by the time they got back, two or three hours later — she'd slip up when she could to get a glimpse of them coming back, if William was out before tea, and if it wasn't one of their long route marches that went on some days till six or seven — there were always a few that hadn't been able to keep up, and came along after the others, limping very often. It made your heart bleed to see them, poor young fellows. Daresay they've never walked so far in their lives. And as soon as one lot got used to it they'd send them off marching with the drums in front down to the station, with everyone waving goodbye, off to the front, and then they'd get another lot in.

There was always something to see now from the upstairs windows. What with the transport wagons and the cars — why, two or three years ago there was hardly a car to be seen passing through Jewsbury — and even a motor bus now, that they were running up to London and back on Saturdays. Quite a lot were taking to travelling that way, instead of the train. It went by at ten o'clock when she was up making the bed. Puffing and rattling — can't say I should like it myself — and throwing up dust over the laurels. Only once she'd managed to catch sight of it coming back, all lit up, nine or ten o'clock at night, but you could hear it rattling down past The Elms, and people calling out good night when it stopped to put down at the corner. And then there was hardly a day the men weren't marching by singing. Sometimes they went out the other way, Toddleton way, but generally there'd be some of them coming past The Elms, one lot or another. You got to miss them when they didn't come. There wasn't a young man or hardly a middle-aged man left in Jewsbury now that wasn't in khaki. Even a lot of the police had gone, and they'd put on special constables to keep order in the evenings, when they got the troops about in the streets; The Reverend Peat had got William to sign on for a special constable, but they hadn't called him out.

Jim got leave again in the autumn, but he didn't come down to Jewsbury. Emily wrote he only had two days and it wasn't worth the journey, she was meeting him up in London. And then the next they heard after he'd gone back he was killed.

Poor young fellow, it did seem hard. A fine, upstanding young fellow like him taken. But there it's always the best that go. And some old man who's no good to anyone left to cumber the ground.

But it's always the wrong ones. And there was poor Mrs. Porter's Albert, he'd gone too, and with the business coming to him, and after the way they'd brought it on the last few years, it did seem a crying shame. It was a pity they couldn't take some that were no use and wouldn't be missed; always the pick of the bunch. That poor Major boy that was a cripple and no good to anyone except for playing on his violin, he was left, and many more you could name if you looked round, and fine upstanding young fellows like Jim and Albert Porter had to be taken.

She shook her head over it coming back from the vicarage, clearing off the kitchen table where she'd left William's tea put out for him on a tray. And he just walking away and leaving it for her to clear. Always the wrong ones. Some that were no use to God or man. Before she'd done she heard the tramp of them coming back down the road, and slipped up quick to take off her hat. She hadn't taken it off yet and as well now as later. They weren't singing tonight, they'd had a long march, poor boys. Tired, they looked. And what a tramping they made in the dark. Tramp, tramp. No wonder they got tired out with all they had to carry on their backs. She could see them lit up, khaki, in a patch down the road: caps and packs, jolting in time, under the street lamp they'd put up two doors down outside The Laurels.

She tidied her hair and ran down and hung up William's cup and saucer that she'd left wet on the dresser, and blew out the kitchen lamp and took her work into the back parlour. She had a big bundle of wool she'd brought back from the vicarage, if she worked hard at it she ought to get three helmets done in the week.

"Mrs. Peat'll be wanting some money before long, for the stuffs."

"Hu. Lot of flummery."

"They want warm things," she said tartly, "poor young fellows. Out there in the trenches."

"Hu."

And it wasn't any good him not liking the noise of the needles, because everyone knew the faster you went the more noise you made, and if she was going to get three helmets done this week she wouldn't have to waste any time about it. She'd done as well as most so far, and she wasn't going to have anyone saying she couldn't do her bit as well as the next. If it hadn't been for Mrs. Porter and one or two of the rest having more time on their hands, she would have done as well as any.

Five to ten and William had his watch out, but there was time to do another row if she was quick. If she hadn't happened to have dropped a stitch she would have done it. Just get that up.

"Ten."

His watch clicked to. He was down on his knees, raking the ashes.

"You go on and see to the door. I've just got this to do."

But the way he wouldn't go, hanging about, fiddling with the lamp, made her drop her stitches as fast as she picked them up, and in the end she had to go out and light the candles and watch him lock the front door; with her mouth shut tight, and the knitting bunched up in her hand to see to while she got ready for bed.

If she could start now with the New Year and knit up her five to six ounces of wool a week regular — that was where it was, the others weren't regular — she'd have done more than any of them by the time the year was out.

They didn't see anything of Emily that Christmastime, she was down the other end of England on her V.A.D. work and they hadn't set eyes on her since Jim was killed. And no time for letter-writing either. Jane had all she could do to keep the house decent, what with seeing to the meals and keeping up with her knitting and getting out in time her three days a week. And as for William you'd never get *him* to write a letter. Sitting in there with his paper and his pipe: it was a wonder what he found to do with himself all day. Out to the door, "Twenty minutes past eleven," and out again to see when she got back. And Jewsbury wasn't what it was either, you couldn't get about so quickly, there was always someone had something to say. She was always telling Minnie Hallet she'd take her into Chirp's one of these days for a cup of morning coffee, but the only time she met Minnie without it was too late she hadn't any money of her own with her. And didn't know what they'd charge. Fancy prices, you could depend upon it. And she didn't altogether like going into Chirp's, where everyone would know her: even though it *was* only up the stairs by the side of the shop. It didn't seem quite right for her to be seen there drinking morning coffee with poor Minnie. If she could have got out now in an afternoon, when the cinema was going on, that was a thing she would dearly have liked to see, whatever she'd had to pay for it. But she had enough to do, with getting

William his meals, and her mornings out, and her knitting, and her Thursday afternoons at the vicarage, and having to slip up to see the boys go by, poor young fellows: always just when she was in the middle of something. It kept her busy. She hardly had the time to count her money even; not that it mattered so much now that girl was out of the house, there wasn't so much chance anyone would stumble on where she put it.

Nearly four years the war had been going on now. Four years in August. Over four years it was, and didn't look as if it was ever going to stop. You'd think we should have driven off those Germans before now. All these poor young fellows having to go out there and get killed, and many that could well be spared.... Younger and younger they took them, nothing but boys. And even quite elderly men too, if they were any good. It was only those that weren't that got left behind. In October they called out William for a special constable. It showed you they must be hard put to it if they had to call up an old man like him.

More nuisance he was than anything else, with his having to get out by five in the evening, wanting his tea early. For all the good he was doing walking up and down the street. He wouldn't have caught a thief if he'd been right under his nose. It was more for the form of the thing than for anything else, just so that they could say they had someone there.

She had to hurry up and get his tea soon after four, or he'd be stamping in and out of the kitchen in a fret for fear he'd be late; and then hold his hat for him while he got into his coat, and put up the chain on the front door after he'd gone — "All these scallywags about" — with him waiting on the step to make sure she did it. She'd hear him go blundering off over the gravel out to the road and she did get a couple of hours then, which was more than she did as a rule; but by eight o'clock they let him off and put someone else on, and she had to listen and unchain the door for him, and get him a cup of something hot because he'd had his tea early. And as if it wasn't enough, he hadn't been at it three weeks before he caught a cold with standing about.

There was only a week to go before his time was up for this once, and they wouldn't be calling him out again for two or three months. He could just as well have said he was laid up. Come to that she could easy have gone into the Town Hall and told them herself on the Monday morning; but he wouldn't hear of it, you might as well save your breath. So out he had to go, coughing and sneezing, standing about the streets again on the Sunday night, and by the next day she had him on her hands, ill in bed.

It was a lucky thing she was strong; toiling up and down stairs all day with cups of soup and currant tea, and the house to look after and shopping to be done and no one to give a hand. Not a girl left in Jewsbury by now, what with the munitions and the W.A.A.C.s[1] and the land-girls[2]: not one to be got for love or money. Come to that she'd as soon be without them; only have them sneaking out to the gate when her back was turned, or poking round among her things. As it was she didn't know what to do with William up in the bedroom all the time, and you never knew when he might take it into his head to get out of bed and look for something. She'd have to move her money away downstairs.

"I'll just take these down to air," she told him, folding a sheet over her arm and gripping the bag tight underneath it.

William only grunted, he did seem in rather a bad way. His breathing was so funny, and he didn't fancy his food; but it didn't seem right to go troubling Dr. Trent, when he was the only doctor left in Jewsbury and would have retired anyhow, before now, if it hadn't been for the war.

She took her money down to the back parlour and hid it in the bottom of her workbag. It was about the last place William

---

1 Women's Army Auxiliary Corps.

2 Members of the Women's Land Army.

would ever look, even if he should take it into his head to get up and come downstairs.

She had to miss her Thursday at the vicarage, though it went to her heart to do it, the first week she'd missed all the time the war had been on. But William was so hot and tossing she really didn't like to leave him. If he wasn't better by the morning she'd have to go round and see Dr. Trent about him, even though it wasn't her day for going out. She brought her knitting up and sat with him, over on the other side of the room with the candle by her on the chest of drawers. For he never had that gas put in. As if he thought he was never going to be ill, nor anybody else. And there was nearly everyone in Jewsbury, now, with the electric light.

He looked as if he was asleep. She sat and peered at her stitches in the candlelight, waiting for him to wake up, and after a bit she heard the troops coming back from their march. Tramp, tramp, coming nearer, past the house now, going on up towards the town. Lifting the blind an inch at the corner she could see the last row with their packs and the two officers walking behind passing under the lamp. Poor young fellows, how glad they must be to get back to the camp and get those things off their backs. And then they give them the evening to themselves, by all accounts, to go to the cinema or what they like.

All over the town, enjoying themselves.

She looked across sharply at William. He was still asleep, but he really did look queer. Perhaps after all she oughtn't to wait for the morning before calling in Dr. Trent.

She put down her knitting uncertainly. Her face was hot. After all it wouldn't do any harm for him to have a look at him, even if it *was* the evening.

Once she'd made up her mind it didn't take her a minute to put on her hat; though she could hardly get the pins in straight she was so afraid William would wake up and say she wasn't to go, and it wasn't fair on her, no it really wasn't, making her take the responsibility, all alone with him like that. The wardrobe drawer creaked while she got out her jacket, and William grunted, but he didn't open his eyes. He was too bad really, to take notice. She slipped out as quietly as she could, with her gloves and purse in her hand, and got downstairs and out of the house. Whatever William would say if he woke up and found she was gone, and the front door left unlocked....

It did seem funny being out of doors in the dark. She could hardly remember when she had been before, except with William on a Sunday evening, and you couldn't count that. What a funny feeling it gave you, to be coming under the lamps and going on in the dark again, just like she'd seen the troops doing. She stopped at the crossroads. Some ways it might be nearer to go up past the church. But it looked dark along there, and that would make her slow. Now if she went straight on up the High Street and round it would be light all the way with the shops, and she'd get along quicker. She ought to do that.

It wasn't so very light, only one lamp lit out of two, and that painted black at the top, and yet it made you feel quite gay. Fancy, you never would have thought Jewsbury would be gay like this at night. Not that it was late, the shops were only just shutting. Porter's was all shut and dark, but some of them, the sweet shops and tobacconists, were still open: you could tell the lights were on inside, for all they had to have the dark blinds, against air-raids — not that they got any, out here — and you could tell the gramophones were going, through at the back. There seemed to be almost as many about as in the daytime too — soldiers walking up and down and standing, and the girls giggling at them, brazen young hussies. Well, and if Chirp's hadn't still got their upstairs room open and the music playing, though the shop was shut up. They must be giving suppers up there. Such goings on! Whoever would have thought it of Jewsbury.

It was too far to see down Market Street whether they were standing yet outside the cinema, but the Jewsbury Arms was full, you could tell that: plenty of khaki in there, *and* outside, and laughing going on. It was quite an adventure to take the plunge round the corner out of the Market Place, where it was darker: all along where there was a queue waiting — just like Minnie Hallet said! — in the dark, outside the Fish Café.

Dr. Trent was out, but she left a message for him when he came in.

"Where you been," William wanted to know.

He didn't so much say it as mutter it. He did look bad. It was a good thing she'd been for the doctor.

"Only to ask Dr. Trent if he'd look in."

William tossed and muttered, but she couldn't hear what he was saying. She could see him in the glass while she took off her hat. Well I *am* glad to have seen that. Might never have had a chance to see what it was like.

After a minute he got his mouth clear of the sheet. "Nothing but expense."

"Never you mind, you lie still."

It did seem funny for her to be talking to him like that, but he'd only make himself worse if he got worrying. Luckily he didn't seem able to keep his mind on anything for long, and it was only about half an hour before Dr. Trent was there.

"He's got this 'flu," he said. "There's a lot of it about."

He took William's temperature and felt his pulse and looked at him as well as he could by the candlelight. What he must think....

"I'll send you round a bottle of medicine. Give him a dose three times a day and keep him quiet, and I'll look in again in a day or two."

William muttered something — it was most likely some rubbish about the expense — but Dr. Trent didn't wait to hear what it was, which was a mercy. It was seven o'clock at night and he'd been on his feet since morning. He was the only doctor left in the place, barring the military doctors up at the camp, and half Jewsbury was down with the 'flu, it seemed, the last few days. Though Jane hadn't heard of it, not having been to the vicarage that week and being in such a hurry on the Wednesday morning she hadn't stopped to speak to anyone.

But Dr. Trent was a nice, pleasant gentleman. "You oughtn't to go sleeping in that room," he took time to say as he was going out. "Or you'll catch it."

Well there was the bed in the little room that was still made up, where she'd got it ready for the poor young officer that never came. And *that* was William's fault. Two or three years, three years ago that must have been. How time did go.

It seemed a shame to use it. There were the sheets, sweet and clean as anyone could wish, all ready turned down under the cover.

So there she was in a room by herself, only with the doors open in case William should call out: wonders would never cease. She hardly knew herself. When she'd blown out the candle she lay there stiff and straight in the little bed — that belonged by rights to some poor young officer that never had it, stiff and cold most likely by now, out there among those Germans — and thought what a funny feeling it gave you being on your own. It seemed a pity to go to sleep and not know where she was.

There wasn't much time for thinking when she woke up. Over-slept herself, the first time in years. Out on the floor almost before her eyes were open. What with getting William's breakfast, not that he could swallow more than a cup of tea, and giving him his medicine and seeing to the house. When she'd done she took her knitting up and sat with him, close up against the window, watching through the curtain the lorries going up and down, and waiting for the men to come by.

Saturday morning she just managed to run up to Peel's for the meat and say she most likely wouldn't be that way on Monday, with the doctor coming and everything. "This terrible 'flu," Mrs. Peel said. Mr. Peel was down with it, too, and she with the dining room to serve as well as the shop, and only a girl to help her. She said if Minnie Hallet should come in she'd tell her about Mr. Chirp being laid up.

William lay breathing as if he was asleep most of the time, but he seemed easier in himself. Dr. Trent looked in in the evening, busy as he was. "He'll be all right," he said. "Go on keeping him quiet. I'll send you round some more medicine."

Jane sat and clicked her needles — even if it was a Sunday she wasn't going to sit with her hands in front of her — and listened to William breathing. She'd see if she couldn't slip round to the vicarage next Thursday, if it was only to take what she'd done and fetch some more wool. He'd be better by then. There wasn't much going by in the road once the bells had stopped, only a few cars going up towards London, which would be officers who had the day off. Jane got on with her knitting and now and then she took a look round the room, with William in it. It looked different, sitting over here. How it showed up where the plaster had gone from the ceiling. Years and years ago. And never been put back. And the paper hanging away from the wall. Well, William only had himself to thank for it. If she'd had *her* way. And now there he was lying in bed and having Dr. Trent come in and see it. Whatever Dr. Trent must think of him.... She was really ashamed to have him see what it was like.

In the afternoon there were some couples walking in the road, Tommies with their girls. She could hear them laughing. After a bit she had to light the candle and draw down the blind and get William his tea. The church bells started. There was a lot of walking about outside, but when she pushed the blind a chink she couldn't see much: only a couple passing under the lamp, the Tommy swaggering with his cane.

When she came to take her hair down at night she wondered why she hadn't moved her things into the other room altogether.

William looked asleep and she might as well settle him down for the night. She picked up her brush and glass and took away the candle. And then waking up the next morning it looked so funny with her own things about the room, the brush on the dressing-table and her clothes hung over a chair. Like having her own room. Tidying up later she found a clean runner for the table and fetched in the toilet-tidy and hung it up on the glass, just to see how it would look. There might be some· vases in the cupboard, that would go on the mantelpiece.

William was better by the Wednesday, sitting up; only complaining he felt weak, and had a bit of a pain. As if that wasn't to be expected.

"He'll be all right now." That's what Doctor Trent said. "He'll want feeding up. Go on keeping him in bed."

What with Doctor Trent coming in so late she only just had time to slip round to the shops before dinner. Fast as ever she could go, too. Without a minute to so much as pass the time of day. And Mrs. Peel coming out while the girl was wrapping up her parcel, all ready for a chat you could see that, got news I expect from her nephew that's out there, and she just having to nod and run. It was a downright shame. Still, if William was making up his mind to get better at last that was something to be thankful for.

And then Thursday if he wasn't taken bad again; saying he was, at all events. She having to miss her Thursday afternoon the second week running, how vexed she was. It did seem really as if he did it on purpose. Sitting up as bright as you please when she *would* have been glad to have him laid down quiet of an afternoon.

"Do you want your newspaper fetched," she asked him.

Because she could have fetched it, perfectly well, and thought nothing of the trouble either if it was going to give him something to keep his mind on for an hour or two. But no, he'd rather save the penny, that was all it was. He'd rather sit there doing nothing, fancying himself worse than he was until he *did* work himself into having a bad turn. He was well enough to jump on her if she so much as took a peep out of the window, or stayed downstairs a minute to look through her workbag, quiet, to herself. And then starting saying he felt queer again on the Saturday morning, so that all she could do was send a message up to Peel's by the milkman when he called.

But Monday morning she really did manage to slip out, round about twelve, Doctor Trent having popped in early that day: just time to pick up the things she wanted. And, as luck would have it, ran right into Minnie Hallet, round the corner into Market Street.

"More than a week now, isn't it, you've had him in bed?"

"A fortnight today, and still there. Looks as if he'll go on for ever, like the war."

"What!" says Minnie. "Don't you know? Haven't you heard? About how they've got a narmistice? Why, they stopped fighting eleven o'clock this morning!"

No! It couldn't be a fact the war was over. Why, it had gone on so long no one could remember what it was like without. So now they'd be bringing all the poor young fellows back, all those that hadn't been killed; and what a jubilation there'd be when they came marching in. Like when the troops first came to Jewsbury.

No! She really couldn't get over it. And to think that if William hadn't been so mean as not to spend a penny on a paper she would have known about it all along. But there you were, that just showed you. Fancy though, the war being over. Just think of that.

And then she had to run. She brought William up his dinner: which he wouldn't eat, for all the doctor had said about him having to be fed up. "The war's over," she told him. Not that he deserved it.

"Eh?"

"The war's over. They're stopping fighting."

"Hu. Bad business. Bad business."

"You ought to be glad they've stopped killing our poor young fellows."

141

Bad business, bad business.

It wasn't any good telling him anything. He'd gone half silly with the 'flu, if you asked her. She sat him up for his dinner and laid him down again after, because he said it hurt him when he sat up. But by the evening, when she came up, having had her own scrap of tea at the kitchen table, to give him his medicine, he seemed more like himself.

"All this physic. Expensive stuff. Time to put a stop to it."

"Better ask Dr. Trent. I daresay you've had enough now."

He was quite well enough to be left by the Thursday after-noon. There wasn't anything she could do, after giving him his medicine and settling him down, and she'd slip away in time to get his tea. She had to find out all about the war stopping; and what she didn't hear at the vicarage she wouldn't hear anywhere.

Well it seemed she'd missed the service for giving thanks, but that was to be expected, being tied like she was. But there'd be big Armistice celebrations, fireworks and all, out at the camp, before they broke it up. So they'd be doing away with the camp, it did seem a pity.

Well, Mrs. Mace said, they'd be leaving a few there just to keep it going, for a bit, but most would be moved out, it might even be next week.

Oh dear, wouldn't it seem quiet when they were all gone. Jewsbury *would* be quiet.

"Well," said Mrs. Mace, laughing, "you couldn't find any place much quieter than Jewsbury was before the war, could you?"

Yes, indeed, so it had been. There hadn't been much going on.

Year after year, with nothing but Jim and Emily coming for Christmas. And now Jim had been killed in the war.

Jane said she must be going; but she couldn't get away before tea, everyone said, because Mrs. Peat was going to make a speech.

They passed the cups round, and then Mrs. Peat got up and said she'd like to say a few words to thank everyone there that had supported so generously what they'd been trying to do, and she knew everyone had put their heart in the work knowing it was for our poor boys out there, and now it was all over and the boys were coming back we were all very thankful, and we were all very glad we had been able to do something.

And Mrs. Porter got up and said — and everyone looked away, thinking of her Albert and how he hadn't been one of those to come back, but she had to get up and speak owing to Porter's being by now quite the firm with the most standing in Jewsbury — how we all wanted to thank Mrs. Peat for all she'd done, and how no one could have done more, and the splendid lead she'd given all the way through.

Then Mrs. Peat got up again and said how there'd be a business meeting on Thursday week to read out the accounts and see what was to be done with the clothes that had been made and left over, and how she'd always be glad to see anyone present that would like to drop in any time for a friendly chat, but there wouldn't be any more work meetings, since, as everyone was thankful for, the time had gone by.

Jane sat as if she'd been stunned. To think it was all over. There were people all round getting up to shake hands and say goodbye and how we all ought to be thankful.

She got herself up, though she didn't know how she was ever going to do it, and said how she must fly because she'd got Mr. Chirp ill in bed, and shook hands with Mrs. Peat and got out quickly before anyone could say anything to her.

And whatever William was going to say, her being late like this....

She had the presence of mind to pop into the kitchen and put on a kettle before she went upstairs to him. He was still asleep, luckily, or he would have called out.

Why, whatever was the matter. Why — what — was it.

It wasn't anything. He must have been trying to get out, that was it, and come over faint.

She sat him up again, from where he was fallen over all huddled up on the side of the bed. He opened his eyes while she was laying him back. That was all, it wasn't anything. Must have started to get up and fainted, he was so weak from lying in bed.

He looked at her but didn't say anything.

"You lie there and don't try to move again," she told him, "and I'll pop round for Dr. Trent." Lucky she hadn't taken her hat off. She was quite white when she went past the hallstand on her way out, but as soon as she was out in the air she could feel the blood rushing back to her head. She really didn't know what she *had* thought, finding him like that.

"It's his heart," Dr. Trent said, putting down William's hand where he'd been feeling his pulse. "After the 'flu. Keep him quiet, he'll be all right. I'll send you round a different sort of medicine and you can give him a dose twice a day in water, and any other time he wants it."

"He was saying it hurt him somewhere, didn't you, William?"

And a lot of nonsense about stopping his medicine. He can tell that to the doctor if he wants to, I'm not going to. He'll find he's got to take a lot more now.

William grunted.

"Ah," said Dr. Trent, "felt a slight pain? Ah yes, he probably would. Well," he said, picking up his bag which he'd put down by the candlestick on the commode, there being nowhere else for him to put it, "give him a dose any time he feels it coming on. He'll be all right."

When the new medicine came she poured him out a dose and it seemed to pull him round. Though all it did was give him the strength to grumble. Nothing to his liking. She went and got her knitting and sat with him for fear he should try to get out of bed again. And then when the candle flickered and she had to bend to see a stitch, it reminded her, and she dropped the work in her lap. It wasn't any good going on knitting, because the war was over.

Well, she thought, picking it up again, sharp with herself, it wasn't any good leaving things half done. No good to anyone. Mrs. Peat was having a meeting to see what was to be done with the things that were left over, and she'd get this finished up and take it with her, to show she hadn't been idle. She went on with it almost without looking up, until it was time to settle William down and go across to her room. And he in a fidget, wanting her back in there, as if he couldn't call out with the doors open.

He was dreadful now he was able to sit up. Sitting there with his watch in his hand, letting her know if she was a minute late with his meals, and grumbling over the medicine. "All that money going to waste, and looks like nothing but water."

But he was glad enough of his physic when he felt it hurting him, when he sat up too fast. Calling out, so that she'd have to put down her knitting and go over to the washstand and pour it out, and the water on top, just so much — and really you couldn't tell the difference — and take it over to him. On the Saturday morning he didn't want her to go out, only that she said she had to go and ask Dr. Trent to send round another bottle.

'Hu. Expensive stuff, expensive stuff."

"Twenty past eleven," he said, he was well enough to say that when she'd got her hat on: pulling out his watch from under the pillow.

Sitting there, timing her. Getting too well, that was what was the matter with *him*. She hardly dared to stay a minute anywhere, for thinking of him: afraid he should try to get down to the door.

"They're having the fireworks Tuesday, up at Jewsbury Park," Minnie told her.

And to think she was missing it all. Not that she would have been able to go, an evening like that. But to think she was missing all the very last of the war. She could have cried.

She hadn't been working more than half an hour after tea before she'd finished the socks she was on, and only half a ball of wool left, enough for a pair of cuffs, if that. And when that was done....

It wasn't that she hadn't got enough to do, in a manner of speaking, what with cooking and fetching William his meals and cleaning up the place that had got like a pigsty downstairs; thick with dust, with her kept waiting on him. And she would hardly have started on a job downstairs before she'd hear the boys marching by, singing and whistling, and have to run up to her room to catch a glimpse. Might be the last she'd see of them, you never knew. Or else William would call out, wanting something, fretting because she wasn't up there with him, and up she'd have to go again. It was lucky she'd always been strong. Up and down, up and down. But sit there with her hands in her lap, looking at him and listening to him grumbling, she could not. Wanting her to bring back her things in there like it was before, though Dr. Trent had hinted she would be as good as dead, but that was all he cared; and wanting her to tell the doctor he needn't go on coming, and wanting to stop the medicine because it was too dear, and then wanting it brought to him because he thought he felt his pain coming on. It was enough to drive anyone crazy.

And then Tuesday night the fireworks were on, over at Jewsbury Park. If you looked hard you could see the sparks now and then when there was a high one, right up over the houses in Vicarage Road, and when the wind turned that way you could even hear the band, very faint, and them cheering. She sat by the window in William's room with the candle up behind her on the chest of drawers and a pair of socks in her lap that wanted mending, and held the blind out an inch to the side so that she could see if there should be a high one.

"What's the matter with the blind," William grumbled.

She dropped it and shut her mouth tight and drew out a thread to darn the socks. After a bit she couldn't stand it any longer; she went down to rake out the kitchen fire and started bustling round, cleaning the stove for the morning. And tomorrow the troops would be going: this time tomorrow they'd be gone for good. Whatever Jewsbury would be like without them...? She could hardly believe they really were to go.

When she woke it was only eight, and she couldn't think for a minute what the tramping was and calling-out down the road.

It was them! Going already!

She had her head out of the window before she knew what she was doing: right out, and her hair down too. Down in a plait on her neck, tied with the bit of pink ribbon she'd used for more years than she could remember, till it was worn grey with washing. But she didn't care. She could have cried. There was Mrs. Mace out at her gate, and all of them out of the cottages down on the corner, calling-out and waving. And the boys calling back too, though the officers pulled them up now and then, and laughing. Not like when they came in first, all stiff and military. They were so glad at going home, and having won the war for us.

And to think they'd gone off before she was up, and she not able to so much as go and see them off. Because she would have, whatever anyone had to say.

She could have cried while she was dressing and getting the fire lit, she was in such a fret to get out and see if they'd all gone, and William keeping calling out, making her later.

No, that wasn't nearly all, Mrs. Peel said. They'd be going down all day in detachments. Fast as they got one lot off from the station they'd bring down some more.

And then, just when she got back into Market Place, she couldn't believe her eyes, there was a whole detachment coming down the road from the camp, right down towards her, and the drums in front banging.

She stood there on the corner until the very last one had gone round: right round into High Street, so close she could have touched the nearest ones, and the girls running alongside knocking into her while she stood there. When the last line came by, and before she knew what she was doing, she'd taken out her handkerchief and waved to them, and then she had to wipe her eyes with it.

Well, just fancy.

She could hardly get dinner she was shaking so, she was so happy: to think she should have happened to be there, out in the street, just that very minute: it mightn't have happened once in a hundred years. And she'd no sooner had her dinner and fetched William's tray down than she heard the drums again, and there was another lot.

She had her head right out and didn't care by now who saw it. There was no end to this lot, it must be all of them that was left, you never would have thought they could have got so many in the camp. Lovely it was, and then just when she'd pulled her head in to breathe a minute and put herself straight, if William didn't have to call out.

She went across to him, leaving the door and window open so that she could hear. Wanting his medicine.

"You've just had it," she told him. "You don't want it again," and started to go back.

He was all white and shaky. "You give me some more."

She sighed and turned back to the washstand and picked up the bottle to pour it. Stood listening. That would be the last of them going by now. If that wasn't William all over....

That was it, they'd have another band at the end. She jerked the bottle down and got out of the door, "You don't want it so soon," she called over her shoulder, "it's a waste."

No it wasn't, it was the beginning of another lot. Just fancy. This must be all, there couldn't be any left up there now. That was the end of them, right away up the High Street, you could see through the trees where the leaves were off. And cars coming down after them. Too big for cars. The ambulances, that would be, or the trucks. They'd be taking them off too. It was the ambulances, you could see now.

She stepped back to take a look through the open doors at what William was doing. Lying back, white, and moving his head about.

"Well, what is it?" He *would* choose just now.

"Physic," he muttered.

"You don't want it." Just doing it on purpose. "It isn't an hour since you had it."

Oh well. She hurried in and over to the washstand. Give it to him and have done with it. Must almost have got to the corner.

He roused himself as she came by. "You stay here. Don't go off."

Well that *was* the last straw.

She really didn't know what she was doing, except that she was so vexed with him she would have done anything. She took up the water bottle and poured some in the glass, the size of a dose, and took it to him. Well he's always saying there isn't any difference.

There, she could hear the rumbling now. That would be the ambulances turning.

William swallowed the water, he was lying back with his eyes shut. "More," he muttered, hardly taking the trouble to open his mouth.

And there weren't so very many of them, won't take long to get round.

William grunted at her.

She ran back to the washstand. Shouldn't wonder if they'd gone, by now.

"Here," she said, furious, "here you are." She snatched up the water bottle in one hand and the glass in the other, and as fast as she could pour out the water she pushed it into his mouth. "Here you are. Here's all you want. Here's enough for you. Drink it up." Gone. There wasn't a sound. "This is what you want, this is all you get, you can't have anything else it's too dear, too expensive, it's too much expensive stuff."

149

William's head fell sideways away from the glass, so that the last of the water went on the pillow.

She didn't know however she got along the road, it was all empty, there wasn't anyone about, they'd all gone in, all gone down to the station after the troops because the troops had gone. She didn't know whatever she was going to say when she got round there, the vicarage, and the church, round to Dr. Trent's. She didn't know whatever she was going to say. She was so worried about how she was going to say it that she said it right out when the girl came to the door.

"He's gone," she said.

Chapter IX

Whoever would have thought that he would go like that. But that just showed you. Here today and gone tomorrow. It made you think. And to think of all she'd done, nursing him, up and down and up and down, indoors from one week's end to another. Never grudged herself the least bit of trouble....

"I'm sure nobody could have been taken better care of, Mrs. Chirp. At least you have nothing to reproach yourself with."

Mrs. Peat, that was. She meant well, no doubt, calling round, but Jane could have done with the time to herself, she had enough to do getting things straight, all put right for the funeral; and it was as much as she could do to get it done, upset like she was. She wasn't sorry when Mrs. Peat said she must be going. Oh dear no, she didn't want anyone there sleeping in the house with her, thanking you all the same. She wasn't one to go fancying things.

She saw Mrs. Peat out and shut the door after her and put up the chain. And that was the last, she hoped. Didn't want any more coming round to help, poking their noses in, for that was all it meant. Minnie Hallet would have come there to sleep fast enough for the asking, and she wasn't the only one either. Sooner be without: doing nothing but make work, and there was enough to do as it was. Some might like it, but she didn't. At a time like that you wanted to be quiet to yourself. Whoever would have thought.

She shot the bolts top and bottom and went to shut up the front parlour. Her hand was on the door when she thought, Might as well turn it out now. Have everyone in there, day of the funeral. Sooner done the better.

She fetched the brooms and clanked down the dustpan in the fender and bustled about, moving out the furniture to sweep behind and getting down to polish the boards in the dim light that filtered under the drawn blind. It did her good to be getting something done. It seemed so quiet in here and funny, with all the blinds down and William lying so quiet there upstairs, never calling out. Something quite fresh. Well if anyone had told her, a week ago....

She set to work rubbing up the brass. No one should say she didn't keep things nice. She didn't know when she'd worked so fast. Before it was time to light up she'd got the parlour done and locked and was out in the kitchen, washing up the best glasses from the bottom cupboard of the dresser. Two more days before the funeral, but you never knew when she might be hindered, people in and out. Many that hadn't been near the place for more years than she could remember. Not that you could blame them for that, for William was never one to encourage a lot of visitors. Liked to have things quiet, poor William.

She got down the big plated dish-covers from the wall and began to rub them up. Quite hot she was with all this work, it kept you busy. Not much time for fussing and fretting. Not that she'd ever been one to fret.

She'd have her hands full the next two days. Porters' coming, first thing in the morning, and Minnie Hallet to give her a fitting.

She might have got her mourning from Porters', too, only that it all meant more expense, and she not knowing where she stood. Yes, and that Mr. Bream. Not that he'd be coming back now till the funeral. Whoever would have thought that William would have put his business with Bream's the solicitors out of Toddleton, will and all, and she never knowing. He was a deep one. And that was where it had been, tucked away all these years, and she left to wonder. After the funeral Mr. Bream was staying on to read it out. It wouldn't be right really to open it up before. But she wasn't to worry, Mr. Bream said, for William had done the right thing, done all as he ought. And anyone could tell what that meant. Of course he might have left Emily a trifle to remember him by. Even though she *had* got her pension now Jim was killed it would be only right as you might say for her to come into a pound or two. Or some little thing out of the house, William might have thought of that, a bit of furniture. That great sideboard now, out of the front, some of that big, heavy furniture, Jane could well do without that, she'd be the last to complain. And it was a good, solid piece. She'd get herself something new, more up-to-date, brighten the place up a bit. It could do with a bit of brightening, it was as dark and quiet as the grave. And not far from being one either, come to think of it, with William lying unburied there, upstairs.

She pulled the door to as she went past to the dresser. Now the lamp was lit on the kitchen table it made the hall dark: all the rest of the house was dark and chilly. She poked the fire and drew a chair up to the stove and made herself a cup of tea. Rest herself a minute while she was getting it.

It seemed funny not having William coming in, calling out for his tea the way he always did. Calling out for her the very minute he was in the house. Always wanted her there, at his beck and call. She stirred her cup and put her feet up on the fender. It seemed funny to be there taking her ease, with no thought for anyone. To think of all the times she'd been up and down the last few weeks, up and down and in and out, it made you appreciate a quiet sit-down by the fire.

But she couldn't rest. There was too much to be done. She had barely emptied her cup when she was on her feet again, looking out the best china that that young hussy that used to be there had broken two handles off and put back without saying. And what business she ever had to be touching it, seeing Jane had always made a point of washing up herself the days the Reverend Peat came to tea. Poking round in the cupboard to see what she could find. But they're all alike, more bother than they're worth.

After a bit she remembered she'd have to find the money to pay Minnie Hallet in the morning when she came to fit her dress. Better have it ready, she didn't want to be looking it out with Minnie there. She took the lamp with her into the back parlour, to fetch her work-basket. The blind hadn't been drawn down, this room facing to the back, and when she put down the lamp and went over to get her basket from the chair the sky was light and cold through the bare window. She'd cleaned out the grate, days back, when William took to his bed, but it was dusty and stale in here, wanted a good turn-out. She picked up the basket and lamp quickly and hurried back into the warm kitchen.

It wasn't until she'd found her money in the bag at the bottom of the basket and tipped it out carefully, with a cushion under, on the table, so that it shouldn't chink, that she remembered William wasn't about to hear it. It did seem queer, not having to be careful. Though it was all for the best, taking care; you never knew who might be about outside, listening to hear what was going on. Jewsbury wasn't what it had been, since the war. Tramps and all-sorts.

Nine pounds five and four, a shilling less than what it should have been, she having missed the last two Sundays. She put aside a sovereign and a half sovereign. Thirty shillings she had to give Minnie for the stuff and making: half as much again as before the war, it was coming to something. It did go against the grain, having to spend all that out of her own money, but what was she to do. There hadn't been above one and sevenpence in the pockets of William's suit, that he left when he died. All the rest was locked up. In the bank most likely. But Mr. Bream would know about that. And then there was the week's housekeeping money in her purse, that William had given her last Saturday, but she didn't like to touch that. Not that it wasn't all her own money now, but it seemed so funny to think of. She'd need what was in the purse for the refreshments after the funeral. No one should go away saying she was mean. Poor William, if he'd known it was the money for his own funeral that he was counting out last Saturday.... Well, we've all got to go.

She slipped the two gold pieces into an empty canister on the dresser and put the rest away in its bag, in the work-basket. Then she took the bag out again and fitted it in the pocket under her skirt. You never knew, with so many strangers about the house.

It wasn't everyone who would have liked to light their candle and go up to bed, all alone in the house with a corpse upstairs. It was a lucky thing she wasn't one to have fancies.

The hall fell back below her into a dark well. Her candle lit up the stained dirty wallpaper and the worn carpet and a piece of dark polished banister that ran up beside her until she turned the corner on to the landing. All the doors were shut and it was as quiet as the grave. There was the little third room along at the end, that the girl used to have. Minnie could have slept in there, if it was wanted. But Jane would as soon be on her own, she didn't want anyone round, she wasn't that sort. For all the harm poor William could do anyone, dead and cold like he was. The candle shone up brighter in her little room. She locked the door behind her and started to take her hair down and get ready for bed. But when she'd got her nightdress on and her hair screwed up behind into a plait, tied with the same bit of pink ribbon she'd used since she didn't know when, she couldn't get straight into bed, she didn't feel easy. She couldn't help taking up the candle and unlocking the door again and going across and opening the other door very quietly, to take a peep at him.

Well, there he was, all laid out, like Minnie had helped her to do — she having been in before to see everything was as it should be — with a clean pillow under his head all nice and sweet. No one would ever think.

She came in and shut the door quietly behind her.

Not that there'd ever been anything. All dried up before ever anyone came. And even if it wasn't, who was to say. She'd be perfectly within her rights, him all feverish and asking for water like he was, hot in the head. Dr. Trent, he hadn't thought there was anything wrong. "So he's gone, poor soul." Writing out the certificate, how it was his heart that went. You mustn't fret, he'd said. You couldn't have done any more than what you did.

She came round to the foot of the bed and stood looking at him, with the candle in her hand making a bright wide splash between him and her, on the clean, straight counterpane.

As quiet and innocent as a babe. No different than if he'd passed away in his sleep.

And so he did, in a manner of speaking. He wasn't himself, hadn't been for days. Lying there half asleep the best part of the time: half silly, with all the physic he'd drunk. He didn't really know what he was saying. She ought to get the room tidy for when Porters' came. There wasn't much to do, give it a dust. She hadn't got her duster up here now. Do it first thing in the morning.

She moved around the room, setting things right; picking a pin from the mantelpiece and dropping it behind the paper in the grate, moving the chair an inch, crossways in front of the corner of the chest of drawers, twitching the curtains to make them fall straight. She had the candle in her hand; every now and then a blob of wax plopped into the candlestick, flat and transparent, with the blue enamel showing through, and in a minute it would be white and solid. Taking the light with her round the room, it was as much as she could do, time and again, not to turn and see what William was doing, lying back there quiet in the shadows. Silly of me, she scoffed.

She pulled the runner of the toilet table into place and moved on quickly past the glass, to fold the soiled towels on the towel-rail.

But it did give you a funny feeling, him lying so still, that was so fidgety towards the end. Such a fret and fidget, nothing suited him. It was his heart, that was what it was, that made him like that. It was a mercy, really, he'd been taken. His life couldn't have been any pleasure to him, being like he was. It was the kindest thing that could have happened.

The slops had been emptied — she'd seen to that yesterday — the fat china jug stood white and solid in its clean basin and the tumbler was turned upside down over the water bottle. And there was his medicine stood beside it, just like it had been when he was alive. The bottle was three-quarter full. There was a waste of good money for you: and how that *would* have upset William. She uncorked the bottle and tipped it over the tin lid of the water-receiver until there was only a dose or two left; she heard the medicine drip through the hole in the lid, down into the pail, and pushed back the cork. Silly, as if anyone would ever have given a thought. Suddenly she pulled open the little drawer under the marble slab, smelling stuffy and strong of soap and shaving brush, and pushed in the bottle. Have it all tidy and nice when people come.

Somehow she felt easier, taking a look at him again before she went out, lying so straight and tidy in his bed. All as nice as you please, no trouble spared. She gave a yawn as she pulled the door to quietly behind her and went across and shut herself into her own room, hardly troubling to turn the key. She was tired out, she hadn't got any time to go imagining things. Plenty wouldn't like it, she thought, opening out the clothes, tucking down her legs wrapped in the long flannel nightgown. Being alone in the house like that, alone with the dead.

She blew out the candle. Poor William, she thought, turning over, it may have been all for the best.

Before she knew where she was it was the next morning, and she'd hardly got the fire lit and had her breakfast when there was the man from Porters', come to measure William for his coffin.

She didn't have a minute to herself all those two days, with people in and out. First there was Minnie Hallet to fit her for her expensive black — and not half the quality stuff it used to be either, and for less money, and she promising faithfully to have it ready tomorrow night, and running out to order the sherry and cake for the funeral and fetch any little things she wanted: which she couldn't have done for herself, the funeral not being over.

Jane gave her the thirty shillings for the dress. And ought to be glad to get it.

"Oo, Mrs. Chirp," said Minnie, "wherever did you get a gold sovering and half sovering from? There isn't one left in Jewsbury hardly, with them all being changed for the paper notes on account of the war."

Which Jane hadn't thought of, though she had seen them in the shops, nasty dirty things, William having paid her the housekeeping money each week in silver.

"Mr. Chirp had them put by," she said stiffly. "He never would have the notes. He used to say whatever would happen in the case of a fire."

She put out her hand and took back the two gold pieces which Minnie hadn't picked up. "I'll give you your money in silver," she said, "it'll be easier for you. You mightn't be able to get it changed." The silver she'd got, nearly four pounds in big money, was heavy, dragging down her skirt. And gold was never going to lose its value, you could depend upon that, notes or no notes. "You run up to the shops," she nodded. "I'll have it for you when you get back. I've got to get it out from where it's locked up."

Just as well, not to have anyone knowing too much. Even if it *was* only Minnie.

As soon as Minnie'd gone she went upstairs and got out the thirty shillings in half crowns, from her pocket. She had some five shilling pieces too, four of them, but it wouldn't do to give Minnie those, might make her wonder. It was lighter, with the gold back in the bag.

Minnie came back with the slab of cake, and the gloves and handkerchiefs, which she'd left to be paid for, out of breath as if she'd run all the way, and saying they'd send round the sherry today for certain.

She'd hardly gone — saying she must fly and get on with Mrs. Chirp's black or it would never be done in time — when the sherry came; and after dinner there was the Reverend Peat to ask about the funeral service and what hymns she'd like sung: it was a mercy she'd got the parlour turned out when she did! She sitting there with the blind down and in her old black, on account of her mourning not being ready. The Reverend Peat was very kind and considerate. She mustn't overdo things, he said, she must think of her own health. He and Tom Higgs would see to all, and she wasn't to worry: everything would be done as it ought.

And then just when she was thinking there wouldn't be anyone else coming and she'd make herself a cup of tea, Mrs. Mace called in to see if there was anything she could do, so she said. She could send her girl in, if Mrs. Chirp liked, to help with the cleaning and handing round. "I know what it is, having a lot of people in, when you've got trouble in the house."

Jane thanked her, but she wouldn't dream of putting her to the trouble, she'd got it all seen to. Emily would be there to help her on the day, Dr. Trent having kindly sent a telegram when he went away after giving the certificate.

Jane didn't suggest Mrs. Mace's going up to look at him, though that was what she'd come for you could depend upon it; she didn't think it was called for. It was a bit funny when you came to think of it, her coming in like that: someone Jane hadn't seen to speak to a dozen times in as many years, unless it was at Mrs. Peat's afternoons.

Mrs. Mace got up to go. "Jewsbury's so quiet now," she said, "you wouldn't know it, it does make a difference now the troops are gone. But you wouldn't have seen anything of that," she said, "what an excitement there was with them marching out. It must have been the very day poor Mr. Chirp was taken."

It was a mercy Jane had her back to the lamp. She could feel herself go as white as a sheet. Whatever could Mrs. Mace have heard, with all the windows open and she out there at her gate as she was…. She drew herself up. "I did hear them shouting and calling out," she said with dignity, "but things being what they were and Mr. Chirp about to breathe his last, I wasn't in a frame of mind to pay any attention to it."

Silly of me, how could she have heard, with all the noise that was going on. And all that way off.

"He went very suddenly, didn't he?"

"Oh dear. Yes, he did. I just turned round and there he was fallen over, all white, and before I could hardly get to him he was gone. You could have knocked me down with a feather. Not but what Dr. Trent had said it might happen any time, but you know how it is."

It did upset her having to talk about it. She couldn't get it out of her mind after Mrs. Mace had gone, how she'd asked all those questions. She ought to have known better. It wasn't like the Reverend Peat who had a right as you might say, and showed a proper respect. It was different with someone like Mrs. Mace, that hadn't any standing in Jewsbury but what she could get by making herself welcome: always with a bit of tattle to pass on.

It preyed on her mind, even after she'd locked up the parlour and bolted the front door for the night — if anyone else should come they could ring and go away — and made herself a cup of tea by the kitchen fire. And not before she wanted it.

It was funny in a way, her saying all that.

That about how the troops were marching and it must have been the same time.

And not too nice, if you came to think of it, showing so much curiosity and William not yet underground. It didn't show nice feeling.

Sudden. As if it wasn't always sudden, with heart disease. For that was what it was. It was all very well to talk about the 'flu, but if he hadn't had something wrong with him it would never have taken him that way. Had it for years, very likely. If it hadn't been *that* day it would have been some other time. You couldn't expect anyone with heart disease to go on for ever. And we all had to go when the time came.

Mrs. Mace wasn't any class, the Maces never had been. Mace's always was a nasty little shop, it never was thought anything of: nobody knew how the old man came to leave so much money as he did. Mrs. Mace able to come and settle at The Lilacs, with a girl to do for her as if she was quite somebody. It showed what she was, coming in and gossiping like that and William hardly cold in his bed, she never would have dared come near the place if he'd been alive. Never had, all the years she'd lived next door. It wasn't so much that there was anything Jane would have minded telling her if she'd wanted to know, but it didn't show a proper respect for the dead.

Next morning there was Porters' back with the coffin, and before she could look round they had William tucked away and brought downstairs and set out in the parlour behind the blind. She watched them from the kitchen door bringing him down on their shoulders, easy round the corner: and a fine job they'd made of it, you could say that for them; good brass handles, all of the best. Porter's always was a good firm. She followed along and showed them where to put him down, and watched them lower the new polished wood on to the middle of the parlour carpet. And the head-man straightened up and touched his hat, respectful. She could hardly wait till she'd showed them out, to be upstairs sweeping out the room that was empty now for her to clear. Sheets in a heap for the wash, and mattress turned back airing over the end of the bed, and the key turned in the lock: not that anyone was likely to come walking round, but you never knew, and with the plaster off the ceiling like it was.

It was dinnertime before she'd done, and the dining room to turn out for the next day, and Minnie Hallet round at teatime to bring home her new black and help her lay out the glasses. There wasn't time to do anything to the back parlour, and no one wanted to be going in there: she turned the key in the lock and left it at that. Before she knew where she was it was the next day and she in her mourning with the prayerbook on her lap, and Emily by her on the parlour sofa, waiting for them to come back from the church.

"You might have written, Ma, and let me know he was bad."

"What time did I have," she retorted, "with him in bed, and the house to see to. I haven't got more than one pair of hands."

Emily had a black band sewn round the arm of her yellow fur coat, and a dyed skirt that stretched across her knees where the coat came apart. If that was all she could do for her Pa, with all her talk of sudden

"What'll you do now, Ma? You won't want to go on living here alone. Pa'll have left you the house, I suppose?"

So that was it, was it. Wanted to know how it was left. Jane couldn't help a smile to herself. She got up to see to the fire that she'd put a match to a minute ago: they'd be chilly when they got back, wouldn't look well not having it lit. It was turning to rain, she could hear it on the bushes outside the blind. "Mr. Bream's staying to read the will, when the rest have gone."

Emily pushed back the hat from her face. Stout she'd got lately, coarse-looking. "What's the use of that," she said, fidgeting crossly. "There's only you and me to read it to, and you know it already don't you?"

Jane sat again with her hands prim in her lap and crossed her ankles. She had her best slippers on, with the beads on the front, that she'd hardly worn since her wedding if at all, and *that* was a good time ago. Quality stuff, that was it, that was the thing to last. Emily with her cheap patents, that showed a crack across the front. And too small for her too, you could see that.

"Well you do, don't you," Emily snapped.

Not so fast, my lady.

Jane unfolded her hands and folded them the other way about. "If you mean have I read it," she said, quite quiet and dignified, "you're making a mistake. I shouldn't think it seemly to pry into such a thing, before the proper time!"

Emily shrugged her shoulders.

Anxious, eh? You'll know it fast enough.

"All I can tell you, is what Mr. Bream told me: and without me asking, mind you. All has been done, he said, *as it should be*."

Emily bent down and eased her shoe with a finger. "And what's that mean? Share and share between us?"

Jane went pink. "What it means," she said, with perfect dignity, "we shall know *all in due course*."

It was a mercy it wasn't lighter, or she would never have been able to hide what she thought. Share and share, indeed. The impudence. She his lawful wife, that had spent the best part of her life waiting on him hand and foot, and this young chit that had gone off.... It was a lucky thing William had some sense of his obligations, he always knew what was due. William was a just man in his way, you could say that for him, poor William. If he could have heard such a thing said, and he barely underground....

Emily yawned. "Isn't there anything to do, getting things ready?"

"It's been done," Jane said quietly. A bit late in the day to think of that, with me slaving day and night ever since he breathed his last. And at a time when most would expect to fold their hands and have all done for them. But that was never *my* way.

Emily sighed. She got up from the sofa and went over to a chair, where there was more room to stretch. She'd seen the bottles put out on the dining table as she came in. She could have done with a glass now, to keep her going, only she'd never hear the end of it. It wasn't too lively sitting in here in the half dark, only the old lady'd been so set on her staying; if it hadn't been for that she'd have gone off with them to the church, to see the last of poor Pa. It was raining harder now, you could hear it dripping from the bushes, down on the gravel. "They'll get wet," she said, and yawned again.

Lounging there with her legs apart. It wasn't the way to behave. And what a time they were, coming back. Jane fidgeted on the sofa and recollected herself and set the prayerbook straight on her lap. They sat there and listened to the rain dripping. *All as it should be*, it couldn't mean anything else, there weren't two ways about it. It didn't take a lawyer to see who should be the one to benefit. Even though Emily *was* his only child, that wasn't the same thing as being his wife; it wasn't as if he hadn't married again. That would be another matter. Altogether.

The book slipped from her lap; she bent to pick it up and the blood rushed to her head from stooping. He wouldn't be likely, would he, to have made some sort of conditions like you heard of people doing? Such as that she and Emily must live together and share the house between them? Or so much a year to Emily and the rest to her? You did hear of such things. But William would never do a thing like that: he'd never had much opinion of Emily and her ways. And that Jim. Jim ought to have provided for her by rights. Even if he *was* killed in the war. You'd think anyone could do just what they liked, just because they went to the war. He ought to have been saving all those years before; instead of the two of them spending it as fast as it came in: easy come and easy go: leaving her with nothing but her pension. All the same, William wasn't to know that, he must have made his will years back. Made it new when they married, very likely.

She sat up and patted her hair straight and shut the book and laid it on the sofa at her side. Emily had jumped up to answer the bell. Through the open door Jane could see them moving in, slow and heavy in their black, through the dark hall into the dining room. Emily was in there serving, she could hear the chink of plates and glasses. She sat there with a hand in her lap and one on the book by her side, while they came in one at a time to pay their respects. "Yes, indeed, it was a sad shock. In the midst of life, as you might say...."

Minnie Hallet slipped up behind her to whisper, "It was a lovely service, lovely," with a sniff into her handkerchief, and slipped away quickly to make way for the Reverend Peat.

"I can't tempt you to take a little refreshment, dear Mrs. Chirp?"

Jane shook her head sadly. She didn't fancy anything. She was wondering how the food was holding out in the other room, and if Emily would have the sense to go out and cut bread and butter if they ran short; or Minnie might see to it. But it wasn't long now before they'd all gone and Mr. Bream was bending down, holding her hand, and she could see the end of the envelope sticking from his pocket.

"Where's Emily," she said, quite in a flutter. "We can't begin without Emily." She explained, "My dear husband's daughter by his first wife."

Emily was across in the dining room talking to Minnie, who'd stayed behind to help clear up. Talking out loud, and just then she gave a laugh: it made Jane quite ashamed. You'll laugh on the other side of your face in a minute, she thought sharply, with fierce, sour rancour avenging the dead.

Mr. Bream went out into the hall and coughed. "If you'd step this way for a minute Miss ... er Madam?"

Emily put down what she was holding and came across and Mr. Bream shut the door behind her, shutting out Minnie Hallet with the trays of stained glasses and crumby plates.

"Won't you take a seat, Mr. Bream," Jane twittered. She really felt quite ill; it was the shock, and all the strain she'd had put on her the last few days.

Emily threw herself into one of the armchairs, and Mr. Bream, easing the envelope deliberately out of his pocket, sat down in the other.

Jane could hardly hear what it was he was reading, she had the buzzing so bad in her head, she thought her heart would choke her.

To my wife, Jane Caroline Chirp....

He might have said my *dear* wife.

...for her sole use and benefit, so long as she shall live.

How beautifully he'd put it all. Mr. Bream was going on reading, but she didn't need to hear any more. It was all right. It was all as it should be. All to her for her life, and Emily after her. Poor Emily, she thought happily, he might have left her a trifle to remember him by!

Mr. Bream had shaken hands and gone, with Jane smiling him out, and she and Emily were out in the kitchen with Minnie Hallet, piling up the plates. Minnie wouldn't look at either of them, she kept her head turned away. She was dying to know, but she didn't like to ask.

Jane told Emily, "Of course if there's any little thing you'd like to take, any bit of furniture."

Minnie looked up and gave her such a nice smile.

Emily said, "That's all right, Ma."

"There's the bookcase in the dining room, that's had your lesson books in it all this while. You might like to have that for the sake of old times. And I can make do without it."

It was almost as if Emily gave a laugh, over her wiping up. Jane looked at her sharply. "It's a nice bit of bamboo. Light and handy. It'd be easy for you to take away."

"That's all right."

"But if you don't want it you can leave it."

Jane went back to set the chairs straight in the front rooms. What did she expect? Think I was going to give her the best piece in the house? With all it's going to cost, doing the place up.

She pushed back the horsehair sofa against the window and drew up the blind. All this old furniture, it was dull and out of date, but it was worth something. It wasn't likely she was going to part with it to Emily. Whatever would William have said. If such had been his wish, such he would have written down.

It was bad enough having to have Emily in the house that night, saying she'd got time off till the next day and there wasn't a train back. All the evening alone with her, once the washing up was done and Minnie gone home and they'd made up the bed for her in the little room the girl used to have at the back. She wanting to see the room where he died.

"Why, Ma, you haven't got it turned out already?"

"I don't believe in leaving things half done, it isn't my way. Even though there *was* only me to do everything single-handed, and I've had my time taken up I can tell you."

Anyone might have thought she'd have come a day sooner, to give a hand.

"Poor Pa," Emily sighed.

It was on the tip of Jane's tongue to say something, but she kept her mouth shut. Emily'd be glad enough to turn it round the wrong way, whatever it was she said. Like to make out she was the only one that felt for him. For all she'd ever done. Like to make out I was only after his money, all these years I've slaved, working my fingers to the bone. Be making out I hadn't got a right to it, if she had half a chance. Not that she ever could do that, but it isn't a nice idea.

She shut the door of the big room firmly and turned the key.

"What do you do that for?"

Jane gave her a sharp look. "Don't want the dust blowing in, just when I've done it."

They went down again into the kitchen.

"It was a great shock to me, when your Pa died," Jane said, taking up her sewing. "He was very much attached to me. There was hardly a cross word passed between us all the years we were married."

Emily said, looking round, "You ought to have someone here with you. You don't want to stay alone all the time, it isn't good for anyone."

Yes, I daresay!

"I can manage all right. I daresay I shall be getting a girl in later on."

Like to come and live here, that's what she'd like, give her half a chance. Likely I'd have her sitting here waiting for me to die so it would all come to her. Bad enough her staying on tonight, giving extra trouble.

It was a relief when Emily said she'd go up to bed. Jane saw her into her room, and on the way back to her own she slipped the key quietly out of the opposite door and took it in with her. She could sleep easier.

She gave Emily her breakfast and saw her off to an early train. "Well, you've got a nice day," she said, standing on the step. Nothing lost by being pleasant. "Let me know how you're going on."

Emily was tying a silk scarf round her neck under her coat.

"I hope you don't bear any grudge," Jane said in a low voice, the front door being open, "me coming into all. It was as your dear Pa wished."

Emily picked up her attaché case. "That's all right, Ma. I've got a job waiting for when I'm demobbed, forewoman in a laundry up in Birmingham. Boy I nursed, his father owns a big chain of laundries up that way, promised he'd keep it open. Before you can look round I'll be manager*ess*." She nodded. "Well, cheerio." She went off down the drive with her big ankles turning over on top of her high, patent heels and a yellow side of the coat flapping out against her swung arm. When she'd got through the gate she waved, and bobbed out of sight behind the next door bushes.

Jane stood a minute after she'd gone. It was a nice day. The sun was up, shining on the wet gravel, where it hadn't dried up from the night before. It did seem funny to think it was all hers, the house and everything. It didn't seem real. Poor William, if he could have known, only a week ago.... She sighed. Well, it's the same for all. She moved to the side of the steps and began to pick dead bits off the laurels, dropping them on the weedy drive.

Saturday, this was. She ought to have been going out by rights; but it didn't seem as if any day this week had been what it ought to be: all upside down. Only middleday Tuesday, William had gone. What a time it did seem. And all the same she hadn't had a minute to herself to see where she stood.

Well, better get on, there was the breakfast to clear. She went in and put up the chain: shut herself into the empty house.

The back parlour was just as it had been, excepting that William wasn't in it. There was his chair square with the fender, and her own straight-backed one at the side, pushed between his writing desk and the window. Nothing in the drawers but a lot of rubbish; clear it out one of these days. And the room wanted a good turn-out too. Sitting in there meant using his chair, and she didn't quite like the idea of that. Or else sitting with it empty in front of her. Enough to give you the creeps. Not that she was the kind to fancy things, never had been; but it wasn't a nice idea, she didn't like it. Unless she was to change things round. But the room wanted a good clean, in any case, and she couldn't be bothered with it now.

She shut the door and turned the key again, mechanically.

Might as well use the front parlour, now she was by herself. Where was the use of keeping it shut up from one week's end to another, keeping two rooms going. Just for herself. It wasn't like William leaving his tobacco smoke about, spoiling the curtains. It would do the furniture good to keep a bit of fire in there in the afternoons, and look better too, if anyone should come. When she'd got the washing-up done and Emily's room turned out — and glad to see the back of her, for all the help she was — and had a bit of dinner, she fetched her work-basket and settled herself in there on the sofa, with a towel to mend; that William had cut, weeks ago, with his razor, and she'd never had time to see to. It was a nice little room when you came to look round it, even though some of the chairs *were* gone in the springs. It was a nice enough little room just for her to sit and work in, and for all the visitors she ever had.... And it did you good to make a few changes: took you out of yourself. One of these days she'd get some new things and freshen the house up, but she'd have to see first where she stood. And that she couldn't know before Mr. Bream had been next week and gone through things with her, to see how much William had had put by. Well, it must be a tidy bit more than ever he spent, you could depend on that, knowing William as *she* did.

In the basket there were the khaki socks and cuffs that ought to go to Mrs. Peat's. Next Thursday, that was. But Jane couldn't very well be expected to go, it would hardly look nice. Even though you might say it was a business meeting and not really what you could call going about. But it wouldn't show proper feeling, to her mind. And it wasn't what she felt like doing either. Sympathetic they might be, but you could have too much of sympathy. It would be as much as she could stand, just now when she'd got the funeral over, to have anyone more coming up and feeling they had to ask and pass remarks. Too much of a good thing altogether. Minnie Hallet could have the woollens, when she ran in after church tomorrow and take them with her to Mrs. Peat's.

It wasn't till the end of the week that she could bring herself even to go out, and that was after Mr. Bream had been in to see her. Mr. Bream was as kind and helpful as you could wish: he had it all straight in his mind by now, what William had done with his money that he got when he sold the shop, and what he'd had put by; and it seemed it was all tied up so Jane couldn't touch it; but that was all to the good, for no one else could touch it either, and it was bringing in a very nice little sum, two hundred pounds a year.

Two hundred pounds! My word, but that was a lot of money.

Well, said Mr. Bream, it wasn't half so much now as it was before the war, but still it went a good way in a place like Jewsbury, and then there was the house and furniture. Mr. Bream explained how she wouldn't be able to take money from the bank just yet; but he could let her have some, that would be hers really, to go on with; would ten pounds be enough?

Oh dear! But she would never think of having all that amount of money in the house!

It was on the tip of her tongue to say she didn't want any, on account of what she'd got tucked away safe in her skirt: but you never knew, she mightn't get the chance another time. She said she'd take five, in case. And Mr. Bream handed it out in notes, which she never had handled before — and whatever would happen to those things in case of a fire? — and went away saying he'd come back before long with more papers to sign, and then she'd be able to get what she wanted for herself. Or she could come and see him if she had a mind to, now they'd got the new motor bus running into Toddleton.

Saturday it was such a nice day it did seem a shame not to go out. Best part of a fortnight since she'd put her nose outside the door, except for running up to Dr. Trent's, and you couldn't count that. And she'd got her new black, and the odds and ends Minnie had fetched for her, gloves and black-edged handkerchiefs and all complete. And all those bills mounting up, it really wouldn't be right not to go and settle them, whatever her own feelings might be. Peel's, in any case. And Mr. Peel having been at the funeral, he wouldn't feel called upon to have any more to say.

She took two of Mr. Bream's notes from where she'd locked them away in her bottom drawer and put them in the housekeeping purse. The old purse never had had so much in it! Get them changed for silver, the sooner the better, she didn't altogether like having all that paper money about. Her hat wasn't too tidy, she thought, fastening her veil in front of the window in her little room. If they should have something nice in Porter's.... She might see what they'd got.

It seemed funny to be out again, and Jewsbury did seem quiet, there was hardly anyone about. It was going to make a difference, with all the troops gone. She went up and settled with Peels'. Mr. Peel was very quiet and respectful: it was a nice day, he said, sympathetic in his way but nothing prying. It had always been a good class shop, Peels'. And across at the baker's there was only the girl serving, never did have anything to say for herself. At Porters' she owed them for the gloves and handkerchiefs Minnie had fetched. You wouldn't think, really, how the money went, with all these bills: it made a big hole out of her two notes. She ought to have a regular widow's cap really, with a crape veil, only it did seem a waste, for she wouldn't want to go on wearing a thing like that. And people didn't so much, nowadays. And yet she didn't quite like to go asking for an ordinary hat, just yet, it didn't look quite nice. But as she was on her way out she stopped. She knew what she'd do, she'd get a nice length of crape veiling, freshen up the old one; it made a lot of difference, a good-looking veil. And more suitable, too, being crape. That would do for a bit, until she knew where she stood. You never could tell how long Mr. Bream might be, getting the papers for her to draw at the bank, and if she was to run short he mightn't be so ready to put his hand in his pocket a second time. Once get over Christmas and she could find a nice light hat that would do for spring and go on through the summer.

They did have some tempting things in Porters' window, in the furnishing. It was as well not to spend too much on herself if she meant to do up the house later on. As soon as ever Mr. Bream had got it all put right for her. She didn't know anything that would give her more pleasure than getting rid of a lot of that old rubbish and having in a new lot of things. Not that some of it wasn't worth money, she'd see what she could do about selling it. Turn in a bit to help with the new.

She would sit there with her work — old petticoats that she was taking in and taking up, skirts not being what they were, and though she had expressly forbidden Minnie to make her new black one of those tight, nasty things it wasn't so long or so full as what she'd been accustomed to — planning how she'd have the parlour done up when the spring came on. A nice bright paper with bunches of flowers on, and a new plush suite: a nice green, *that* would look nice. Why, it would make it so you wouldn't know it was the same place! And come to that why didn't she sell the piano and buy a gramophone, the way a lot of other people had done? She never could do that though. Whatever William would have said...!

Though after all, whatever you might say, it was hers now to do what she liked with, there was no getting away from that. But it wouldn't do to be making too many changes all at once, it wouldn't look nice. She'd see, when it came on for spring, what she could do.

It did seem a bit dull sometimes, in the evenings, having no one to speak to, but you couldn't have everything. She didn't believe in encouraging a lot of visitors, only making work; and half the time all they wanted was pick up some bit of tattle they could go and pass on. That Mrs. Mace had tried dropping in again, to see if Mrs. Chirp wasn't lonely, so she said. But Jane had soon let her know: quite nice and quiet, no offence meant or taken. "I'm much obliged I'm sure," she said, quiet, but so that anyone could see she meant it. "But I've got my work to do. I've got no time to sit about talking."

She didn't so much mind Minnie Hallet running in on a Sunday, the way she'd taken to do, to ask if anything was wanted: on account of Jane having a touch of the lumbago[1] which prevented her attending church as she always had done. No, she didn't know that she'd ever had such a thing before, but there you were. She could feel it coming on even when she was getting up on a Sunday morning, when the bell was going for early service. And in the week-time it must have been the same, only she'd manage somehow to get about and do what she had to, the same as she always had. As for Minnie coming down to do her bit of shopping for her, she wouldn't hear of it; Minnie had her own work to do, and Jane was quite well able to look after herself. She didn't believe in depending on other people.

And she wasn't sorry when Emily wrote she wouldn't be coming for Christmas, she was asked to friends. Though it didn't seem quite nice her gadding off, so soon after her Pa had passed away, but that was her own affair. Jane would as soon have her room as her company. She didn't altogether like Emily's manner.

She wasn't one to mind her own society, never had done. She had the house to keep straight, the front parlour and kitchen and her bedroom; the rest was shut up, only made work. And twice a week now, Wednesdays and Saturdays, she would dress herself in her best black and go out to get what things she wanted. Twice a week was enough, just for herself, and now she was on her own there was no reason why she shouldn't go out any time

---

1   Mild to severe low back pain.

she wanted, come to think of it, if she should run out of anything in between whiles. Not that she ever did do such a thing, always having been a good manager — and whatever they would have done, without! — but it was something to know she could. And being able to take her time, too, when she was out, not having to be particular to five minutes or so. Not like when William would be waiting for her on the doorstep. Poor William! She had time to plan now what she wanted to do, and look out her money overnight so that she could get off in good time. She quite enjoyed herself when the fine spring days came on, and she knew she could get her money from the bank if she felt like it, planning what she'd do to brighten up the place, and pricing things in the windows. She needn't settle on it all at once, there wasn't any hurry, she'd think, screwing up her veil in front of the glass in her little room, trying the bottom drawer again and slipping out the key and pinning it to the lining of her dress pocket. Take her time. Time to look round and suit herself.

Prices had gone up since the war, really dreadful. If only William had bought then, when she told him.... But that was William all over. And now she'd have to give twice what he would have done then, and it wasn't for want of telling. Porters' had some lovely suites this year, but it did seem a wicked lot of money to spend all at once. And the money did seem to go, too, even being careful like she was. When it all had to come out of what she'd got: when the housekeeping money wasn't coming in regular.

But the first time she brought herself to go to the bank, which she hadn't had to do so far since Mr. Bream had told her she could, but she didn't want to go too hard on her own bit of money that would come in for a rainy day: when she came out, quite hot in the face, and only just next-door to Porters', with the notes folded in her purse, she really couldn't resist looking for some little thing to brighten up the place for the summer.

It was really more than she ought to have done, and she didn't feel quite easy about it in her mind, but she couldn't resist it, it was such a nice little stand. And bamboo was so light and handy, you could move it about in dusting; she wouldn't give a thank-you for those big heavy things. And the pots thrown in, which was a help, pink china pots: a big one on the top, and three little ones hanging down on chains. And they had some lovely plants out now down at Williams's, the young man told her. Not that she was going to spend good money on plants, that grew for nothing, but he wasn't to know that. When they sent down the stand that afternoon she had it put in the parlour window, with the sofa pulled out, and out she went there and then with the little trowel William used to use, that was put by under the sink, and dug up four lovely ferns she found down in the hedge at the bottom of the garden. Lovely they looked, when she'd got them hanging in the pink pots, and hadn't cost a penny, and what a difference it did make to a room. Now you never would have got William to do a thing like that.

She would sit there with her work on fine afternoons, with the fern-stand up against her between the sofa and the window, and plan how she'd have the room done up as soon as ever she was out of her mourning. Suites did seem a wicked price, perhaps she oughtn't to spend so much money all at once. There were those loose cover things they had now; she might let Minnie make her a set of those to cover up the old chairs. One of those nice bright cretonnes[1]. Minnie oughtn't to charge her half of what they would at Porters' for the making, and be glad of the work, too. She'd have to see, later on.

And there was another thing, you didn't want to be too quick over making changes, it didn't look nice, it only set people talking. It was a funny thing how ready everyone was to talk about what

---

1 A heavy cotton fabric, typically with a floral pattern printed on one or both sides, used for upholstery.

didn't concern them, settling other people's business for them. Always plenty ready to do that. Mrs. Peat, when Jane did bring herself to go to church, for Whitsun, wanting to know whyever she didn't have a girl to live in and help her, with her lumbago and everything. Didn't like to think of her being there alone in the house. Though Mrs. Peat did mean well by it, it wasn't like some.

These girls, nothing but a worry and trouble. And not only that, directly you got a girl in the house, you got gossip.

It was bad enough as it was, everyone wanting to know why she didn't. As if it wasn't her own business. And of course they all knew it wasn't that she couldn't have afforded it, they knew that well enough.

Once having done it she felt she had to go to church once of a Sunday, if she didn't feel too bad, so long as it was good weather. Though she couldn't say she was too fond of it. Mr. Peel they had now, helping Tom Higgs to take up the bag. Mr. Peel was a big, fine-looking man when you saw him like that out of the shop, but not half the class William had been. And it wasn't a thing she liked, sitting there and watching someone take his place. And having to find something for the bag, week by week: it was a regular tax. And as if it wasn't bad enough it was said the Reverend Peat was going to retire in August and they'd be having a new young man there, with a lot of fresh ways. And then Mrs. Mace coming up to her after the service: "However you can stay there all by yourself at night...."

And when it came to Emily running up for a couple of days: "I do think you ought to have someone with you, Ma...."

It was enough to drive anyone crazy.

"I can manage my own business. I don't want any telling."

Run up to see what she was doing with the house, that was what it was. What else should she have come for. Keeping an eye, to see she didn't get rid of anything. That was what it came to, the way William had left things; he ought never to have done it.

Putting her at the mercy of Emily, having her poking round just to see what she could find out. It was enough to give anyone the creeps to have her sleeping there along the passage, knowing she was keeping her eyes open, waiting for a chance to get what was coming to her. Waiting for you to die. For that was what it came to. It wasn't nice. It was a mercy she couldn't get off from her work for more than a night, and that was bad enough.

But it wasn't till Emily'd taken herself off, and she was sitting alone in the parlour one afternoon, that she really thought of it: whatever did she want with a great house like that all to herself? Half of it shut up, no good to her or anyone else. It was too much of a good thing altogether. If she got into a smaller place there wouldn't be any *room* for Emily to come and stay.

Jane couldn't help laughing. She couldn't keep still, now she'd once thought of it. Whyever hadn't she thought of it before. She got up from the sofa and fetched her duster and started wiping over the ornaments on the piano. There was no law, after all, that said she had to go on living here; she could live where she liked as well as Emily could. If she were to sell the house a lot of this old furniture could go, and it wouldn't cost half so much to get new if she was in a smaller place. You didn't want a great barn of a place these days: look at those nice little houses they'd started building again up Station Road: two rooms up and two down, and she didn't even want so much. She wouldn't know herself if she got somewhere like that! And this was a good solid-built house, it ought to fetch a nice bit: more than what she'd have to give to get what she wanted. One of those little houses like they'd built up Station Road. It would never do for her to move to another house in Jewsbury, though; think of all the talk there'd be. Get somewhere different, over Toddleton way. Somewhere right away. Make a change. And then she *might* get a girl, for it wasn't that she was so anxious to have the work to do, but in a place like this everyone knew your business better than you did yourself. That was what she'd do. Get somewhere quite different. Somewhere fresh.

Once she'd thought of it she wasn't in any hurry. Take her time and look round. She didn't want anyone remarking on how ready she was to get away, and not out of her mourning yet. But that was what she'd do. It was a funny thing she'd never thought of it before. Then she wouldn't trouble about getting new covers made, before she moved. Go on quietly till her year was out, and then get right away and set up fresh in a new place.

And Jewsbury wasn't what it had been, either. With the new houses they were building, bringing a lot of strangers in, and the buses running every day now up to London, coming and going all the time. It spoiled the character of the place. It used to be a nice quiet little town, but it wouldn't be long now before it was like a suburb of London, the way things were going. Building right away up the London Road, out past The Oaks. Come to that you might as well *be* in London. Not half so many busybodies up there. More people about, and they had their own affairs to see to. And more going on. After all, where was the point of spending your whole life shut up in a poky little place like Jewsbury. Especially now, when she was free to do what she liked, there wasn't any point in it.

And then the Peats going, that had always been so nice and friendly. It wasn't the same thing, having fresh faces up at the vicarage. And a young man like the Reverend Wilson, coming in and changing everything in the parish from the way it always had been. Whatever William would have said…! Poor William, it was a mercy he'd gone. Starting these new-fangled envelopes for everyone to take home and put their offertory in, instead of in the bag like it was in the old days. Free-Will Offering Scheme, he called it. Such as had never been heard of in *Jewsbury* before. A fine lot of free-will there was about it, with your name put down and everyone knowing what you put in. It wasn't reverent.

It was almost a lucky thing, that with the dark days coming Jane's lumbago got so bad again she really couldn't get to church. For it upset her, to see the way they were going on, so different from the old days. It was time to be moving.

She went on quietly for a bit, and not a word did she say to anyone of what she intended. But that was what she'd do: get away up nearer London, where nobody knows who you are. And the end of November, as soon as ever her year was up, she took one of those rattly buses that ran from the Market Place into Toddleton on a Wednesday morning, and asked Mr. Bream to see about selling the house for her.

Chapter X

And what a relief it was to get away from Jewsbury! To get away out of that great house into somewhere she could feel was her own. Such a nice little house, too, even if it was in a row. You hadn't got to be too particular nowadays. And even if she had got people next door, no one was going to bother *her*, and there was the bit of garden, to keep anyone off the front door. *I* think it's a very nice little house, myself. And such a pleasure to be able to go out in a new place and see something fresh around you. It had made a new woman of her. She really felt she could breathe, for the first time in years!

Parlour and kitchen, just what she wanted for herself — and there was no one else to consult, so far as she knew — and two upstairs. She'd have a girl in that little back room, one of these days, and that would settle it. No more of Emily's popping in, any time she wanted a day out. Impudence, that was all it was.

She didn't quite like not to let Emily know she'd moved, it would seem so funny, though it did go against the grain to give away where she was after all the trouble she'd taken. But there you were. When she'd been settled in for a week or two she took her courage in both hands and sat down to the dinner table, which was in the parlour now, there being only the one room in front, and wrote off to Birmingham that she'd moved to such a nice little house at Dalton Park, but she was sorry to say that she hadn't got room now to put anyone up.

That was enough for her. No need to go into details. It wasn't any business of hers, whether Jane had bought or rented. And anyone would tell you nowadays it wasn't the time for buying house property. With the rates what they were, and not a small house to be had for love or money; nothing but great barns of places that everyone wanted to get out of, with so many going into flats to live, like they were. And Jane knew enough by now not to get herself saddled again with something she couldn't get rid of when she wanted. Three months it had taken her, getting The Elms off her hands, and she was lucky to do it then: it was only that with all the strangers coming into Jewsbury since the war it was bought by a new young man from Toddleton wanting to set up as a dentist, which Mr. Bream had happened to hear of. Which was going to put Mr. Gilpin's nose out of joint, and not before it was time. Yes: it made you shudder to think your money might be tied up in property like that, and no way to get at it. She was a whole world easier in her mind since she'd got it all safe in the bank: Dalton Park branch, and she wasn't too sorry to make a change there. Too well known in Jewsbury by half: too many people knowing your business. You could say that for a place like Dalton Park, you could go out and come in and nobody any the wiser.

It quite gave her something to do at first, exploring round the shops to see where to buy things. It was really a pleasure on a fine day, and spring coming on, to take a stroll up the High Street — the Parade, as they called it here — and price things in the windows.

It wasn't the same kind of shops as in Jewsbury, either. Branches of big concerns, most of them, grocers and dairies and all: no farmers here, to bring the milk round. And the shops weren't so ready to send, inclined to be a bit off-hand, it wasn't the same thing as where you were known. But never mind, you could put up with a little thing like that. It was all to the good, for then you could walk along and take your choice, buy where it was cheapest. Jane got herself a new shopping basket and took to her three mornings a week again. Mondays and Wednesdays and Saturdays she was out, as regular as the clock, round the corner by the Dance Palace and up the Parade, as far as ever the shops went: after that there was the cemetery, with some works facing, and then more houses; where the trams went on, up through Webber's Lane, — that was shops again, but not worth the penny for the tram — getting up further into London.

But this was good enough for anyone, you didn't want anything better than this. If butter was up a penny at the Imperial Stores it was sure to be down at the Dominions, up on the cemetery corner: that was what you got by being in a big centre like London; competition did that, that was what you never would have got in a little dead-alive place like Jewsbury. When it was a nice day she'd go on as far as the cemetery and take a stroll along the paths. Beautifully kept up it was, it was a pleasure to see all the graves laid out so nice and tidy. Different from what it would be in Jewsbury when the young Reverend Wilson had had his way for a year or two: all for missions and new-fangled preaching, and not a thought for the good of the parish. Poor William. And to think she'd had to pay seven-and-six to get a good class wax wreath, something that would last. Which she'd done on leaving, not wishing to have it said she'd left the place and no provision made. Seven-and-six, it did seem a wicked lot of money. Even though it *was* a very nice wreath, as good as anyone could wish. And so it ought to be. If they didn't let the grass grow for a year or two and choke it all up.

She was quite tired by the time she got back along the Parade with her basket, and when she'd had her dinner she was ready for a sit-down on the sofa, where you could watch, over the fern-stand, people going by outside the railings. Different from The Elms, with those nasty great bushes shutting you all in. It was a pleasure just to sit there and watch what was going on.

And then if Emily hadn't got to answer that she was ever so surprised and running up to see how Ma'd settled in, and Ma wasn't to worry, because she'd got friends would put her up, up in London.

It was enough to try the patience of a saint. And there was Jane having to put on her hat and run out to the registry in the Parade to see if they could let her have a girl to come in that very next week. For if Emily was once to see that little room empty at the back, you would never have got her out of the place again.

And there she had to sit, giving Emily her tea in the front room, and she worried out of her life to know what the new girl was up to out there with no one to keep an eye on her. Gossiping, I know, out at the back. And the coals coming in, that had to be most particularly watched that he didn't go giving short weight. Emily couldn't have chosen her time worse, if she'd tried ever so. And *loud*, Emily'd got. "Hullo, Ma, how's life?" That was a nice way to talk.

Though to give Emily her due she did try to make herself pleasant.

"I expect they're missing you, back in Jewsbury!"

Well, yes, Jane couldn't say she wasn't missed, by some that she could name. Poor Minnie Hallet was very sad, almost in tears when it came to saying goodbye. "But then I've been a good friend to her, always giving her any bits of work I could to help her on. She'll find out the difference." And the Peels, that they'd been such good customers of, so many years, they'd find out the difference too when they got the dentist young man there from Toddleton. "And Mrs. Mace, that I haven't set eyes on for the best part of a year, so sorry.... You really wouldn't think how many there were, all so sorry I was going."

She poured Emily her second cup. It was quite a change to have someone to talk to for half an hour.

"Of course the worst-hit would have been the Peats, that we'd known for so *many* years. Only that as I expect you've heard they were the first to go, owing to the Reverend Peat retiring back last summer."

And it wouldn't have gone off so badly, if Emily hadn't suddenly started looking round.

"I see you had to get rid of the piano then, Ma. Or have you got it in another room? You haven't got another room, have you?"

Well, just fancy. Looking round as calmly as you like.

"No I have not, not downstairs. I brought away what would fit in here, and the rest had to go. I couldn't be cluttered up with a lot of rubbish."

And it won't be long before I'm rid of what's here, if it interests you, and got a new lot in. Such impudence. As if I couldn't do what I liked. And just when we were having a nice little chat.

Emily was up, looking round. She'd finished with her tea. "So you let the sideboard go, and the piano, and brought the table in here, with the parlour chairs? But how about Pa's desk and what was in the back room? You never sold that, did you?"

"I hadn't got any choice in the matter," she retorted stiffly. "It wasn't a case of whether I wanted. There wasn't room for it."

And not in too good taste asking, either.

"Poor Pa, how he did like to keep his own chair to himself. And how about upstairs, then?"

"I had to let the big suite go. It was too big for these little rooms."

Well really, for two pins she would have said exactly what she thought. Coming here and sizing things up, for all the world as if the place belonged to her. And wanting to look round. Well this was the last time. No more. Upstairs too; as if Jane could have brought that great bedstead, that weighed half a ton if it weighed an ounce: why, there wouldn't be room to stand by the side of it. *And* that great suite. People didn't have such things nowadays. She was well enough satisfied with her room as it was, with the things she'd been using for the last year or more, and luckily there was a wall-cupboard, so she never would need to buy a wardrobe.

"And that's the girl's room," she snapped, jerking her head to the other door that she could see Emily was staring at. Just as well, to let her know. Have no mistake about it.

Coming downstairs, Emily said, "Well, Ma, I expect you were right to make a change. You never would have been happy back there at The Elms, all by yourself."

And who asked you, whether I was happy. "I'm happy enough." And why shouldn't I be, I should like to know, after a life of slaving and scraping that not many would have put up with. And who asked you to give your opinion, coming nosing round, poking into what doesn't concern you.

Well really, of all the impudence.

She was so angry, after she'd seen Emily out — "Goodbye," she said stiffly, and she didn't say Come again, either — that she could hardly bring herself to go and see what the girl was doing with the tea-things.

To think of it. Coming here and telling me what I can do.

She couldn't get it off her mind all that evening: she sat there worrying, long after she'd sent the girl up to bed.

Coming and asking what she'd done with William's things. As if *she* hadn't got a right to say what was to be done, if anyone had. As if she could have kept that great desk, in a little house like this. Taken up half the room, and no use to anyone. And it wasn't as if he'd ever sat at it to speak of. Never had, all the years she could remember. When he had to reckon up his accounts he always did it on his knee. Coming there and arguing where was this and where was that. Poor William, if he only could have known! And as for that nasty old chair, she always had wanted to get rid of that, nasty, dirty old thing, years and years before ever William went. If she'd told him once she had fifty times. If she'd had her way he would have thrown it out years ago and got new, it wasn't fit to be seen.

She was sorry now she hadn't sold the whole lot, like she'd meant to at first. But things were such a price to buy, and the move cost so much more than she would have thought. And really when you came to see what things fetched it was as good as giving them away, it seemed a shame: good solid furniture that had years of wear in it yet, and twice the quality of what you could buy new: nasty rubbishy stuff, a lot of it, painted up to sell, and no wear or value in it. Just the dinner table she'd kept, and the chairs that went with it, and the horsehair suite out of the parlour. For there was no reason at all why she couldn't get it covered later on, and even have the springs done up, if it came to that. Later on, when she'd got over the move. And then the fernstand that she'd bought herself: she was glad she'd got that, even if it had been a bit extravagant at the time; it looked well in here, in the low window, better even than it had done at The Elms. But having Emily coming in and finding fault, it made her want to sell up the whole lot tomorrow. It was the calmness of it, thinking she could walk in…. But never again! She was going to put her foot down. She *would not* have Emily there again.

Once she'd made up her mind about that she was determined not to think about it, she wasn't going to let it worry her; but she was going to be quite firm.

For she couldn't think — putting on her hat to go out the next morning — why ever she should let that chit of an Emily worry her, seeing she had no more claim upon her than the tomcat.

And she really would see, now summer was coming on, about making a change from this heavy crape veil. Hot and stuffy like it was. And now she'd come to a new place there was no reason whatever for her to go on with it, no one was to know. Even if it hadn't been that her year was out in any case, but you knew what it was in a place like Jewsbury, have everyone talking. But there was no reason, here, for anyone to know anything at all about it. No one be any the wiser.

She unpinned the rusty folds of crape and went through the drawer for a piece of her old veiling.

And it wasn't even as if she was any relation. Never had been. Only a connection by marriage. No blood relation. It was nothing but impudence, her following her about.

She found the veil and pinned it on; and as she was passing the Drapery Stores on the Parade, she went in and got herself a nice new bit; though there wasn't half the choice there used to be, many not wearing them now: but Jane did like to see a nice tidy veil, it always looked good. Nice and ladylike. And then she wouldn't need to get herself a hat just yet, with all the expenses she was having.

Keeping that girl there, there was a wicked expense for you! Wanting wages that would never have been thought of before the war. And all the times-out. Whatever William would have said...! And wasting half their time as it was, out gossiping at the back. And sitting out there in the afternoons: just sitting down, in a chair, doing their own sewing, which they never would have dreamt of doing. It was enough to make William turn in his grave! And this was the second girl that had given notice at the end of her month, just because she said the place didn't suit her. Little chits that ought to be glad to have a roof over their head, let alone a comfortable home. Too well off, that was what was the matter with them. Why, in the old days.... Too much done for them, that was the trouble with all the lower classes now. Didn't know when they were well off.

It was nothing but worry and bother. She never would have had a girl in the house, if it hadn't been that she had to have the room taken up. Having to keep everything locked away, and be so careful when she went out, it was more bother than it was worth, she would rather have done the work herself fifty times over. She didn't like to leave her money in the drawer, even if it was locked, when she wasn't about; for you never knew when one of these hussies might get hold of a key. And there she was, having to drag about with all the money she'd got out of the bank for the month — let alone her little nest-egg, that she wouldn't have risked for the world — pinned into her skirt. For she didn't like to keep on drawing cheques, it came expensive. And even then how was she to know the girl wasn't up there trying on her clothes the minute her back was turned, or passing food out to her friends and relations.

The third girl did stay out two months, to the end of July, before she gave notice — seeing it was summer and next to no work to do: they didn't want *work*, nowadays — which brought her to the end of August, and when she went Jane wasn't having any more of it. If anyone *should* come, which Jane was determined they should *not*, it was easy enough to say it was the girl's day out, and who was to know. Come to that, she could leave a few things about in the back room, to look as if the girl was still there.

It was a weight off her mind when she was alone in the house again: being able to put up the chain on the door and feel she'd got the place to herself. She could almost take pleasure again in going out and looking round the shops, knowing all was locked up at home. Though she never dared to leave her money there, even now, and she never felt quite safe, with so many girls about the district knowing the ins and outs of the house and where she kept things. It wasn't a nice idea. And not only that, she lived in a constant dread Emily would write and say she was wanting to see her. The heart came into her mouth, whenever she saw the postman stopping at the gate. Which wasn't often. For she never had been one to waste her time writing letters, or expect other people to, either.

Then it got on through the autumn — and Jane having to lay her own fire again: not that she minded doing that, do it any day sooner than have one of those hussies about — and sure enough one day the postman that she'd watched go past for weeks and weeks turned in, up the path, and there was her letter on the mat.

Her heart was beating so she didn't know how she ever got it open. She really did wonder if she wasn't going off one of these days like poor William. But it might have been worse. Only to say Emily'd been wanting to come up, but hadn't seen her way to manage it. And hoped to do so before long. And was Ma taking good care of herself?

Oh dear. But it did make you think. All alone there in the house, and it might be anyone coming, just as well as the post-man, and even with the chain on the door whatever would she do. And you did hear such things, nowadays. It was safer in flats, the way a lot of people lived, all upstairs. And wouldn't be so much work either, for her to do by herself. Only she'd got the lease of the house now, till next February. And what a mercy she hadn't bought it! But when the lease was up she really didn't know that she wouldn't look round.

It was that feeling of all those girls that had been there, know-ing the ways of the house. She never felt quite easy. And then hav-ing a room too many, making work. Even if she did keep it locked up. Which she didn't quite like to do, for fear Emily should come some time she wasn't expected. And then Dalton Park. She'd never felt quite at home there. It was a nice enough place, but it wasn't what she was accustomed to. She'd be better off in rooms, really, further into London, where she wouldn't have so much work, and everyone couldn't get at her so easily. Unfurnished rooms.

She took to treating herself to tram-rides up the main road past the cemetery, so that she could have a look round. Even if it did cost a bit in fares. She'd save it if she got into a smaller place. Got into rooms.

And then there was another thing. You never knew when Emily might take it into her head to get married again, a young, healthy woman like her. And there you'd be. With a *husband* looking round, to see what he could get. Fussing after his wife's expectations. And only too glad to find a house where the two of them could stay. It was too much of a good thing. Just standing up to be shot at.

She was on thorns that Emily would say she was coming for Christmas, but she didn't. And that pointed to it, too: to the fact of her having connections elsewhere, more than she'd ever spoken of. No laundry was so busy it didn't give her more time-off than that. And who were those she was staying with back in the spring, up in London? Well, London was a big enough place, that was one thing to be thankful for. And if Jane was to move again she wasn't going to give away where she'd gone to, this time. Get right away from the lot of them.

Get into a smaller place she might have a chance to look round and enjoy herself for a bit, which she never had had, yet.

She was lucky enough, getting on for the end of January, to find a couple of nice rooms that just suited her, right away up past Webber's Lane, almost what you might call right inside London; and she gave notice, then and there, to leave the Dalton Park house as soon as ever the lease was up. It did go against the grain to have the rents overlapping by a week or two, and it was as much as ever she could manage it; but otherwise she would have risked losing the rooms, which she didn't want to do. And you never could tell when Emily might take it into her head. Sooner away the better, once you'd thought of it. And she wasn't having any bothering lease this time. Take it by the month. Not be so tied up.

191

Chapter XI

It really was a relief to get away. She never had cared much for Dalton Park, it wasn't her kind of a place. There was only one thing to say for it, there wasn't a soul there that knew her, or knew she'd gone. Or cared, come to that. She'd always kept herself to herself, ever since she'd gone there; and that was more than you could have done in a place like Jewsbury. If it hadn't been for those girls that had been in and out of the house, she didn't know that she would have troubled to move. But it was a blessing in disguise, for she would only have had that house hanging round her neck; she was much better off here with just the rooms she wanted.

Two such nice rooms, too; and she could go from one to the other without going out on the stairs, which was an advantage, seeing there were strangers up and down. Not that they were going to bother her much, out at business the best part of the time. From her sitting-room window she could see the buses going by: My word, it was more buses than you'd see in Jewsbury in a twelve-month! Or even at Dalton Park. The trams, they had out there. It was a nice wide street, too. Out at the back you could only see across the yard into the houses opposite, but who wanted to look out of their bedroom window? She'd got a nice thick bit of curtain she could put up, to make sure of not being overlooked.

It seemed funny at first, having to walk right over to the window and look down before you could see the street, but she'd soon get used to that. And there was one thing about it, if she couldn't see *out*, nobody else could see *in*.

And then she'd got the use of the kitchen downstairs, for when she wanted it, though there was a gas ring in her room where she could just boil up a kettle. Really, with the gas cookers and electric light there was nowadays there was no work left for anyone to do. No wonder everyone was managing for themselves. It wouldn't be long before all those young hussies of girls were finding themselves out of a place, and serve them right. No work in them. Nothing but gossiping and days out. Everyone in this house did for themselves, and very well they got along too. Even though there were two lots of tenants as well as her to use the kitchen, not to mention Mrs. Mossy herself with her daughter, who lived down below stairs. There was only a single gentleman up at the top and two ladies on the first floor, and so far as Jane could see none of them did much in the way of cooking. Though she took the precaution of getting her own meals in between times, so as not to run into anyone. It was all the same to her, whether she had her dinner at one or two, and the days she went out it meant she hadn't got to hurry back. She'd kept her own pots and pans from Dalton Park — what she'd had back at The Elms, as long as she could remember — and took it down with her, whatever it was she was going to use. She didn't believe in cleaning other people's dirt. Some might have thought it looked funny, the kitchen dresser with her pots and crocks on it in the sitting-room along with the dinner table and the parlour chairs, but for all the difference it made to anyone…. It wasn't for the number of visitors she was going to have.

And how she did laugh to think of Emily's face if she was to turn up at Dalton Park and find her gone. Poor Emily, she supposed she really would have to write to her one of these days.

And kitchen furniture like that cost a mint of money to buy, even though it didn't look much. She wasn't going to let it go for a song, which it would have done, and perhaps have to buy it back another day if she ever got into a place of her own again. Not that she meant to move again in a hurry, but there was never any knowing. It was worth a bit of trouble getting it all to fit in. By the time she'd got the table in the middle and the armchairs one each side of the fire, and the sofa against one wall and the dresser on the other there wasn't too much room to move about, but she did manage to fit the fernstand in between the windows. It was better in the other room, because she'd only brought the things from her own bedroom: let the rest go, that used to be in the girl's room. Those she *had* got rid of. For she never meant to have any of *that* again. Wherever she might move to in the future, she meant to have the place to herself. The only thing that bothered her a bit was there being no cupboard in here: what wouldn't go in the drawers had to stay out, or else in her boxes. But that was just as well, for a box you could lock up and make sure no one should come prying. For you never knew, in a strange house. And she didn't mean to spend on a wardrobe, that was one thing certain: a great clumsy thing that mightn't be any good to her another time, she'd sooner save her money to get the chairs done up. And that was what she'd do, too, as soon as ever she got settled in and found out where to go for things.

What a pleasure it was, going out now on her mornings and seeing new faces all round her! And a new lot of shops to look at, such good shops too. She might have lost a penny or two the first weeks, not knowing where to go; but she soon found out the streets in behind the main road, where the shops were smaller and a good bit cheaper. And better value, too. For what you paid for half the time in those big places was nothing but the name of the shop.

It wasn't only food, either. Lovely things you could get, in the way of clothes and furnishings, and not half the price they used to be in Jewsbury. She was about due for a new pair of boots. Three or four years she'd worn these, or more: it was a good two years before William went that she got them. The best part of five years, and only mended once. That was what came of taking care of your things. But really they were so reasonable up here she might see what she could do about getting herself some more later on, when she'd got over the expense of the move and could let herself go a bit. And there was one thing, she wouldn't have to throw away her old ones this time, they'd go on for ever in the house. To think of all the good boots, with months of wear in them, that she'd had to go out and bury in the ash-pit, just because her newest had got kicked out in the heels and toes and she was ashamed to be seen in them of a Sunday. It was a wicked waste; only if ever William had seen more than two pairs lying about he would have wondered. A wicked waste it was. But that was in her young and giddy days!

It didn't take her long, either, to find out that Mrs. Mossy — who no doubt knew these parts, having lived round about here for the most of her life — did her shopping in the evening on a Saturday, when the prices went down, so she said.

Well, Jane would never have thought of that. But she'd noticed how Mrs. Mossy was going out, once or twice, when she was frying something for her tea latish on a Saturday evening — getting on for six or half-past, since the rest of the house, that didn't go out to business on a Saturday afternoon, would be having theirs between five and six — but it wasn't for a week or two that she thought to remark on it. And even then she didn't quite like the idea for herself, going out so late in the day, it wasn't a thing she ever had done. Even though it was tempting.

She didn't do it the next week, but the Saturday after she took her courage in both hands and out she went after her tea: giving Mrs. Mossy time to clear off out of the way, for she didn't want to have to walk with her and have someone taking her mind off what she was doing.

And how glad she was, that she had taken the bull by the horns and done it! It was like a fairyland with all the shops lit up; and things so cheap! Round in the smaller shops, that was, where they had meat and fish on slabs in the window and no glass in the way, so that you could see what you were buying. They even had some barrows right out in the street, but she didn't quite like the idea of that. She got a lovely little joint, that would last her right through the week, just by having happened to stop at one of the butchers' the minute he was coming out and holding it up to know who'd have it cheap. It was wonderful what you could get, being in a big centre like London.

After that she never did her shopping except on Saturday nights if she could help it, unless it was for one or two little things that she might want, that she ran out for on the Mondays and Wednesdays. But Saturday mornings she'd stay in and clean up her room, so that she'd be all ready to get on her hat and gloves the minute she'd had tea. It really made shopping quite a treat, to stroll out on a warm evening and see all the shops lighted up and all the people about, you wouldn't think there were so many people in the world. And even after she'd got used to it she couldn't help feeling a bit excited, going out at such a funny time of night. A thing she never would have thought of in the old days.

It was as much as she could do not to laugh, thinking of Emily's face if she could only have seen her. Whatever Emily must be thinking by now.... The best part of six months! And serve her right, coming and interfering. Jane hadn't written yet, and didn't mean to, what was more. She was so happy, having got away to herself, away from all that peeking and tittle-tattling, you wouldn't believe. It wasn't likely she was going to give away where she was, and have them all coming round again, like flies round a honeypot.

She would never have been so happy in her life, if it hadn't been for one or two little things she didn't quite like about the house. It wasn't so much Mrs. Mossy, though even she wouldn't have been above satisfying her curiosity if she got the chance, but Jane could have sworn it was that daughter of hers. A brazen faced little hussy, if ever there was one. With her hair cut up short over her ears, like a boy; it wasn't decent. That was who it was, you could depend upon it. With the powder on her face as if she'd rubbed it in the flour-bag, and her sniggering round corners. It was just the kind of thing she'd do.

For Jane could swear that her things were being turned over. It wasn't that anything was missing, but she never could be sure that things were folded like she left them. It was more a feeling than anything else: she could *feel*, the minute she unlocked the door, when someone had been in there while she was out.

And she didn't like it. It was all very well to say nothing was taken, but it wasn't a nice idea even having someone poking round trying on your things. Because that would be what that little chit would be up to. Just the sort of thing that would appeal to her. To see how she looked.

And even with being careful like she was, with the keys a regular weight on her that she had to carry about. There was the key of the drawers, and a key to each trunk, and then the door-key. And for all the good *that* was.... That young hussy'd got one that fitted, you could be sure of that. Daresay she's got a key to every door in the house, if the truth were known.

It went to her heart, too, to have to keep all her best things laid by in her boxes, getting crushed. Just on account of that little wretch....

She shook out the folds of her black silk mantle that she'd had ever since she was married, and always been so choice over — and she could swear *she'd* never creased up that sleeve — and folded it back as well as she could. It would come to that, presently, that she'd have to put on everything she'd got, so that no one else should!

It really took away all the pleasure there was in being out, not knowing what was going on behind your back. She'd see that wretched little hussy sometimes as she was coming downstairs: watching for her to go out, pretending to hide behind the kitchen door. And that was another thing, the way things went from the kitchen. If there was so much as the size of a pea of butter left over from what she took down she would be obliged to bring it back upstairs. For if it was to be left down there, even from dinner to tea, you could depend upon it she would never have seen it again. And that young madam standing about and fiddling, with her back turned, trying to look as if she wasn't watching what went into the pan and what came out. With her skirts half-way up to her neck, a grown woman, it wasn't nice. Jane passed her, on her way in, wiping up something on the stairs, which was just a nice excuse to be hanging about where she'd got no business. And if she hadn't been at that drawer today, putting her great hands into those best black kid gloves, then Jane didn't know anything.

I'll serve you, she thought. And the next time she was going out, she just rolled the gloves one inside the other and popped them into her pocket. Ah-ha, my fine madam! Sneaking away inside the kitchen. But *I* can see her nasty skirts fluttering out around the door!

Though really, when it came to having to carry two pairs of gloves on you, for fear your best kid were going to get pulled right out of shape.... And for all you knew she might go and tear them, she'd be quite capable of it, and then where would I be? It was too bad.

But Jane wasn't going to be got the better of. She did a thing she never had done before, and didn't expect to do again; and that was to buy from a street barrow. Right through the back, to where they had the barrows out in the road on a Saturday: and there last week she'd seen them, hanging up, and she'd been half tempted then: only one-and-eleven-three, and the loveliest big bag, that would hold everything she had to take about with her. Waterproof too, and shut with a clasp. It was dirt-cheap at the money. Though why ever she should have to go to the expense of paying out even one-and-eleven-three for a handbag — a thing she never had carried before in her life — just because that wretched little chit.... But it did make a difference having something to put your purse and keys in, and any little thing. She fetched the gloves right out of her pocket then and there and popped them in, she didn't care what people thought! And then she wouldn't need to carry her basket except for her big shopping. But better not to put her money in, excepting for the bit that was in her purse, in case she *should* happen to drop it. Though she wasn't likely to do such a thing.

She really felt quite proud of herself, having got such a fine big bag so cheap. And all it would hold, too. It was going to pay for itself, if she could stop that nasty brazen-faced little beast spoiling all her best things. There was her newest pair of stockings, that Minnie Hallet had bought for her for the funeral, and that she didn't want pulled about; she'd pop them in, too, to make sure. And her bank-book, that she didn't like anyone prying into. It was getting cold enough now to wear her cloth jacket, and though she would really rather have put on her mantle, to keep it out of harm's way, she didn't want to get it worn, the most valuable thing she'd got, just on account of that hussy's thieving ways.

And there she'd be, sniggering round behind, out in the kitchen. Jane could hear her all right. Always with a snigger on her face as if no one knew what she was up to. Jane gave the front door a bang. It was a comfort to her, anyhow, to know that what little she had got of valuables was safe on her arm.

But it was getting on her nerves, knowing that her clothes and things that she had to leave were being turned over: her boxes being gone through, not once but a hundred times, as soon as she so much as set her foot outside the door. It wasn't that she'd got anything to hide, but she didn't like the idea of it, having her things fingered over. And reading her papers, finding out what she'd got. And you never knew what sort of roughs a girl like that might be in with. The next thing would be, she'd be murdered in her bed.

And she'd been there quite long enough. You didn't want to stay too long in one place, in that sort of a house. Nobody did. She'd been there the best part of ten months now, and the first-floor had changed hands twice since she'd come. And no wonder, if they were served the same way she was. It was only what you might call a place for passing through, never was intended for more. And it wasn't the sort of thing she was accustomed to. If she gave notice now she'd get out at the end of the year.

And how it did make her laugh, to think if Emily tried to come after her then what a job she'd have! She wouldn't be surprised if Emily should take it into her head to have a try, coming on for Christmas time. But she'd find her hands full.

And next time she wouldn't have any more of that business of sharing kitchens. Have a place to herself, that she could shut up, and no landladies' daughters poking round. Come to that, she might stretch a point and move out the middle of the month, if she could find something that suited her. Wait over Christmas and you'd never get any business attended to until after the New Year, and that was when her notice was up. That's what she'd do, get right off as soon as ever she'd found something. There was never any point in waiting about, once you'd made up your mind to go.

Chapter XII

Oh the relief of being in her own place again!

Even if it was small, it was big enough for what she wanted. Two nice enough rooms, too, if it hadn't been that one was taken up with being made into the kitchen. But that was all to the good, that was what she wanted. No more of that going downstairs and having someone prying into every little thing you did. And able to go from one room to the other too, without going out on the stairs. Not that there wasn't another door out of the kitchen on to the landing, but she had a good stout bolt put on that on the inside. Even if it did cost a shilling or two, she'd soon save that on something else. And it was well worth it, it made you feel safer having only the one door that would unlock. And one key less to carry, too, which was something: for there were plenty of little things she didn't like to leave about, not knowing who there might be in a strange house.

Not that she'd seen anyone coming up the stairs, not to notice, but there were plenty in the house, you could tell that, from the prams down in the passage and the washing hanging out when you looked down from the back window. And it wasn't in every way what Jane was accustomed to, but you couldn't have everything. The rent wouldn't have been so reasonable if it hadn't been that it wasn't such a quiet kind of a street as where she was before. But she didn't mind a bit of life going on outside the window, it made a change in a way. She wasn't one to complain, so long as she was left to herself. And there was another thing, being up at the top you didn't have people coming by. No one that hadn't any business there. And so far as she could tell, excepting for the landlord that called round for his rent Monday mornings, there wasn't anyone that had. Which was a mercy.

It made her laugh, the way she'd had to fit the furniture in, to get it into the one room. What with the bed and the chest of drawers and the dresser and the dinner table and the parlour chairs, it was a proper mixture! But that was what you had to pay for being on your own, and well worth it too; and so far as she knew it wasn't anyone's business what she chose to do. And then her own little fernstand, that she just managed to fit in between the dresser and the chest of drawers. There wasn't any place to stand her trunks excepting in the kitchen. But that was just as well, for it meant that anyone would have to go through the front room before ever they got there, and with the door in between, that she was able to lock and take the key, that made it doubly sure.

Come to think of it she might have sold some of this big, heavy furniture and got smaller, when she moved, if it hadn't been that she didn't quite like the idea. For there was no denying it, you always lost over selling, never got half of what the thing was worth. And as for what you could buy now, it wasn't anything like the quality it used to be. Nasty, shoddy, gimcrack stuff; and the prices they asked! Better by half to hold on to what you'd got, even if it was a bit big for the room. After all, so long as she could just get around to do what she wanted, she didn't want to be dancing jigs in the middle of the floor. And there was another thing, this old furniture had value. Good solid mahogany that would always turn in a bit, you'd never come to want so long as you had that by you. It wasn't like this nasty stuff nowadays, fit for nothing but firewood in a year or two, only got up showy to sell.

And it was the same with the clothes. It went to her heart to think she'd have to throw away her black alpaca, even though it was gone a bit along the seams. It was more than she could do to discard it, for you'd never get that quality stuff again. Pop it back in her trunk and see if she couldn't mend it up one of these days, for it was a thousand shames to throw away good material. Always looked good. Ladylike. Not like what you could get now. And come to that, she'd keep it out and wear it while she was indoors. For all anyone was going to see it here. No need to be spoiling her best new funeral black, which she'd save for going out. And as for her serge, you might as well wear out the oldest first.

She didn't believe in waste, and she couldn't afford waste, what was more. With all the expenses she'd been put to, moving. And then she had to save a bit for a rainy day. It wasn't as if she had anyone but herself to depend on.

And didn't want to either. She was happy enough, so long as she was left alone. Cooking her bits of meals and giving her room a sweep out once a week — which was all it wanted, there being no one but herself to stir up the dust — and going out to do her shopping.

It was quite a little expedition, by the time she'd locked up all her boxes — because you did like to be sure — and got on her hat and jacket and gone all round to see if there was any little thing left lying about that anyone could have picked up, and popped it in her bag, and fastened up the doors; and then got herself down four flights of stairs.

But it was well worth the trouble. For after the first few days when she didn't quite know where to go, having moved to a new district further into London, and no doubt gave a penny or two more than she ought to have done, she found out she was quite near to a street-market again: a lot bigger than the one where she'd come from, too, and going on all the time, not only Saturdays. Clapington Street Market, they called it. And really the things you could buy, and so reasonable, it was a pleasure just to walk up and down!

Even clothes she could have bought there if she'd wanted, and every bit as good as in the shops. It was lucky she wasn't given to be extravagant, or she really might have been tempted. But she was quite content to look. Excepting for one day when she went higher up than usual and came across a barrow that had cards and cards of lovely veiling! Well. And you could hardly find it now, in the shops. That would show you. Well, she did let herself be tempted then. All different patterns too, and so reasonable, and time to take your choice. That was the way to buy, nowadays; no more of these shoddy shops that could hardly be bothered to serve you. If they weren't careful they'd soon find out their mistake.

And spring coming on too. It did her good to have the feel of a new bit of veiling all crisp on her face. And looked so neat and ladylike. Well that was where *she* was going to shop in future, and if anyone had any sense they'd do the same. And as for Saturday nights it was a hundred times better, even, than where she was before. Almost giving things away. And all so gay and bright when it was lit up. It really was a pleasure to see how bright everything looked.

It really seemed as if she'd found somewhere she could settle down at last. She was so happy, doing her bit of cleaning on a Saturday morning and having her little outing in the evening, and a stroll out, just to take the air and price things up, on Mondays and Wednesdays, and no one to worry her: no one ever coming up those stairs but the landlord ten o'clock Monday morning, as punctual as the clock, so that all she had to do was have her money ready on the dresser and open the door to him; and all he'd say would be Good-day, and sign up the book: she was so happy she couldn't believe her luck. And then one afternoon, in the middle of a week, just the very minute she was on the point of making herself a cup of tea, like a bombshell out of the blue, *Emily* must come knocking at her door.

She knew who it was all right, even before she opened; and she was in two minds whether she'd open to her at all. She never could think why ever she had done so, excepting that Emily having once found out where she was she'd be sitting on the stairs day and night and no peace until she was let in. Better to open to her and let her see she wasn't wanted. And after all it mightn't be her, though whoever else.... She slipped back the tea-caddy into the drawer.

That was who it was all right. Following her about.

"Oh, so it's you."

"Why, Ma! Wherever have you been hiding yourself all this time!"

And didn't wait to be asked in, either. Inside she was, and nothing for Jane to do but shut the door after her or else have all the house listening to her business.

"I haven't been hiding myself," she said with dignity. Of all the ideas. As if it was likely. "I suppose I had the right to move, if I wanted to."

She was so upset she really didn't know what was happening, until she saw Emily'd sat down, all by herself and without being invited, and thrown open her coat. For all the world as if she meant to sit there till doomsday. But ask her to have a cup of tea Jane *would not*. Even though she did give a look at the kettle that was beginning to boil. Jane pushed round behind her and took it off the fire. And she knew what was coming next.

"You might have written, Ma, and not given me all the trouble to go round asking where you were. I had ever such a job to find you. I only heard it from the bank."

So that was it. But Jane knew what to say all right. She'd got it all ready. For she'd had it in the back of her mind that this might happen one day. She picked up the cup and saucer she'd put out for herself on the table and took them back to the dresser. "I did write," she said. "Didn't you get it?"

She could feel herself going quite pink, but she didn't care. It was all the same to her whether Emily believed her or not.

Sitting there looking round as if nothing was good enough for her. Think I was going to live in a palace so she could come to stay? In her fur coat, that wasn't the same as she'd had last time either. Such extravagance.

"Is this the only room you've got?"

Looking down her nose. And what if it was.

"Have poor Pa's investments gone west then? I know how it is with a lot of people these times. I don't know that I could do much, but...."

"I can look after my own business, thank you."

It really was as much as Jane could do not to fly out at her. Coming following her round like that, and all she'd got to ask after was the money. You would think, that seeing her after all that time.... But no, it was the money she'd come after, and hadn't even got the sense to hide it. But if she thought she was going to find anything out she was mistaken.

"I can look after myself all right, and I don't want anyone poking their nose in."

It wasn't often she spoke so plainly, but it really was too much for flesh and blood to bear. Well, she'd said it, and it wasn't a bad thing she had. She'd said what she'd got to say, for once, and she just stood and looked at Emily, as much as to say that she could have said plenty more if she'd had a mind to.

"Oh, all right," says Emily in her coarse way, getting up in a huff, "you can stew in your own juice. If that's all the thanks I get I'll go back where I came from. I can't think why I bother about

you, you aren't my mother after all. And you led poor Pa the hell
of a life, nagging at him all the time."

"That's enough," said Jane, holding the door open. "You don't
need to go blaspheming against his memory."

"Memory fiddlesticks," says Emily, right out on the landing
too. "For all you ever cared...."

But Jane had got the door shut at last.

Well really. She was shaking so much she could hardly get
back to a chair and sit down. To think of it. Coming there. To
think. Well really. And what a thing to say. And as if she couldn't
do bad enough insulting the living without she must come and
talk like that about her poor dead Pa. Poor William. Oh dear. And
to think he was always so considerate. Well, there was one thing
certain, if he could have heard how Emily spoke to her just now
he would have turned in his grave. He would indeed.

But that was the end of *her*. She never would dare to come
again after that. That was one thing. After she'd shown so plainly
what she was coming for. It was too bad. And there was Jane so
happy, in her nice little flat that she'd only been in just over two
months, and now she'd have all the trouble and expense of moving again. It was really too bad.

For she couldn't stay there, after that. It had poisoned the
place for her. And besides you never knew. Just to think of her
coming there and saying those dreadful things. And where she'd
always been so happy.

And right out there on the stairs, where anyone could have
heard her.

She couldn't bear to stay there another minute.

Saying she was *hiding* herself.

And I should like to know what for.

And then to make it worse, as if that wasn't bad enough, she
couldn't find another place that suited her, all in a hurry. For she
was determined not to go far from that district, where she was so

well-off and happy. And why ever she should be driven out, just because that hussy took it into her head....

But she couldn't rest until she'd found something, and it wasn't long before she did. Tucked away on the other side of Clapington Street, and where Emily would never think of looking. Up Broughton Road, which was a little road where no one would ever think. And if it wasn't quite what she was used to, being accustomed to looking down on the passers-by instead of up, it all made a change; and there was this to be said for it, a basement had its own front door and there was no excuse for anyone to be coming through, nor looking at her either, going in and out. And she'd take good care she didn't give her address to anyone this time, even if it *was* only the bank. It just showed they couldn't be depended on. It was easy enough for her to walk in and cash her money when she wanted, which she wouldn't need to do more than once in two or three months if she was careful, without them knowing where she lived. They needn't ever know she'd moved. And as for the people here, once she'd paid up her week's rent on the Monday morning no one was going to ask any questions, and needn't be told if they did.

But to think.... Well it was a mercy she had the move, to take her mind off it. It really was. Just to think, of her coming there and saying.... Just to think of it.

Chapter XIII

Oh, but to have got away at last! Got rid of all the lot of them. For no one was likely to come after her *here*. Have a job to find it for one thing: have to come down Clapington Street and round the corner, for there wasn't any way out the other end of Broughton Road. Not that she was any too fond, all the same, of leaving things about even now, for you never know, with their crafty ways. And down in the area too, it was easy enough for anyone that meant it to come prowling round looking in the windows. But she knew what she'd do, she'd pull the blinds down when she was going out, and there wouldn't be any seeing in, then.

Such a nice little place, too, just suited her down to the ground. With the front room that was every bit as big as what she'd had before, if not bigger, for all the rent was so reasonable. And if there wasn't room for her boxes in along with all the furniture, it wouldn't be the first time they'd stood in the kitchen, and no worse for it either; and it was all to the good, for the kitchen window giving on to a wall not more than a foot away, *and* having good solid iron bars to it, there wasn't much chance of anyone getting in *that* way. And as for the wall making it a bit dark, that wasn't going to trouble her. For all she wanted to be seeing, just to cook her bits of meals for herself. And there was always the gas if you were put to it, and had a mind to slip some coppers in the meter. None of these electric lights here, and she wasn't sorry, nasty glaring things. Lamps used to be good enough in the old days. A nice soft light that was, and quiet too, not noisy like the gas. Good enough for her and William. But the way people went on now you'd think nothing was good enough. Like that hussy with her fur coats. But never mind her. Soon put a stop to *her* coming round. Of all the impudence. Come to that there was one of the old lamps put away in the dresser now. If she was just to get it out and buy a drop of oil next time she went out to market she could *save* the price of the gas.

And as for the front room, she'd found that if she kept the blind down only half-way even, no one could ever see in from up in the street, they would have had to come right away down the steps. Which no one was likely to do, so far as she could see, excepting for the upstairs' tenants coming down to the dustbin now and then, what was over in the corner where she could easy keep her eye on it; and a nice thick bit of net curtain would soon settle them.

Of course, when she was out, that was a different matter.

But just to think, she muttered, putting on her hat. To think of her *daring*, coming there and saying....

She fastened up her veil, neat and nice, and screwed it in under her chin, bending forward to look in the dark glass over the chest that was pushed back alongside the grate away from the window: which was the only place it *could* have gone, if she was to get in the dresser and the bed, and how she could have done without either she would very much have liked to know. She took her gloves and shopping bag out of the top drawer and pushed in the empty drawer again. Empty it was, and so it should remain. For where was the sense of unpacking and spreading things about, when it was a hundred times easier to get them out of the boxes when she wanted, and boxes could be kept locked up, which drawers couldn't.

She wasn't going to show anyone where her keys were, you could be sure of that; never did get them out before she was through the door into the passage, for you never knew, curtain or no curtain. But once she was out there in the dark inside the front door she reached down and fetched out the bunch from her under-pocket, and then she went on into the kitchen, to her boxes, that were stood up against the sink.

Yes, it was these two things that she didn't really like leaving, her feather boa and her best silk mantle. And if it hadn't been that it was such a warm day she would have put them both on. But she really didn't think she could bring herself to wear more than the boa over her cloth dress; and if she was to wear the alpaca., which she might have done, or her serge, it would mean leaving the cloth, and that was a good deal newer. But she knew what she *could* do, she could just slip the mantle over her arm, for you never knew when it might turn chilly at this time of year. And then she'd have it with her.

And then her best gloves, and newest pair of stockings, pop into her bag; and the rest would have to take its chance.

She locked the trunk and went round the kitchen, with the keys quiet and tight in her gloved hand, putting things to rights. Margarine into the cupboard: and that ought to do till Wednesday, get a quarter on Wednesday it ought to do out the week: and spoons and forks popped in her bag. Two of them rattled when she shut the clasp; she dug to the bottom and pulled a stocking between them.

Even with standing as close as ever she could to the window she couldn't see up above; not more than to the top of the wall when she got right up close to the bars, and that was where there was a tuft of grass hanging over. It was a bit of garden up there, and it wasn't likely anyone was coming looking down over. And if they did there wasn't much that they could see, excepting a bit of floor, and not more than a stone or two of that.

She gave a twitch to her boa and went out and locked up the kitchen, and out in the passage she slipped the keys back in her under-pocket and got out a half crown to put in her purse. Now there was only to feel her way up the stairs, where it was nearly dark, and make sure that door was shut at the top; and then the front room blind to draw down, behind the fern-stand, and pick up her umbrella and lock the door; and then the front door into the area.

There we are!

And up the steps, which wasn't too easy, they being narrow, with a turn, and she with her bag and umbrella and her mantle on her arm; and a look back to make sure she hadn't dropped anything, for her pocket with her keys and money would knock against the steps on the way up and give her a turn, even though she did know it was all pinned in; and a last look down over, and there she was out on the pavement. And only just along Broughton Road and round the corner by the public house, and here we are in Clapington Street, with the barrows all along.

And it *was* hot, too. You never would have thought it down there in her own little flat. That was the place to live in! Always nice and cool when she got home.

And hotter it got, as time went on. It got like that that she had to take her boa over her arm when she went out, along with her mantle, for she really couldn't stand it. But she wasn't going to give up her regular shopping days, for if you once did that you soon found you didn't know the prices; and what was more there were days some things would be cheaper than others, not for any reason that she could see, but there it was. Vegetables and so on. Sometimes a whole penny a pound difference from one day to the next. And if you didn't keep your eyes open you had to take what you could get. And it wasn't always Saturday nights it was cheapest either, sometimes on her Mondays or Wednesdays she'd find a real bargain. Especially if it should happen to have rained and things on the stalls were wettish. Pretty well give them away, on account of them not keeping no doubt. Oh yes, she was always glad to see a nice shower come down, early of a Monday or Wednesday morning.

And then there was another thing, all the barrows didn't sell at the same price, you had to keep your wits about you. She soon got to know. If it wasn't up on the corner facing Woolworth's it would be back down the street by the grocer's where they had the stall outside, and you couldn't say before you'd seen the two. And no harm in looking on the way up, keep an eye on all. And for her bit of meat she had to go right away up the other end, past where the clothing barrows were, second-hand clothes and such: a shop, she had to go to for that, for all the meat they had in the street was the cat's-meat stall. Not that that didn't look good enough very often, as if anyone could have eaten it, but there it was. And for all she wanted, being by herself, it didn't hurt her to go into the shop for it once or twice a week, and then she could stroll right away back down the street and price all there was, before she bought.

Often she'd go up and down as much as two or three times before she could be sure she'd found just the thing she wanted. But she didn't mind that. She never was one to spare herself trouble. It was quite a pleasure really on a nice day, after a bit of a shower to lay the dust, just to stroll up and down and see things. Especially in the mornings, when it wasn't a crowd like Saturday nights. When they really had time to attend to you. It was a pleasure to stand there in the sun and pass the time of day while they were weighing out the carrots or potatoes or whatever it might be. Potatoes it was, and one of them rolled to the ground, right under her feet. And the woman was reaching out for another, if she hadn't picked it up already and put it back on the scales. "Waste not want not, as my poor husband used to say."

Poor William, how pleased he would have been if they'd had anywhere like this to shop in Jewsbury. How he did hate to see extravagance, it went to his heart. And only today she'd had to give a whole threepence for a new paper carrier to take home what she'd bought, the handle having come off her basket last week, and the bit of string she'd tied it on with wouldn't hold. Not that you could call a carrier extravagant, considering what she saved on buying. But still, threepence was threepence, and it didn't last more than a week or two. And baskets the price they were. She knew what she'd do, she'd look through her things and see if she couldn't find a piece of stuff that would make a bag. Something strong, that would last. Oh dear, it was hot, she had to stop a minute to rest her carrier against the railings, half-way up Broughton Road. But it wasn't far now. And how lovely and cool it struck, when she got down home into her own place again.

She couldn't quite make up her mind about the bag. There was a nice little piece of ticking, that she'd got once for mending up an old pillow and never had done: right back at The Elms that must have been, and the old pillow got rid of among the stuff that was sold. Never been used. A lovely strong bag that would have made, only that she didn't quite like the look of it, being striped like that so funny. But the only other thing that she *could* have done…. Well it seemed a thousand shames, cutting up good clothes. But there was her very old black that she had down at the bottom of her box, what she had for her wedding, think of that, how it wore. Purple it was, and dyed for the old Queen. A thousand pities, for dyed stuff never did wear the same; if it hadn't been for that it would have been as good as ever it was.

But there you are: gone all under the arms, and past mending, and been turned too. And a lovely bit of stuff: the very best quality, and always pays in the end. And yards of stuff in the skirt, good as new. More than what you'd ever get now. Nasty skimpy flimsy things.

She couldn't make up her mind. She couldn't quite bring herself to cut it up. But there wasn't any hurry, she'd think it over while she had her dinner.

She popped a penny in the gas and boiled her potatoes and got out her bit of meat from yesterday, from out of the cupboard: when the potatoes were done she put on the kettle to make herself a cup of tea. And after all, who was to be any the wiser, if she did make herself a bag out of the ticking. With it on her arm under her mantle and everything.

She carried her meal into the front room, there being no table out in the kitchen, and sat down where she could keep her eye on the area, to make sure no one should come poking down there that hadn't any business.

There was only one thing to be said for cutting up the black, and that was that she could make it big enough to hold anything she wanted to take with her besides her shopping; not have so many things to carry. Slip her boa inside of it. But then on the other hand, she couldn't very well be putting in potatoes and so on on top of her clothes. It was a problem.

She carried back her plate and knife to the kitchen sink, leaving out the teapot on the table in case she should feel like another cup later on, and got out the ticking and the black dress.

No, it really did seem a thousand shames, even gone like it was. And there was the ticking just a handy size, and never going to show, once it was on her arm, wouldn't make two penn'orth of difference. That was what she'd do.

She folded the dress back into her trunk and poured herself out another cup and set to work making up the ticking.

And come to that she'd still have the black. Could make it up another time if she wanted.

And glad she was of it too, when it came on for winter and bad weather. Yes, winter again. Seven months she'd been here in Broughton Road, think of that. And it really did look as if that Emily was going to leave her alone this time. Got tired, I expect. Found there wasn't enough to be got out of it. Though you never could tell, sly like she was, when she might be going to pop up again like a bad penny. In a way it wasn't a bad thing to have a bit of rough weather, for no one was coming walking along Broughton Road that weather that hadn't got to, you could depend on that. With the rain coming down like a river, down those area steps, so that she would have to go with her broom and sweep the water away to stop it coming in under the front door. Many wouldn't have liked it. But she didn't mind a bit of wet, so long as it meant peace and quiet. What she *was* thankful for was that she hadn't cut up her old black, back in the summer. For how she ever would have managed with her boa and mantle over her arm, once she'd taken to her heavy jacket, without them getting soaked through, she really didn't know. And now she did bring herself to sacrifice the black, for it meant saving her better things: made a most lovely bag, just the skirt, with the bodice cut off: big as a sack you could have carried coals in, or bigger! And with her mantle folded inside, flat and neat, and hung over her arm, no one was ever going to know even that it *was* a bag. Might just as well have been a coat she'd got with her. And come to that, if anyone was to know, it wasn't any of their business. And what was more, if they knew you'd got things with you, they knew it wasn't any good them coming down here to find them.

For there was just one thing she never had liked about this basement flat of hers, and that was those stairs with the door at the top. Where it used to be joined on, all one house, you could tell that. But it was all very well, even if the door was always kept locked as they said; and so it was, so far as she could ever find out, but how were you to know who might have the key? She'd have had a bolt put on, only that it meant having someone in to do it, showing the ways of the house. She did drive a good stout nail up against the join, and tied the handle with string to a nail in the wall, but you never could tell how far that would hold. It was the first thing she did, every time she came in, to go up and see if that string hadn't been moved. It was the bane of her life. She never felt really safe.

And it was important for her, someone in her position, to have the place well locked up. It wasn't only people nosing, that ought to have known better. But having to fetch money from the bank for months ahead like she did, you never knew. For she didn't like going there too often, and it wasn't only that it cost her fourpence in bus fares to get there and back. She didn't altogether like their attitude the last time she did go. Wanting to know if she hadn't moved away.

"And why should I have?"

Posted her pass-book, and got it back through the post-office.

"Well, then, it was a mistake. And you needn't post it anymore, I'll ask for it when I want it. You mind, you keep it till I come."

For she didn't *want* that thing hanging about, for everyone to see. A nice thing, showing up where she kept her money, so that anyone that liked would know where to go....

No, she didn't altogether like it. Didn't like the look of that young clerk. Some young jack-in-office, jumped up. Hardly take the trouble to be civil. It wasn't like that in the old days.

Well, she wasn't going there any more than she was obliged to. For there was another thing, you never knew when someone might see where you were coming from, and follow you back. And you did hear such things. Anyone knowing she'd got all that money on her. She wouldn't have gone there at all only that she didn't know how to do without. Just enough for the rent, she took, for three months ahead, and five shillings a week over. With the little that she ate it need never come to more than that, being careful like she was. And that was quite enough to have about even with keeping it under her hand like she did day and night. And then her little nest-egg, for a rainy day. She really didn't like to go to sleep, those nights after she came from the bank, for thinking how someone might have followed her and marked down the house, waiting for night to break in and murder her in her bed. Oh dear, what a dread she did have, that one of these nights, sooner or later, someone might break in and she be murdered in her bed. It was a dreadful thing to think of. And then at last she thought what she *would* do; she'd get an iron bar, like what was on the kitchen window, and screw it over the door at the top of the stairs. It cost her nearly half a week's money, and what a business it was too, getting it screwed on: when she'd seen the ground-floor out to work in the morning, they being the only ones that could have heard. But it was well worth the trouble. After that she did sleep a bit easier, even though she'd have to save that two shillings somehow.

Which she did do in time, through being careful and watching out where she went for things. And it wasn't any particular hardship to her, which was something to be thankful for, having to make the most of what she'd got. Always did have to do that. Never had anything to squander, like some, And no better off for it either. Easy come and easy go. See them up Clapington Street of a Saturday night, with their skirts up to their necks, and their fur collars, and their silk stockings, such nonsense: and paying out good money for tomatoes and messes, coming from abroad, all at the wrong time of the year. Even if it did cost less than the shops. No thrift or sense about them nowadays, nothing put by for a rainy day. She never had believed in that sort of shiftlessness, always liked to know she had her little nest-egg put by. And so long as she'd got that safe and could just rub along, with a shilling or two left over to put by with her savings when it came round to her day for going to the bank again — which she was obliged to do, like it or not — she was as happy as you could wish. And well enough satisfied to eat what was in season, wouldn't give a thank-you for some of their outlandish stuff. A potato or two or a few carrots was good enough for *her*, good healthy natural food; or it might be a cabbage now and then, though she never did care so much for greens. Unless it was getting on in the summer and peas so cheap it seemed a shame to leave them on the stall. Or marrows, that they'd almost give away. But she wasn't so particular, you had to take what you could get. When you were all alone in the world, and having to look out for yourself, like she was.

And then one day, all unexpected, she had a bit of luck. And a thing you never would have thought of. One Saturday night it was, half-way up Clapington Street on the left-hand side, near the corner by the public convenience, and she having all she could do to make her way through the crowds that would keep banging into her things — all in such a hurry nowadays — and keep her eye on the stalls as well, and for all her trouble she'd get pushed out time and again almost off the pavement: when suddenly, looking down, what should she see but a most lovely cauliflower, rolled right down in the gutter. Really, it seemed a shame not to pick it up.

Well really it did. And it didn't look as if anyone had dropped it or was looking round for anything. Just rolled right down, and everyone busy about their own business. So far as she could see, there was nothing to stop *anyone* from picking it up. Unless it was rotten underneath; you couldn't tell.

Well really, for all the notice anyone was taking....

And get down and pick it up she did, for all they might bump and push, pretending they couldn't get past. There, a lovely big cauliflower that would cost sixpence any day that time of year, and that she never would think of buying! What had rolled off a stall, or someone had thrown it out, though it was only the teeniest bit gone on one side.

It must have been on account of that. Must have been thrown out. There wasn't anyone taking any notice, even now she'd got it in her hand.

Well, at the finish, into her bag it popped. For she couldn't stand there holding it for ever. And might just as well. And if that was what you got by looking down, she'd look some more! For she wasn't one of those to go walking gazing up in the air and miss what was under her nose. And if the gutter was where you found good food for nothing, the gutter she'd watch in future, and not ashamed to do it either.

And she could see what it was, when she came to look round. Some of the stalls would throw out anything they didn't fancy, or what a customer objected to. Not that there was any more just now that was any use: a half rotten apple — she turned it over with her umbrella — and a bad potato or two and a heap of loose cabbage leaves. But you never knew when there might just happen to be something really worth having. And to think she'd been there the best part of two years and never seen that before. She'd keep her eyes open after this.

For if she could pick up good food for nothing, she was going to be happy for the rest of her life!

Chapter XIV

For it really did look — what was it, two, three, best part of four years — it really did seem as if when she came here she'd found somewhere at last that she could settle down and not be bothered.

And not before it was time either, for she wasn't getting any younger. All this being driven about from pillar to post. Not that she couldn't get around and do her work with the best of them. Tuesday for her lamp and Thursday for sweeping up the area, and a dust round the front room Saturdays, and her bit of washing, if she felt up to it, before her time for going out on a Monday morning. Not that she was such a stickler for that, there being no one but herself to wash for and little enough needing it. A sheet a week they'd always changed in the old days, regular as the clock, top to underneath and underneath to the washtub. But with only her using it it didn't need all that. Only wear out in washing, and soap costs money. And it was a backbreaking job, standing over the tub. If there was a Monday morning she didn't feel up to it she'd just let it slide till next time, for all the harm it was going to do anyone. It was much more important for her to be at her best for when she was going out: very much more important it was, having to look out for herself like she did. For if you weren't up to the mark, there was always plenty ready to take advantage. Ten to one you'd miss something good, if you didn't get downright robbed, starting off feeling worn right out and with a pain in your back.

For she did feel her back a bit lately, she couldn't say she didn't. It wasn't that she couldn't get round her work, but she did have the lumbago in her back coming on if she'd been down on her knees any time, giving a wipe over to the floor. — Let it go for now, for all anyone was going to see it. — And that lumbago was a thing she hadn't felt for years hardly till last winter, not since she left Jewsbury. For that was a nasty rheumaticky place for you. A good day it was for her, when she made up her mind to go from there. It might have been that it was a teeny bit damp in the kitchen here, though nothing to speak of; but you could tell there was damp about, the way there were mildew marks on things in her boxes when she opened them up, now it was the spring, not liking to leave all shut so long without a shaking out, for fear of moth. And a lucky thing she had done, and a pity she never had thought before to turn those boxes right out. For there were her boots, right down at the bottom, that she might just as well be wearing: only her second best and nothing wrong with them except for being a bit down at the heel. And now she'd come across them she might as well take to them again and save her best: that had a hole right through the sole and was only fit for fine weather. And her nice smart bead slippers, as damp as damp. And her muff, that she never had been able to carry for years past, her hands being taken up with other things; but that didn't mean she wanted it ruined, what with moth and wet. Leave it all open to dry up a bit, while she was in the house. Oh dear, and on her alpaca too. And she'd been wearing that only the other day, only back in the autumn. And what a good piece of stuff that always was. And only sewed up a bit along the seams. But if she was to wear it again for a bit, which she easy could do with her jacket over, the air would soon take the damp off. And then her cloth, that was her newest, and always had been too hot for this time of year — on account of the funeral having been so late as November — could go into the bag, along with her mantle and boa and so-on.

But it was when it came round to winter again that it really began to weigh on her mind: however she was to stop her things from getting spoilt worse by the damp. For keep a fire going out there, she would not; with coal the price it was, and the trouble it was to bring it home, even sixpenn'orth at a time. And with the gas-ring to do her cooking on, which didn't take five minutes, it was a wicked waste to go lighting a fire. Though she did have a bit in the front room of an evening when she was sitting down quiet, but that wasn't so much waste as what you might have thought. For she'd found out lately that by going up along Clapington Street latish in the day, when the barrows were moving off, you could see the most lovely pieces of wood lying about sometimes; and one or two bits popped in her bag, that no one was ever going to miss, would keep a handful of fire in, with a lump or two of coal, a whole evening almost.

It was quite a little adventure going out at that time of night, and not at all what she always had done, even for her Saturday evening shopping. But you live and learn! And when you thought how you never knew what you might come across, lovely bits of wood, and things dropped from the stalls sometimes, it was a regular treasure-trove! And no one ever said anything, never noticed very likely. Who was going to notice, if you were just strolling along. Even if you *were* to stumble on a find and just pop it in your bag. Not that there was anyone about to notice, excepting for a few, and they were up to the same thing very likely if the truth were known. And with what she had to carry no one was to notice a thing more or less.

For she had to do it, she hadn't any choice in the matter. She couldn't leave her things to rot in those damp boxes, it was only common-sense, and there wasn't any other thing she *could* do except have them with her, all that was any use. And by keeping out her mantle and hanging it over her arm there was plenty of room; and not only that, but having the mantle hanging over, her bag didn't show so much, and you didn't want everyone knowing what you'd got. Not that it made much difference, for anyone could think what they liked, they couldn't get at what you'd got so long as you had it on you.

Though she did wonder sometimes what she must look like, with her black bag so full — not but what once you'd got a bag with you it might just as well be full as half empty — and her handbag and her shopping bag. Though that had toned down a bit with use, it didn't show so much what it was made of. Didn't show at all come to that, no one would ever have known. And even if they did it was her own affair. And she was always careful to dress herself nice and ladylike; never would have dreamt of going out without her veil put on tidy and her gloves on — one of these days she'd sew up that finger, before it showed — and her umbrella rolled up as good as the day it was new. Though she would dearly have liked to know who it was had knocked the knob off, and when it was they'd done it: that was a thing she *would* have liked to know. Pulled it off, you could depend on it, in the street, one time she hadn't had her mind on it, and sold it for what they could get. Someone had that for their honesty. For it was always a good umbrella, what William had given her for her wedding present, and if the knob wasn't real gold it was good quality brass. She took good care now to see she had it in her hand and not loose under her arm, or they'd be having the whole thing next. For you couldn't be too careful these days, with everyone out for themselves. Poor William, whatever he would have said if he had been spared, the goings-on there were now. The pushing and shoving. Only yesterday, when she was stopped by the stall up at the end and taking out her purse to buy potatoes, there not having been any worth picking up for days past ... pushing round, pushing at her black bag fit to have it over. And that would be the next trick, push it over and pick up what fell out. If I hadn't had my wits about me. Oh, my word, you have to look out for yourself nowadays. Whatever William would have said....

And then the young fellows at the bank, this last time she went. Taking such a look at what she'd got as if the next thing they'd be slipping it in their pocket. Educated young fellows too, in a position to know better. What it was coming to.... But there was one thing she was thankful for, that she'd caught them out looking as she had; for that had given her the idea to do a thing she never would have thought of. And she didn't know to this day how she dared to do it. A whole twenty pounds she'd drawn out — and stare if you like young fellow — more than she ever had done in her whole life, and however she was to get home.... But how glad she was, when she did get home safe and sound, and got it snug and safe in the sole of her stocking — for no one was very likely to come looking for it *there!* — to think how she'd got free at last from those impudent young fellows at the bank. Why, just with her rent and her little drop of oil and being careful like she was, she wouldn't need to go back there for many a long day. Make it last as long as ever she could. Hardly needed firing, or light even, with the hot weather coming on again.

And it was hot too, hotter than ever it was, and heavy, getting up the steps with all her things. But it was well worth it, to have all safe and sound. It was worth something, to have your mind at rest. And once she was up in the street she wasn't in any hurry, she could take her time. And as for all this pushing and shoving there was nowadays, hurry-scurry, well, they could push all they liked they couldn't walk over her, nor yet through her that she knew of, and if they couldn't take the time to walk round they could wait till she was ready.

For she didn't believe in all this hurry-scurrying. She liked to take her time and look around her. Always had done and always would. That was the way you missed things, being in all this hurry. And what's the hurry. And William was like that too, you never could have got him to hurry. What's the hurry, he'd say. What they want to be in all this hurry for. Want to get there before they arrive? In his humorous way. No hurry that I know of, what's the hurry.

And there you are, if she'd been all in a hurry she never would have seen those two lovely oranges that was rolled down. Not that she ever had cared much for fancy food, but beggars mustn't be choosers. Leave good food lying in the gutter, flying in the face of Providence. Oh dear, my back, how I do feel it nowadays. Now then, what's the hurry, pushing like that. What's all the hurry about.

What a blessing it was to get in quiet and put down her things. Empty out her bag. Bit of wood into the bucket, and two nice carrots she'd found that would do for her dinner, along with what was left of the six-penn'orth of meat she got yesterday. And not much for it, either. Really it went to her heart sometimes to see what lovely meat they sold at that cat's-meat stall so-called, and what a lot you could get for a penny or two. If only she dared to try it. And a penny dug out of her pocket to make the gas burn. She'd have her dinner presently, when she'd had a bit of a sit-down. All this hurry and flurry.

But take your time as much as you liked, you couldn't keep the clock still. There it was winter again, and spring, you couldn't keep pace with it. And that twenty pounds that she thought was going to last the rest of her life as near gone as made no difference. Just with the rent, and the little bits she had to spend. And how it did vex her to think she'd have to go back to that bank again.

But have to go she did, and she made up her mind to serve them the same trick. Draw out another twenty, and make it go further this time. If she dared she'd draw double. And then when she got there, all ready to face up to those young fellows, if the manager didn't have to come out — an elderly man he was, *she* knew him — and instead of speaking sharp as he should have done to his young clerks to make them mind their business, there he had to come ... would you believe it, peeping round himself, from the end of the counter, while the young fellow was coming out to serve her: as curious to see what she had got as if he was the errand boy instead of master there. And there she was with the pen in her hand ready to write, and him peeping round.... She never did know to the end of her days what came over her, but to see him peeking and poking.... She really as near as fainted when she saw what she'd written down. One hundred pounds. More money than she ever had thought of. It was all she could do to keep her hand from shaking when she passed it over to the young man. But once she' done it, she would abide by it. And there was one thing, never more — that must have really been what brought her to do it — never more would she have to come back here as long as she lived.

It gave the young man a turn too, when he saw what she'd written down. He had to go off and show it to the manager — who'd come out into the open now for all the world as if he hadn't been there peeking all along — and whisper something. Not allowed very likely, to pay out a big sum like that by himself. And then he came back and started counting it out of a drawer.

And up comes the manager, washing his hands as if butter wouldn't melt in his mouth. "Ah, good morning, Mrs. Chirp, I believe we have your address now, let me see...."

"You've got it," she told him, picking up what the young man was pushing to her.... "Here, what's this, you give me proper notes." Nasty flimsy....

That did make the manager jerk up at last, and see what was going on.

"You'd like it in pound notes?" he said, taking up the bits of paper and pushing them back. "Just give it to Mrs. Chirp in pound notes."

Yes, I should hope so.

So the young man had to hand it over in the end, and there she was outside, though how she ever got there she couldn't have said. And there was one thing she was sure of, that they were watching for which way she went, and if she had taken her bus in the usual place they would have spotted it as sure as sure.

It was quite a long way she had to walk too, before she came to another stop; though it saved a penny, and that was something. And even then she couldn't be sure she wasn't being followed. What she'd do was get off the stop before her own and slip round the back way to Clapington Street, and so she did, and sure enough there wasn't anyone behind her by the time she turned into Broughton Road: where you could always tell, the road being empty most days excepting for when the children were playing out of school. But oh dear what a journey that had been. Even though she had managed to shake them off in the end and get home safe with her hundred pounds and tuck it away: into her stocking, what would go, and the rest pinned under her skirt along with her savings. Oh dear, what a business. But that was the end of it. And oh what a mercy to think she never would, never again, have to go back to that bank and have them asking questions.

And now she really *would* have to economise, if she didn't want to go back there again. She'd have to see what she could do. There was that meat, that was what bothered her; that was by far the most expensive of what she had to buy. Dearest by far. But she knew what she'd do....

There, if that wasn't as nice a bit of meat as you could wish to see. Threepence, think of that. And the very best bit they had on the stall. Every scrap as good as what you got in the shops. It was only that they *called* it cat's-meat, being cut smaller and not what everyone would want. But for all she wanted.... And the very same meat, if the truth were known, and half the price. That would show you how they had you in these shops.

And come to that, if it wasn't nice any time she could always go inside for once and give a bit more.

And it was after getting her meat at the stall one day that she took it into her head, she couldn't say why, to go on up Clapington Street and see what there was higher up where she never had been before — getting adventurous in her old age! — up past the old-iron stalls.... And there, right up at the top of Clapington Street, if she didn't come into a lovely wide road with trees, and seats under, where she was able to rest her things and sit herself down for a minute.

And what a blessing that was, to be able to have a bit of a sit-down before starting back, on a hot day like this.

Oh dear, for it was a hot day, summer again, how it did come round. Summer and winter, and summer and winter, how the years did go by. It was a pleasure just to take your weight off your feet and look around you. And this was a pleasant sort of a road, nice and open. Avebury Avenue, as they called it. With the trees and all. Reminded her of the old days, oh dear, the way it had been at The Elms. Too much of a good thing that was. You couldn't see out hardly in the summer, the way the leaves were out on the trees.

But she mustn't stay sitting about here, time she was getting back to her dinner. But that was what she'd do, she'd come up here one of these days, when she had the time, and sit and take the air. It was a pleasure just to sit a bit and take the air, quiet.

And so she did too, summer or winter, so long as it was a nice day. Though it was a bit of a way, but she had plenty of time, she could take her time about it. Take your time, he'd say, don't go hurrying now, take it easy. She took to going up there sometimes of a morning or afternoon even when it wasn't her regular day for shopping, just to sit and take the air. It was worth the bit of a walk, for the pleasure of putting down your things at the end of it, when you'd been on your feet all day like she was, and her arms aching sometimes from what she had to carry. For it was no good talking like that, you couldn't help it, you had to do these things nowadays, you had to look out for yourself, there wasn't anyone else that was going to that she knew of, you had to keep a sharp eye in your head.

Like that box. A lovely big box, that she never would have seen if she hadn't had her eyes open. Made all of wood, and do for lighting the fire for weeks to come if she could only get it home. And not far, either. Only just down on the corner two streets off from home, when she came back down Clapington Street from Avebury Avenue one Thursday dinnertime with the barrows all moved off for early closing. Just down on the corner where they had the stall with all the tomatoes. Tomato box, that would be; what they got them in from abroad.

If only she could see how ever she was to get it home.

And have to look sharp about it too, for there were street cleaners coming now. Have it swept up in a jiffy, if she wasn't sharp.

In the end she picked it up in her hand, there being nothing else to do; and lucky she had done. For she hadn't got more than half of the way back to Broughton Road when there was an old sack thrown down in the gutter; just the very thing! Torn a bit, but not so that it mattered.

There, with her box in her sack — and no one would ever know what it was — she'd get home easy. And what she'd do, now she'd once found out how it was, she'd have the sack with her another time, rolled up in her bag, in case she should run across the same. A lovely box that would keep her fire in the best part of an evening. If she could find enough like that she never would *need* to go buying coal. Burning up money.

And it was cosy of an evening, once she'd got her fire to go. Never mind the cinders — there's a nice big bit would do again — sweep them out later. Tomorrow. Next time the room's done. A handful of sticks, and it might be a lump or two if she was put to it, picked small, out of the bucket under the sink. Going nice and bright, and she able to take her ease in her chair to the side of the hearth, just to herself, nice and cosy. With the lamp lit, back on the table. It was a pleasure just to sit and take your ease. Come to that she might have been mending up that rent in her jacket; but never mind for now, never show, see to it one of these days. A pleasure just to sit. Never was one for gallivanting round. Nor yet for sitting reading out of a book, like some. William, he was the one for books, always a book to his hand, poor William. And how he did like a bit of fire to sit by.

It seemed a pity almost when it came on for ten o'clock, but there it was. Sitting up meant light and fire; never was one for indulging herself. Rake out the cinders, and light her bit of candle and put out the lamp; and round she'd go, with her candle, and her jacket pulled on for it struck chill out there in the passage, to see that all was as it should be.

Spoons in the trunk and trunk locked, and the kitchen door; and what a climb it was up those stairs, to try that door at the top. Oh dear, what a climb, and down again, and all she could do to stop the grease from dripping, climbing back down. And then the front door. And into her room and lock herself in.

But here she was at last, with her nightgown on for bed, and her hair tied up with the same bit of ribbon she'd used since she didn't know when. Just to see to the window catch — blind, curtains — and then she was ready. The candle away up on the mantelpiece where it wouldn't shine, if anyone *was* to be peeking in, and then she could undo the pin from her pocket and lay it all out on the bed — careful, now — to see all was there. Laid out all separate, not to chink. Three sovereigns, and four half sovereigns and her four crown-pieces; and six of *them*, and nine of *them*, and *that*, and *those*.... And then her gold brooch, that was worth a pretty penny all by itself, good solid gold, heavy, you could tell. Pop it all back in its bag and under her pillow. And then the notes from the bank, out of her stocking into her bedsock, nasty things these notes but handy for putting by. And then she could blow out the candle and crawl in.

And be up with the lark, too: never was one to lie abed, not like these youngsters nowadays. Into her clothes, and starting up the area steps, soon as ever she heard the bottles rattling down the street — take her time, never did believe in being hurried — with her jug, and her penny, for her milk. And then make herself a cup of tea, and pack up her things, and get off, if it was a nice morning, up to her seat up on Avebury Avenue.

For she had a fancy for this seat. There was plenty more, but she had a fancy for this one, and it wasn't often she took a fancy. Never had been one to have fancies. But so far as she could see it wasn't doing any harm to anyone. It was a nice empty road, there weren't many came that way. Like the road up past The Elms, before the soldiers came. Oh dear, that war, that was a fuss and a pother! And what a time back it did seem, sitting here quiet it was like another world. How ever many years would it have been. There was the year poor William was taken off, the end of the war that was. And then a year before she moved. And then all the time before ever she came to Broughton Road, hunted round by that Emily and *her* lot, it was nothing in the world but to see what they could get. Liked to eat me out of house and home if they had half a chance. Like William used to say, in his humorous way. And then the way the time went since; you couldn't keep upsides with it.

Summer or winter, it did you good to get a breath of air. And what she could do, if she was to put her mantle on over her jacket, that would keep her warm. And do it good wearing, no good keeping put by, saving for those that was to come after; and if she had her way she'd burn every stick and rag she'd got sooner than they should get it. Of all the ingratitude. After all she'd done. But it did make her laugh, to think of the job they'd have one of these days finding out where she'd got to.

Not that she wouldn't be spared for many a long year yet, hale and hearty as ever she was, if it hadn't been for her back, and that never had carried off anyone yet that she knew of. The one thing she hoped, she hoped she'd outlive that Emily, after all her plotting and scheming. 'Thought I'd like to see you.' Like to see me underground, that's what you'd like. Not yet awhile, don't you worry, not yet awhile. If it hadn't been for her back; and that was nothing to speak of if it was a nice bright day, able to sit out and take the air. Oh dear, these steps, they'll be the death of me! But if she was to pick up her bit of marketing on the way, if there was anything down so early, or coming back more likely.... No hurry, take your time, sit a bit and take the air. And if it wasn't for getting back to dinner she could have sat there all day, she really could. Twelve-twenty-two on the church, oh dear, she never had been one to notice how the time went. Up we come. Be late for dinner if she wasn't careful.

Chapter XV

Up with the lark, and get on her clothes. Up the steps — oh how she did feel her back these days! — for her drop of milk. Nice bit of sun up in the street; get out, later on, get a bit of sun, good for the rheumatics. Oh dear! And back down the steps, and make herself a cup of tea.

And if that tear wasn't gone worse in her alpaca. Of all the vexatious things, and only sewed it up when-was-it. And always been good stuff, always was good. Pop in a pin, that's what she'd do; with her mantle on, no one any the wiser, hardly show. For all it was anyone's business. Peeking and poking.

And her veil gone again too. What you get now, no wear in it. Now if there was to be a nice new bit of veiling up on that stall today she didn't say she wouldn't treat herself to a bit, with the spring coming on. No harm in seeing what they'd got. It wasn't often she gave herself a treat, and she did like a nice tidy veil.

Well, with her hat on, and her jacket and her mantle, there was only to get her things together. Undo her black bag, that was stood up against the wall so she could take it again easy, and feel down to see all was there. For she didn't need to go looking, she could tell well enough by the feel. Her boots and her best bead slippers and her boa and her muff and her best black and her serge.... Ah, you couldn't deceive *her*. *She* knew which was which well enough by the feel, she would have known if there was so much as a pin missing, without ever setting an eye inside. Tie up the string again, good stout cord, a lucky day when she came across that. And prop it back against the wall, all ready with her umbrella on top.

And spoons in her handbag, and up those stairs to try the door, oh what a climb, it was a crying shame, whoever put those stairs there to make her do all that up and down before ever she could start out. And see to the window and make sure of the blind being down. And pull on her left-hand glove, the right being too gone, but who was to know that so long as she had it with her in her hand; and her shopping bag and the old sack empty over her arm, where they wouldn't notice till wanted; and pick up her umbrella and handbag and black bag, dump out in the passage and turn the key, and then the front door, and here we are and up we go. Oh dear what a climb, how she ever got that black bag up and down like she did it was a miracle, it wasn't everyone that could have done it.

Easy along Broughton Road. No hurry now, take it easy, take an easy by the railings, and here we are, round the corner. Now if she should happen to have a nice bit of veiling up there.... Easy now, take it quiet. What's this, cabbage, never was partial to cabbage. But good healthy cabbage leaves, not to be sneezed at. Oh dear, my back. Flying in the face of providence. Now where's that bag. Now what you pushing for. Here we are. A sin to leave them lying. Never was partial all the same, give me a nice potato any day.

Nice potato. Give me a nice potato.

What I want's a nice potato. None of this any good. Bad day

today, nothing any good. Too early, have a look coming back. Now then, here we are, where is it, here. Now if she should happen to have a nice bit....

"Haven't you got any black?"

Black, that's what I want, black. All these fancy colours. Don't like all these fancy colours. Never would put fancy colours on my face. Can't take the trouble to answer. What they're coming to. What it is nowadays you never would believe. Colour veilings, never did fancy them. Never saw that in the old days. Knew how to dress like ladies in the old days. Never what I've been accustomed to. Nice bit of black. Always looks nice.

"Haven't you got any black?"

"Not today, Ma."

Not today, not today, what's today got to do with it. I want black. Nice bit of black. Always looks nice. Nice and ladylike.

"I want a nice bit of *black*."

Can't take the trouble. What have you got there. What's that over at the back. What they're coming to. I'm sure I don't know. All these fancy colours, don't like it. Never did like it. Like a nice bit of black. Always looks good. As poor William always used to say....

"Well, what is it?"

"I want *black*. You show me some black. My poor husband always used...."

"Not today, I tell you!"

Not today, not today. Always something, always some rubbish. Oh very well, have it your own way. Lose my custom, that's all you'll do. Don't want work nowadays. Don't know which side their bread's buttered.

A nice potato now? Now that's a thing I do like. Oh dear! One nice healthy potato. Must be some more. Must be more round here. Now what you pushing for. Somewhere about. Now that's a funny thing, only one. Isn't often you find only one. Oh well, have it your own way, now where's that bag. Oh my back! Just put down for a minute. Now what you pushing, shoving. Up again. Now here we are. Not far now.

Newspaper. What's the good of newspaper. Lay the fire. Burnt out before you can look round. Sooner have a nice bit of wood. Stuff it in the sack. Better than nothing. Thankful for small mercies.

Newspaper enough to lay the fire for a week or more. Seemed as if no one had anything to get rid of but newspaper. Stuffing up the sack. Throw it out if any better comes along. What's this, orange. Nothing but peel. Of all the rubbish. Oh, and here now, her penn'orth of meat.

Here we are at last. And ready enough for a sitdown too, what with her sack and her bag, and her back off in half.

And then to think. Of all the vexing things. To think there had to be someone, today of all days, on her seat. As if there wasn't any other seat. As if there wasn't plenty more seats without you must choose.... After all the years she'd been coming there.

She didn't know which upset her worse, she really didn't: going on to another seat or having to sit with someone up against her things. For hug them up as she might, if there was someone on the same seat as sure as sure they'd be managing to have their arm push up sooner or later against one of her bags. You had to have eyes all over your head. But sit she did, in the end; for if you were to take the trouble to walk on as like as not someone would be on the next or come pushing in after. Got all safe. Handbag and shopping bag and black bag and umbrella and the sack with her papers in. All safe so far. Oh, to get your weight off your feet for a minute.

Now you just keep off them, my lad. You just keep your elbow off that bag. I can see you if you think I can't. I can see with the back of my head. A great strapping lad that ought to be ashamed of himself, sitting down. In the old days you didn't use to see a great hulking fellow....

A blessing to sit down a minute. Even if you did have to keep a sharp eye. That was the one that bothered her, the black bag that was down at the end, she had half a mind to get up and move it round. Right up against where the young man was putting his arm. If he should so much as lift a finger to that hole in the side....

But in the end he had to get up and move off, couldn't sit there for ever, and then she *did* get a chance to rest herself a bit. Nice and quiet, under the trees, if it hadn't been for her dinnertime she could have sat there all day. It did seem a long way to go back for her dinner. Supposing she was to have her bit of meat for her tea. That was what she'd do for once. And then she wouldn't have to move for a bit. And find better down Clapington Street too, coming on for afternoon. Now that that young man had made up his mind to take himself off. What they were coming to. Able-bodied young fellow sitting about, ought to be at work. Never see such a thing all my born days.

"You all right, Ma?"

What, what's that, what....

Oh!

Handbag and shopping and black and that one.... Oh, oh dear, what a turn. Take no notice, that was the only thing. Take no notice and he'd take himself off. Go off the same way he came.

"You all right?"

Oh. Oh dear. That and this and shopping and.... Oh, so that was all it was. Well, really, if you'd ever told her.... Well really, if she ever had seen such a thing, to think of it, to think nowadays even the police hadn't any more manners or decency than come up and address.... And this one and that....

"Brought all the luggage along, then?"

Oh! Oh really, it was too much, so that was it was it, it was as much as she could do, it really was, to bring herself.... But draw herself up she did, quite quiet and firm.

"Are you addressing me, my man?"

And him having the impudence, bending right down. Right down over the seat, as near as ever so.

"Got somewhere to go, all right?"

She really didn't, she really never had.... Umbrella and hand and black and sack.... She really never, and if it wasn't that she wouldn't stoop to demean herself.... Oh dear! ... to demean herself to stoop, if it wasn't that she wouldn't have dreamt of speaking....

"Sure you know where to go?" he said, moving round.

He really and truly did. Just when she was getting herself up, when she was having all she could do to lift.... Putting out his hand, as if the next thing he'd be snatching something.

And then she *did* draw herself up. Though how she ever did it....

"I'm going home," she told him, "when I'm ready, and not before."

And he must have seen then it was no good him going on. Saw she meant it. And had to take himself off at last.

"All right, Ma."

Grinning all over his face. Thought he was clever. Ma indeed. Of all the.... Of all....

Oh dear, how upset she was. Really if there hadn't happened to be a seat empty further along she really didn't know. Oh what a turn it did give her, having a policeman come up and speak. A policeman, think of it. Not that she'd got anything to hide, never had done, but you never could tell. And what with the weather, and what it was coming to, to think of her being spoken to.... Coming up like that. She really didn't know what she *had* thought....

Oh the relief, to get off her feet for a bit! — Black and sack and shopping and this and you.... — And no one here, that was one thing, pushing and poking. Well, this would be a lesson to her, no more of coming up here, a pack of thieves and rascals. Up to no good nowadays, no one any better than they ought to be. And as for that policeman, call himself a policeman, ought to be reported. The very idea. And that's what she'd do, too, if he so much as tried speaking to her again. Yes, and now you just try, now you just so much as try.

Connecting threads:
Gertrude Trevelyan
and Virginia Woolf
An Afterword by Ann Kennedy Smith

On 29 June 1927, in the early hours of the morning, a total solar eclipse could be seen from parts of the United Kingdom. It was the first to be visible in England for over two hundred years,[1] and Londoners who could afford the 18-shilling return fare took a special overnight train from King's Cross to north Yorkshire to witness the extraordinary spectacle. Leonard and Virginia Woolf were among the crowds who travelled there. "How can I express the darkness? It was a sudden plunge," Virginia Woolf wrote in her diary. "Also to be picked out of one's London drawing room and set down on the wildest moors in England was impressive."[2]

The following day, at Oxford, another extraordinary event took place. At the University's annual Encaenia ceremony held at the famous Sheldonian Theatre, a young student, Gertrude Eileen Trevelyan, aged 24, was presented with the Newdigate Prize for her 250-line poem in blank verse, "Julia, Daughter of Claudius" (later published as a limited edition by Basil Blackwell). The value of the prize may have been small in financial terms - a cheque for

£21 - but its reputation was mighty. Founded in 1806, Sir Roger Newdigate's Prize was given annually to an Oxford University student for the best composition in verse of under 300 lines. It had previously been won by John Ruskin, Matthew Arnold, and Oscar Wilde. Now, for the first time, a woman had been awarded the University's most prestigious literary prize.

The Encaenia is always a special day in the University of Oxford's calendar, but in 1927 few male undergraduates were present to watch Trevelyan collect her cheque. Excitement about the eclipse had been building for months, and most university men had left the city earlier that week, hoping to get the best vantage point. "This," the *Oxford Times* asserted, "doubtless explained the presence in the gallery of many undergraduettes in their quaint hats."[3] But the female students who crowded into the Sheldonian Theatre that day, proudly wearing their academic gowns and caps, knew how hard their predecessors had fought for them to have the right to be there. For them, seeing a woman undergraduate awarded the Newdigate Prize was perhaps as momentous an event as viewing a total solar eclipse.

A few weeks before, Virginia Woolf had been invited by Oxford University to give a lecture to undergraduates, an acknowledgement of her achievements as the author of critically acclaimed novels including *Jacob's Room* (1922) and *Mrs. Dalloway* (1925).[4] The trip was a useful distraction for Woolf, who was feeling anxious about her new novel, *To the Lighthouse*, published on 5 May 1927. She knew that its daring, experimental style might be challenging for some readers and she was waiting to hear the literary critics' verdict. "I know why I am depressed," she wrote in her diary on the book's publication day. "A bad habit of making up the review I should like before reading the review I get."[5]

Good reviews mattered to Woolf. Positive comments would translate into reprints by the Hogarth Press, the tiny publishing press that she and her husband Leonard Woolf had jointly run for ten years.[6] Healthy book sales would also mean a corresponding increase in her income. "It is misleading to think of her as indifferent to financial matters, in spite of her capital and her private Press," Woolf's biographer Hermione Lee writes. "She was intensely conscious of her value in the market-place."[7] Woolf need not have worried about *To the Lighthouse*. It proved to be a turning point in her career, confirming her reputation as a novelist, and its brisk sales meant that for the first time her income was higher than that of her husband.

Her Oxford lecture was entitled "Poetry, Fiction and the Future." Woolf was pleased to see what she called "the youth of both sexes" crammed into the lecture hall, noting that many of them were greatly under the influence of the Bloomsbury group of writers and poets.[8] Male undergraduates still outnumbered female ones, but in Woolf's eyes, having a mixed audience was a visible sign of progress. She had always regretted missing the opportunity to read Classics at university herself. When she was a young woman, her father Leslie Stephen, a leading man of letters and former don, had explained that there was not enough money for Virginia and her sister to follow in their brothers' footsteps to Cambridge. The injustice of this stayed with Woolf for years[9] and she did not hide her contempt for Oxbridge men who, because of their education, behaved as if they were effortlessly superior to her. "Her rage was fuelled by competitiveness," Lee notes. "It was *she*, not any of them who was going to be the great writer."[10]

As a final-year student of English with a passion for literature, Gertrude Trevelyan likely would have attended Woolf's lecture. Because fiction was changing so rapidly, Woolf, said, no one could predict its future but "the next ten years will certainly upset it; the next century will blow it to the winds."[11] Listening to these words, did Trevelyan dare to envisage her own future as an experimental and challenging writer?

Given her conventional background, her early literary ambitions are hard to guess. Born in 1903, she was the only surviving child of well-connected, upper-middle-class parents and she grew up in Bath in Somerset. As a teenager she attended Princess Helena College, a girls' boarding school in Ealing, west London, where she won the school's essay-writing prize two years in a row but gave few other indications of literary promise. In 1923, Trevelyan went up to Lady Margaret Hall without a scholarship but with a view to getting a degree, perhaps unaware of what a significant achievement this already was.

By then, women had been studying at Oxford for over fifty years, but for decades the University's governing body, or Council, had steadfastly refused to accept them as full members or award them degree certificates. After the horrors of the First World War, however, there was a determination among many people to make a better, fairer world, and in 1920, three years before Trevelyan began her studies, a vote was passed by Council permitting women students to graduate with full Oxford BA and MA honours. It was a milestone in the University's history. The special graduation ceremony to mark the occasion took place at the Sheldonian Theatre on 14 October 1920, and the mood was described in the *Oxford Times* as one of "excitement" and "bewilderment." Eleanor Jourdain, the Principal of St Hugh's college, called it "a woman's day, and a day for women to remember."[12] Among the first cohort of graduates was the writer Vera Brittain, author of *Testament of Youth* (1933) and *The Women at Oxford: A Fragment of History* (1960). Years later, in *Gaudy Night* (1935), Dorothy L. Sayers brilliantly captured the lifelong significance of an Oxford degree for her fictional *alter ego*, the detective Harriet Vane: "Whatever I may have done since, this remains," Vane reminds herself. "Scholar; Master of Arts; Domina; Senior Member of this University."[13]

Gertrude Trevelyan arrived in Oxford at a time of renewed confidence among women academics and students, who seemed at last to be catching up with their male peers in meaningful ways. According to the Oxford classicist and lecturer Gilbert Murray, female undergraduates "were certainly more remarkable and interesting than the majority of the men."[14] Trevelyan's peers included Mary Renault, the future historical novelist who studied at St Hugh's from 1925 and spent her spare time practising dagger-throwing, and Elizabeth Pakenham (née Harman), a brilliant beauty who became a historian and the mother of Lady Antonia Fraser.[15] In 1926, four out of Oxford's five women's colleges and halls, including Lady Margaret Hall, were awarded their Royal Charter, officially placing them for the first time on an equal footing with the male colleges. It was another important step forward.

It's revealing that Trevelyan chose to study English, which as a new academic discipline at Oxford and Cambridge was breaking adventurous ground in the study of modern writers. Otherwise, it's hard to be certain of what she gained from her student experience. She later summed up her time at Lady Margaret Hall in terms of her acute sense of difference from her fellow students. "Did not: play hockey, act, row, take part in debates, political or literary, contribute to the *Isis* or attend cocoa parties, herein failing to conform to the social standards commonly required of women students," she wrote.[16]

Trevelyan's rejection of the upper-class Oxbridge female stereotype is characteristic of her refusal to conform, but it may also indicate more serious health difficulties that caused her to take four years, instead of the usual three, to complete her degree. In 1933, living in London, she wrote that, apart from winning the Newdigate Prize, her chief accomplishments at Oxford were developing "smokers' throat and a taste for misanthrophic reflection, which occupation she has since pursued at Fulham, Notting Hill and elsewhere."[17] The "smokers' throat" she so casually refers to might have been the first signs of the pulmonary tuberculosis which would become a more serious condition for Trevelyan in her thirties. Other clues to her unhappiness at Oxford lie in one of her earliest novels, *Hot-house* (1933), in which an older female tutor at a fictional Oxford women's college discusses the unsuitability of Mina, the protagonist, for university life: "Rather unbalanced, you know. Nerves and so on. Not quite the right thing for the college, perhaps."[18]

Although Trevelyan felt as if she didn't fit in at Oxford, her first published poem was about to make her famous there. "Julia, Daughter of Claudius" was inspired by an account in John Addington Symonds's seven-volume book, *Renaissance in Italy* (1875-86), telling the story of how in 1485 a Roman sarcophagus was discovered by workmen digging up the Appian Way. Inside was the body of a fifteen-year-old Roman girl, her beauty perfectly preserved. "Awake! For Julia lives. Awake!/ For beauty is not dead."[19] Trevelyan writes. Her poem is a powerful retelling of the story of how Julia's body was taken to the Vatican City and displayed in a marble coffin, but when growing numbers of pilgrims demanded to see this "miraculous" corpse, Pope Innocent VIII began to feel that his position as leader of the orthodox faith might be threatened. To prevent this new and powerful pagan cult from developing further, he had the girl's body removed and secretly buried at night, leaving her coffin empty.

For a time, it seemed as if the twentieth-century equivalent of a cult was building around Gertrude Trevelyan. The news of the first woman winner of the Newdigate Prize was reported around the English-speaking world, from *The Times* in London to the *Wagga Wagga Daily Advertiser* in Australia. "Miss Trevelyan's verse shows promise and power, and a sweep of diction none too common in modern poetry," the *Spectator* critic wrote on 25 June 1927 and the *Daily Mail* predicted that her "future work will be watched with interest."[20] Trevelyan herself did not take all the fuss too seriously, claiming never to have written verse before and telling the *Mail* that she wrote the poem "for a joke." Years later, recalling the excitement surrounding her award, she drily observed that all the publicity was probably due to astonishment at "evident revolutionary tendencies at work in the University."

The "revolutionary tendencies" that Trevelyan referred to concerned the increasingly contested place of women at Oxford in the second half of the 1920s. In the seven years since they were permitted degrees, female students had been enrolling at the University in ever greater numbers and the male authorities were becoming alarmed. For conservative members of the University, the headline news that Trevelyan had won the Newdigate Prize may also have been a tipping point. On 14 June 1927, a proposal to limit the number of women undergraduates was debated in the Sheldonian Theatre. The Principal of Somerville College spoke passionately against the motion. "We are sick of the disabilities of our sex," she said. "We feel bound to hand on the privileges we have inherited as unchanged as possible to our successors."[21] Many of the more progressive male dons agreed with her, including the Balliol classicist Cyril Bailey, who said: "Many members of the University would feel a deep sense of shame if Oxford said to the world 'No more women need apply.'" But the proposal was passed by the majority and a new statute drafted capping the number of female students at 840, one sixth of the total complement of undergraduates, for the foreseeable future.

Just two weeks later, Trevelyan walked up to the stage of the Sheldonian to claim her prize for a poem that described what happened when a powerful world leader felt threatened by a fifteen-year-old girl, even though that girl was long dead. Trevelyan's "Julia, Daughter of Claudius" might appear to be a fanciful tale, but its symbolism is telling. That month the University of Oxford had demonstrated that the men were still in control and could take away a woman's powers at any time. If she threatened the status quo and the male sense of superiority — as the University's female students had done by their growing presence, insistence on degrees and their winning of prestigious prizes — there would be consequences. Women were still at risk of losing the "privileges" they had worked so hard for, including the right to an equal education. It's hardly surprising that, in March of the following year, male undergraduates at the Oxford Union debating society voted in favour of the motion "That the Women's Colleges of this University should be levelled to the ground."

After Oxford, given her family background, connections and literary promise, Trevelyan could easily have chosen to live a comfortable life on her inherited money. Like Woolf, she had inherited at least five hundred a year and could afford a room of her own in which to write. But — also like Woolf — she valued her ability to earn her own money and live as unconventionally as she wished. In 1927 she moved to London and worked as a private tutor for a few years, while also publishing poems in the *Nineteenth-Century Magazine* and writing articles for literary journals.[22] She turned down the offer of a prestigious research fellowship at Radcliffe College, Cambridge, Massachusetts and lived at various addresses until in 1931, when she and her friend from Lady Margaret Hall, the French scholar Paule Scott-James (née Lagarde-Quest)[23] settled at 107 Lansdowne Road in London's Notting Hill.

The following year, Trevelyan published her first novel *Appius and Virginia* under the gender-neutral name of G.E. Trevelyan, with a dedication to "PLQ." The novel tells the story of an unmarried forty-year-old woman who sets out to raise a baby orangutan as if he were a human child. The protagonist strives to establish a connection with another species but is eventually forced to realize that the divide between them is too great. "It must have required considerable courage to conceive Appius and Virginia and to carry out the conception so carefully," wrote Leonora Eyles admiringly in the *Times Literary Supplement*. "Miss G. E. Trevelyan demands equal courage from her readers."[24]

Other critics were less appreciative, including the *Daily Mail*'s James Agate who dismissed the novel for its "frantic silliness." Trevelyan's next published work, *Hot-House* (1933) resembled more conventional fiction, set as it was in the overheated atmosphere of a fictional women's college. Barbara Pym read it while she was still a student at St. Hilda's in Oxford, dreaming of becoming a novelist herself one day.[25] "Reading Gertrude Trevelyan's novel *Hot-House*," she wrote in her diary. "I desperately want to write an Oxford novel – but I must see first that my emotions are sim-mered down fairly well." Pym puts her finger on why Trevelyan's attempt at a campus novel failed: the subject was too close to her own experiences at university for her to turn it into the imagina-tive fiction at which she excelled.

That year Trevelyan contributed an acerbic piece "On Gar-den Cities" to the collection *Red Rags: Essays of Hate from Oxford* (1933), described as "a counterblast to Oxford Communism." A photograph of the book's launch party shows her in evening dress and wearing glasses, the only woman among the sixteen suited Oxford men (the biographer Renée Haynes was the only other female author to contribute an essay).[26] It is the last time that Trevelyan is photographed at a social engagement; from then on, she appears to have remained in her London flat and immersed herself in writing fiction.[27]

The six novels that followed in as many years were as boldly experimental as they were thematically disparate, and included such ambitious novels as *As It Was in the Beginning* (1934), *War Without a Hero* (1935), *Two Thousand Million Man-Power* (1937), "a twentieth-century literary classic" according to Rachel Hore, who wrote the introduction for the Boiler House Press edition. There was no equivalent of the Bloomsbury group for Trevelyan in 1930s Notting Hill. "She had a small circle of friends, avoided the limelight, reviewed no books, neither taught nor edited, made no trips abroad or otherwise diverted her time and energy from the task of writing," Brad Bigelow observes. "This allowed her to take great risks in style, structure and approach, to create works of imaginative intensity unequalled by any novelist of her time aside from Woolf herself."[28]

There may of course also have been more personal reasons for Trevelyan's solitary dedication to her novel-writing. Archival records reveal what she chose to keep secret from everyone but her closest friends: that she spent periods in London hospitals throughout the 1930s being treated for her pulmonary tuberculosis. She must have realized that if her health allowed her only limited time in which to write, everything else must take second place.

Jane had worked for her money, she knew the value of it. Knew how to save, and knew how to spend, too. All good quality, all of the very best. Mr. Chirp might have done worse for a manager. Gone further and fared worse.

Economic independence – the ability to earn, save and spend one's own money – is, like education, a source of power. The injustice of denying both to women because of their gender is threaded through Gertrude Trevelyan's searingly honest novel, *William's Wife*. First published in 1938, it was one of her last published novels, and develops a motif from *Two Thousand Million Man-Power* (1937) and *Theme with Variations* (1938): the sense of an individual at the mercy of overpowering societal forces. Towards the end of *Two Thousand Million Man-Power*, Robert Thomas thinks of himself as one of millions of human cogs in "one vast, intricate machine, speeding up, quicker and quicker, running on man-power." He and his wife Katherine are figures in an industrial landscape, struggling to survive in a world that constantly threatens to crush them.

William's Wife shifts the focus, developing this theme entirely through the perspective of one woman, covering her story from the late 1890s until just after the First World War. It's a remarkable *tour de force*, striking in its psychological insights and immersion in a character's mind. Jane Atkins is a twenty-eight-year-old domestic servant who, thanks to her sensible, hard-working and prudent principles, has risen to the status of lady's maid. The story begins on her wedding morning, as she prepares to step into an unfamiliar new world. Her mood of excited anticipation as she dresses is caused less by thoughts of her husband-to-be William Chirp (a stolid older widower with a grocery business) than about her wedding trousseau.

> She stooped and lifted her skirts to do up the high new boots. It was a pity, in a way, she couldn't have put on the smart slippers she'd bought, with the beads sewn all over the toes; but they never would do for out-of-doors, even with going in the cab. Have them nice and new for afterwards.

From her fancy straw bonnet to her primrose kid gloves, she is proud to have paid for every item herself with her hard-earned savings.

At first, the new Mrs. Chirp enjoys her status as a married woman. For a working-class girl with no formal education in Victorian England, marriage to a property-owning businessman represented a substantial step up the social ladder. "She was grateful to Mr. Chirp, he'd made her the mistress of The Elms, she hoped she knew her duty by him." There is little work for her to do in her husband's substantial home in the fictional market town of Jewsbury apart from mending clothes and dusting the front parlour every Saturday. Here, she feels proud of "the clock under its glass dome and the pair of china vases and the candlesticks hung with bunches of gilt grapes: it was her furniture now, her ornaments, hers, Jane Chirp's." But her growing suspicion that all is not as it should be is manifested initially in her imagined rivalry with the first Mrs. Chirp. When Jane finds her old sewing basket, complete with its broken scissors, unfinished mending and reels of cotton thread, she carries it to the kitchen to throw it in the fire, but "just before she pushed the basket into the round, red hole of the stove, she took out the reels and slipped them in her pocket."

It's a beautifully economical piece of writing, demonstrating Trevelyan's skill and subtly indicating key themes of the novel. Jane's insecurity and sense of displacement is revealed early in the book by her impulsive action, along with the inner life that she must hide for the sake of appearances. Saving useful reels of thread from the flames shows both her natural frugality and the value that she places on the sewing skills which helped her to rise from household servant to lady's maid.

The thread also has symbolic value beyond the novel by connecting Jane's experiences as a wife not only to her predecessor, but by extension to all powerless Victorian wives. During William Chirp's first marriage, English law stated that a woman gave up her right to her own property and inheritance when she married. Before the Married Women's Property Act of 1882, a wife had no individual legal status, and anything she earned or owned during her marriage automatically passed to her husband. Around the time when Jane became the second Mrs. Chirp, the law had changed in her favour and she was entitled to keep her savings. But because of her lack of education, she has no idea of her legal rights.

By the time she realizes that her husband is a miser who is pathologically unwilling to spend money even on basic household repairs, it is too late. Two years on, when William refuses to permit her to buy the clothes she needs to keep up her respectable appearance, Jane realizes that she will have to develop new strategies in order to survive.

> He drew at his pipe for some minutes, then he looked round at her. "My poor wife...." He cleared his throat. "My first wife didn't go spending on new gowns, not once in ten, no, fifteen years." He put the pipe in his mouth and turned back to the fire.

Powerless to confront William, Jane becomes skilled in deceitfulness, saving pennies from her household allowance and hiding the paper-wrapped coins in places he is unlikely to find. She congratulates herself on her ingenious schemes, but is constantly on a knife's edge of tension, in fear of discovery.

> One day Jane put the screw of paper among her sewing, last place William would ever look, and then she came hurrying back from the town in a prickly heat, for fear the girl might have been at her basket for a needle and thread.

Today we would recognize William's controlling behaviour towards Jane as a form of "gaslighting," or coercive control, making this novel still powerfully relevant.

Jane enlists the help of her dressmaker friend Minnie Hallett to make her a dress that is so like her old one that William never notices the difference. This connection to a woman who is beneath her in social class is of vital significance in helping Jane to survive, as is the affection she gets from her married stepdaughter, yet later in the book she will reject both lifelines.

Instead, the old dress becomes the last thing Jane feels affection for. It symbolizes the last shreds of her independence, frugality and sewing skills as she adapts it for a new purpose: "made a most lovely bag, just the skirt, with the bodice cut off: big as a sack you could have carried coals in, or bigger!" As a respectable wife, she had managed to keep up appearances while William was alive by using skills of subterfuge and resourcefulness. "All she wanted was a bit of what was due to her," she reminds herself. But as a wealthy woman after William's death, free to live as she pleases, she finds that she has internalized his suspicious attitudes towards other people and her paranoia makes her isolated and vulnerable. Yet her tattered dignity remains intact to the end. "Up we come," she tells herself, after collapsing in a gutter. "Be late for dinner if she wasn't careful."

"The ability of Oxford-educated Trevelyan to slip inside the mind, culture, and language of a woman of a different age and class is remarkable and utterly convincing," writes Bigelow of *William's Wife*.[29] We know little about Gertrude Trevelyan's life when she was writing *William's Wife* in the late 1930s, but clearly she paid close attention to, and imagined the inner lives of, people she observed on London's streets, in shops and travelling by bus. The sight of a dignified woman carrying all her possessions in shabby bags, or scavenging for food in the gutter, might have made Trevelyan wonder how far she had fallen.

In *A Room of One's Own* (1929) Virginia Woolf describes looking up "position of women" in the index of *History of England* (1926) by the Cambridge historian G.M. Trevelyan, a distant relative of Gertrude Trevelyan's.[30] Disappointed to find only references to arranged marriage, wife-beating and Shakespearean heroines, Woolf wondered why G.M. Trevelyan could find no room in his book for the lives of real women throughout history. In the late 1930s she began making notes for a very different sort of history book that she hoped to write one day, following the "unmarked tracks" of women ignored by male historians: "the progress of Anon from the hedge side to the Bankside."[31]

But war broke out and Woolf's book survives only in two draft chapters. In September 1940, while the Woolfs were staying in Sussex, their home at 37 Mecklenburgh Square was badly damaged in the Blitz. Returning to London to salvage what she could, Virginia felt a strange exhilaration to be free of most of her possessions, "save at times I want my books & chairs & carpets & beds — How I worked to buy them —one by one — And the pictures."[32] It's a poignant reminder of how proud she still was of her earnings as a writer. The following month, Trevelyan's Notting Hill flat was destroyed by a German bomb and she was severely injured. She never recovered, but died a few months later at her parents' home in Bath. Her death certificate recorded the cause of death as pulmonary tuberculosis, and the few obituaries written about Gertrude Trevelyan described winning Oxford's Newdigate Prize in 1927 as her greatest achievement.

Note:

My thanks to Brad Bigelow; Lady Margaret Hall's Archivist, Oliver Mahony; the Society of Authors; and the Women's History Network. Any remaining errors are my own.

Endnotes

1   Marriott, R. A., "1927: a British eclipse," *Journal of the British Astronomical Association*, 1999, vol.109, no.3, pp.117-143

2   Virginia Woolf, *Selected Diaries* (Vintage 2008), abridged and edited by Anne Olivier Bell, with an introduction by Quentin Bell, p.233.

3   "Timeline: 100 years of women's history at Oxford" in *Women making history:* https://www.ox.ac.uk/about/oxford-people/women-at-oxford (accessed 24.3.23)

4   Woolf was also a respected literary critic and essayist, who began her writing career in 1904 as a book reviewer. See Ann Kennedy Smith, *Cambridge Ladies' Dining Society 1890-1914* website: "Mrs. L.'s cheque": https://akennedysmith.com/2016/11/25/kathleen-and-virginia/ (accessed 24.3.23).

5   Woolf, *Selected Diaries*, p. 229.

6   "...the story of the Press is, in a way, the story of the marriage: Leonard's anxiety for her health, their mutual interests, their areas of division, and reflected in the list, their cultural and political life." Hermione Lee, *Virginia Woolf* (Vintage, 1997), p. 362.

7   Lee, *Virginia Woolf*, p. 558.

8   Ibid., p. 507.

9   In a letter to Lytton Strachey, she described Cambridge as "that detestable place." Virginia Woolf and Lytton Strachey, *Letters* (Hogarth Press, 1956), 12 June 1912.); see also Karen V. Kukil, "Paper Hearts: The Correspondence of Virginia Woolf and Lytton Strachey, 1906-1931": https://www.smith.edu/woolf/kukil%20article.pdf (accessed 24.3.23)

10   Lee, p. 213.

11   Virginia Woolf, "Phases of Fiction" (*The Bookman*, 1929).

12   "Timeline: 100 years of women's history at Oxford: 1920," op. cit.

13   Dorothy L. Sayers, *Gaudy Night* (Gollancz, 1935). Quoted in Kennedy Smith, "Dorothy L. Sayers's Graduation Day," https://akennedysmith.com/2020/10/17/dorothy-l-sayerss-graduation-day/ (accessed 24.3.23).

14   Quoted in Daisy Dunn, *Not Far from Brideshead: Oxford Between the Wars* ((W&N, 2022), p. 118.

15   Daisy Dunn, *Not Far from Brideshead*, pp.119-26.

16   G.E. Trevelyan, "On Garden Cities" in *Red Rags: Essays of Hate from Oxford* (Chapman & Hall, 1933), pp. 133-150, p. 134.

17   Ibid.

18   Brad Bigelow, "*Hot-house*, by G.E. Trevelyan (1933)," The Neglected Books Page website: https://neglectedbooks.com/?p=6657 (accessed 24.3.23).

19   Gertrude Trevelyan, *Julia, Daughter of Claudius* (Basil Blackwell, 1927).

20   *The Spectator*, 25 June 1927.

21   "Women at Oxford: Strong Protests Against the Statute," Western Mail, 16 June 1927.

22   G.E. Trevelyan, *Red Rags*, op.cit., p. 134; other biographical information from Lady Margaret Hall student register.

23   Paule Honorine Jeanne Lagarde (also known as Lagarde-Quest) was born in Paris in 1905, and attended Lady Margaret Hall from 1926-29. She became a French lecturer at King's College London (1943-45) and at the London School of Economics (1945-73). Biographical information from Lady Margaret Hall student register.

24   Quoted in Alison Flood, "'If she was a bloke, she'd still be in print': the lost novels of Gertrude Trevelyan," https://www.theguardian.com/books/2020/dec/10/if-she-was-a-bloke-shed-still-be-in-print-the-lost-novels-of-gertrude-trevelyan (accessed 24.3.23).

25   Ann Kennedy Smith, "The Ascent of Barbara Pym" in *The Critic*, 4 September 2022: https://thecritic.co.uk/the-ascent-of-barbara-pym/

26   Mary Evans Library website, https://www.prints-online.com/new-images-august-2021/gertrude-trevelyan-contributors-red-rags-23463118.html (accessed 24.3.23).

27   "[Trevelyan] was evidently enough of a contrarian to steer clear of the decade's many left-leaning literary networks. Indeed, she seems entirely to have escaped the notice of her contemporaries: quite a feat, given how inquisitive some of them were. Scarcely a trace of her survives in the second-hand bookshops or in scholarly accounts of mid-20th century British fiction." David Trotter, 'Hippopotamus charges train', *London Review of Books*, Vol. 45 No.13 29 June 2023.

28   Brad Bigelow, "The Eclipse of Gertrude Trevelyan," afterword in Gertrude Trevelyan, *Two Thousand Million Man-Power* (Boiler House Press, 2022), pp. 283-4.

29   Brad Bigelow, "*William's Wife* by G.E. Trevelyan (1938)," The Neglected Books Page website: https://neglectedbooks.com/?p=6048 (accessed 24.3.23)

30   Gertrude's father and G. M. Trevelyan shared the same great-grandfather (the Venerable George Trevelyan, 1764-1827).

31   Quoted in Francesca Wade, *Square Haunting: Five Women, Freedom and London Between the Wars* (Faber & Faber, 2020), pp.307-8.

32   Quoted in Wade, *Square Haunting*, p.314.

Gertrude Eileen Trevelyan was born in Bath in 1903. She came to fame as the first woman to win the Newdigate Prize for best undergraduate poem at Oxford in 1927. Starting with *Appius and Virginia* in 1932, she published eight novels, her last being *Trance by Appointment* in 1939. Her novel *Two Thousand Million Man-Power* was reissued in the Recovered Books series from Boiler House Press in 2022. She died at her parents' home in Bath in March 1941.

Alice Jolly is an English novelist, playwright and memoirist, who has won both the Royal Society of Literature's V. S. Pritchett Memorial Prize for short stories and the PEN/Ackerley Prize for autobiography.

Dr Ann Kennedy Smith is a writer and researcher based in Cambridge. Her articles and reviews have been published in the *Times Literary Supplement*, *English Review* and the *Oxford Dictionary of National Biography*.

SAVE YOUR PENNIES

If you only save a penny in one shilling-worth of Goods by paying cash, it may seem small, but consider how many pounds you spend in twelve months, these little pennies will be pounds.

COMPARE THESE PRICES.

And see if it is a penny or more.

Finest Butter .... 1s. 3d.
Creamery Butter .... 1s. 2d.
Pure Lard .... 6½d.
Good Cheese .... 8d.
Best Cheshire .... 7½d.
Best Crystal Sugar .... 3s. 5d. per. doz.
Best Lump Sugar .... 4s. per doz.
Our Double-weight Margarine is of very fine quality, made with the cream of choice nuts and pure fresh Milk.
Best Washing Soda—4lbs. for 1½d. or 7lbs. for 2½d.
Wax Candles ...... 2½d. lb. or 3 lbs. for 6½d.
Now the cold weather is upon us you will need something to keep you warm, and at the same time reasonable.
Try our Soup Squares, at 2d. all kinds.
Pure Soluble Cocoa, 1s. per lb., 3d. per ¼ lb.
Loose Provost Oats .... 2d. per lb.
Scotch Oatmeal .... 2d. per lb.
Fine Oatmeal .... 2d. per lb.
Pearl Barley .... 2½d. per lb.

Bagnall's Stores

CASH TRADERS

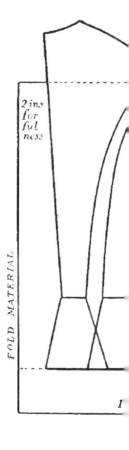

2 ins for ful ness

FOLD MATERIAL

ANALYSIS OF WEEKLY HOUSEHOLD BILLS

	£	s.	d.	£	s.	d.	£	s.	d.	£	s.
Butcher - - -	0	8	0	0	10	0	0	15	0	1	0
Fish - - -	0	2	0	0	3	6	0	4	6	0	
Baker, &c. - -	0	3	6	0	5	0	0	6	6	0	
Butter and eggs - -	0	2	6	0	6	0	0	7	0	0	
Milk - - -	0	2	0	0	4	0	0	5	0	0	
Fruit and Vegetables -	0	3	0	0	4	6	0	5	0	0	
Grocer - - -	0	6	0	0	8	0	0	10	0	0	13
Washing - - -	0	4	0	0	6	0	0	7	0	0	
	£1	11	0	£2	7	0	£3	0	0	£3	1

This average is rather below than above the sum allotted

For true Economy in
WASHING AND CLEANING
USE "COMPO."
Buy a Packet & Prove it for Yourself.

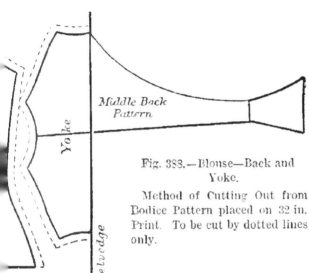

Middle Back Pattern

Yoke

Selvedge

Fig. 388.—Blouse—Back and Yoke.

Method of Cutting Out from Bodice Pattern placed on 32-in. Print. To be cut by dotted lines only.

William's Wife
By Gertrude Eileen Trevelyan

First published in this edition by Boiler House Press, 2023
Part of the UEA Publishing Project
William's Wife copyright © Gertrude Eileen Trevelyan, 1938
Introduction copyright © Alice Jolly, 2023
Afterword copyright © Ann Kennedy Smith, 2023

Proofreading by Lindsay Hause

Photograph of Gertrude Trevelyan by license from the National
Portrait Gallery

The right of Gertrude Eileen Trevelyan to be identified as the
Author of this work has been asserted by her in accordance with
the Copyright, Design & Patents Act, 1988.

Cover Design and Typesetting by Louise Aspinall
Typeset in Arnhem Pro

ISBN: 978-1-915812-06-3

Milton Keynes UK
Ingram Content Group UK Ltd.
UKHW022240130923
428613UK00012B/140

9 781915 812063